CRUDRAT

BY GAIL CARRIGER

The Finishing School Series
Etiquette & Espionage
Curtsies & Conspiracies
Waistcoats & Weaponry
Manners & Mutiny

The Parasol Protectorate Series
Soulless
Changeless
Blameless
Heartless
Timeless

The Custard Protocol Series
Prudence
Imprudence
Competence
Reticence

Parasolverse Tie-in Books & Novellas
Poison or Protect
Defy or Defend
Ambush or Adore
Romancing the Werewolf
Romancing the Inventor
How to Marry a Werewolf

AS G. L. CARRIGER

A Tinkered Stars Mystery
The 5th Gender

The San Andreas Shifters Series
The Sumage Solution
The Omega Objection
The Enforcer Enigma

CRUDRAT

THE TINKERED STARS

GAIL CARRIGER

The Wheel turns and true scions sit its blades lightly –
and close to the center. But those without implants ride
far to the edge where it is easy to fall off.
   ~ From Claudicix's Advice to Young Progenetors

Shink.

The huge blade rotated towards her head, so close as to slice the top off right quick. Just there, above the ears. The blue-tinged metal was heavy and sharp enough to do it, too. Bone wouldn't slow it any more than dust.

Maura ducked, leaped into a flip and landed in a runner's crouch on the other side of the blade. One knee came down too far forward, hitting the cruddy tunnel floor hard. Sharp pain ran up her leg to her hip. Worse by far — her knee made a loud metallic *clang*.

She froze, blood icy and muscles all aquiver.

Now I've done it — gone and dented the tunnel, like some pup on first run. She tipped her head, as though she could hear through the whirr of the blades. As though anyone could hear anything through that. Had foreman noted the knee-down? *He'll kill me deader than spacedross if I damage the scyther. Well, perhaps not that dead — too messy. Hates messes, does foreman. But the smallest dent'll see my license pulled, that's for certain-sure.* Maura reached up and touched the cord that held her run-tag 'round her scrawny neck. There it hung, the chip secured tight and tucked safely down the front of her vest.

No recall alarm sounded. No angry shout rent the rushing air. Naught to hear but the whirr of blades.

Shink. Shink. Shink.

Best keep moving then.

Maura slid to one side, still berating herself. Letting knee touch floor was a right-up-certain stupid mistake. Mistakes in a scyther got a girl killed, and dying bladeside? Now that really *was* messy.

She was getting big and sloppy. Maura shook her head at herself and darted forward, keeping low.

Shink.

This time a blade came at her from the side.

And getting right-up old and slow to go with the sloppy. Maura lunged to the left, spinning up and bouncing off the tunnel wall with one foot. Every blade that came whirring in stacked the odds up against her. Half her life spent crudrat-ting, and she was almost – *what?* She frowned, thinking hard. *Three and ten?* It hurt her noggin to calculate the number of cycles. Past-time always hurts when it's been frittered away running blades and begging for scraps from highstocks. Too old to keep running. Crudrats mostly went in for dying young.

Move.

Maura shifted her weight and dashed up the opposite side

of the tunnel until she was parallel to the floor. At the same time, she snaked out with her scraper, scooping out crud from behind a higher blade where it met the wall. She tipped the long spoon over her shoulder and heard a little slurp as the murmel riding her swallowed happily. She felt whiskers tickle her neck as he snuffled about to see if he'd dropped any crud on her in his enthusiasm.

Shink.

Lower blade. Maura pushed herself off the wall, and jumped to the opposite side of the tunnel. She twisted in mid-air, landed between two blades, and rebounded into a backwards flip.

Breathe, she told herself firmly. Running the scyther always worked best when she timed her breathing to the blades. It was one of the tricks that had turned her from a good crudrat into the best one this portside.

Another blade spun out. Maura leaped forward, curved aside, and balanced against the opposite wall, ending halfway up with her back to it, elbows and knees bent. She sucked in her stomach as the blade passed. Not that there was much to suck. Maura had intimate familiarity with all her ribs – never was a time when she wasn't hungry.

Sliding down the wall, scraper out, she culled crud from behind a lower blade and fed it over her shoulder to the murmel. The murmel made a funny purring noise as he ate. A lightly acrid smell wafted through the air.

Shink.

Upper blade. Near haircut, and she already wore her blue hair cropped short. *Curse my bones, I be getting too tall for this game on top of aught else.* Maura ducked.

The murmel wrapped his long blue tail more firmly about her waist and chittered in her ear in a way Maura was sure he meant as reassuring.

Breathe.

The murmel's chitter became high-pitched in alarm as a blade swished close to her back — and thus his.

Space it, what's wrong with me this shift?

Maura back-flipped over the blade, dodged to the side, and vaulted off the wall forward using one foot, protecting the murmel but keeping her speed up. She scooped with the same movement and passed the ladle-full of crud to the hungry beastie on her back.

A loud animal shriek echoed through the scyther tunnel. It threw her next leap off. She stumbled, missing blade-cut by a hand's breath.

"Tell your wild relations to go easy. Don't they have naught quiet to say?" Maura addressed to her blue fuzzy companion.

The murmel ignored her, intent on digesting his latest scoop.

She'd no worries the wild murmels might interfere with her run. Sure they were mighty tempted by the massive crud deposits in the scythers, but wild ones weren't stupid enough to face blades for it.

If they were, Maura'd be out a job.

Shink.

Breathe. Scoop. Feed the murmel. And repeat.

She moved steadily forward – dancing the three-steps of her entire existence.

***

At the end of the run Maura flipped over her hands out the scything tunnel entrance, landing in a crouch on the engineering yard floor. Not a necessary maneuver, but sometimes she just liked to impress the other 'rats.

Pant. Pant. Pant.

Maura squinted up. The steady bright light in the bay was almost blinding after the dim blue flicker of the tunnel.

"Check in!" barked foreman, wrenching her upright by her ear. *He* wasn't impressed by her stylish exit.

Maura winced. *Heya, that ear's still attached.*

"Four-four-five, sir!" she gasped out the words.

"Weigh out!" He threw her head towards the weight station. He was a big man and while Maura was getting tall she was not yet half his size in pure mass. His throw gave her a good start, motion-wise, and wrenched her neck as a kindly afterthought.

She dashed over, all her limbs loose and comfortable now that she hadn't blades to worry about. She unwound the murmel from her back. The furry blue creature's stomach was distended, full of crud. She cradled him against her chest. He reached one long fuzzy arm up and pawed at her cheek affectionately.

"Stop flirting, you." She pushed his paw away. She wanted to scratch the head of the silly roly-poly beastie but it wouldn't do to be thought soft. Everyone was looking, all the other 'rats wanted to know what her run was worth.

She plonked the murmel onto the weigh scale. Black numbers scrolled across its readout.

Foreman ambled over and noted the weight on his scanpad.

"Sixteen pips more than last time, four-four-five, but your time was off by thirteen ticks. Still faster than any other 'rat this shift by," he paused and checked the pad, "two ticks, and heavier by three pips. Never mess with your pay-rate, do you?"

Maura didn't answer, busying herself about the scale. She fussed over the murmel and tried not to grin in pride.

Foreman grabbed her arm and yanked her towards him. His breath smelled of stale protein packs and caffeine tabs. "Someone will cut you down to size one spin, girl. You're getting sloppy."

Did he hear the knee down? Maura tried not to cringe. Foreman didn't like it when they flinched.

Curled comfortably on the weighing scale, her murmel lifted his blue head and belched. The acrid smell of partially digested crud wafted up. Maura huffed air out though her nostrils and the foreman backed away. Processed crud was toxic. The murmel twitched his whiskers at them.

Foreman continued, "That's poor numbers for you, four-four-five. Very poor indeed."

"Sir!" Maura gasped. She was truly hurt by such a comment. She'd sooner take a blow than a mocking of her run. She was prideful of her work. *It's not like I got aught else to do well.* She bit her lip to keep from talking back. *He'll seize any chance to obedience-me-rough or pull my license just because.*

The murmel squeaked strangely soft. Everyone standing about watching hopped-to. Quiet sounds from murmels meant important business. They meant something might be really wrong.

The foreman let Maura go so she could look to the creature. No one else could touch him without losing a digit, or more. Murmels didn't take kindly to handling by any but their chosen runner.

She lifted the little creature and went to place him with his brethren. His squeak had obviously been meant to get her away from foreman. It wasn't a noise of real distress. She scratched him under the chin in thanks.

"Losing your step or your speed, Maura?" asked one of the other 'rats smugly.

"Shut your face, Ger." Rees elbowed the boy in the side.

Maura nodded to Rees without comment. Half her size and two-thirds her age, Rees liked to play the noble-gallant. *Who am I to clog his fun?*

Rees made a little bow. He fancied himself some long lost lordling, fated to sit parliament. "I come from prog-enetor stock," he always said. Though he didn't look to have a single trigger trait. *Leastways not any visible ones. His voice was awful sweet-like.* Nevertheless, he'd opted Maura as the victim of his court flattery. Using her to train himself up in proper etiquette. He said it was for "when they find me and take me back." All rejects lived with that hope at first. *The sum-total of pup wishes.* Three turns in, his hair gone to blue and Rees still wouldn't space that fantasy.

Maura dropped her murmel to the floor.

The little creature muttered reproachfully. It could be he was greedy for more crud or could be he wanted to stay with her. Then again, could be he was just grumpy. One never could tell with murmels.

She pushed him gently with one bare foot. "Settle," she said, giving him the home command.

He skittered off into a nearby air-duct. Inside, the other tame murmels eyed him suspiciously, pretending they didn't remember who he was. One or two sashayed over, blue tails lashing threateningly. Maura's murmel, alpha of the pack, reared up and shrieked at them at the top of his lungs until they all sat and stared, like progenetor children before a teaching drone. Then he curled up in a corner and went to sleep. Among murmels, alpha seemed to be established by one-who-could-yell-loudest.

Maura took a calming breath and turned back to collect her pay.

The foreman looked her up and down. His expression disgusted and his scrutiny more pointed than usual.

Maura glared at him from narrowed silver eyes. Triggered eyes. She could read it in his face, him noting all her failures. *I ain't naught but crudrat — blue hair from too much tunnel-time and skin likely to go blue soon, too, if'n I keep at it much longer. She straightened her back and looked him full on. What of it? So you've a citizen chip implant and I don't. Five turns scraping the blades and never a single cut. Not one. You can stick that in your implant and process it. I know some 'rats who've lost limbs. Space it, I know 'rats who've lost lives.*

Foreman didn't like it when they stood up to him, even if they didn't say a whit. To him, Maura was nothing more than a scab of society, space jetsam, non-citizen – reject. His expression said it all. She was a waste of air.

"How much you weigh these ticks, four-four-five?"

Maura knew what he was thinking. There's always more reject kids to be got at, small and nimble enough to crudrat. Heavy runners, on the flip side, dent the tunnel, and tall ones die on the blades. Maura was turning both heavy and tall. And getting cocky. Why gamble on her anymore?

Numbers, always on Maura's side until now, were starting to weigh in against her. *Whatever else my genetic stock, and surely I've the weirdest eyes going, I've been triggered tall.* For months she'd been starving herself down, trying to battle adulthood — not that crudrats ate well to start. But bone weighed what it weighed no matter how little she ate. Not to mention the fact that tunnel running had built up her muscle and muscle read-out heavy.

"Don't know my weight, sir."

"You've been running my tunnels how long?" Foreman narrowed his eyes.

"Five turns sir."

The foreman looked genuinely surprised at that.

Well, everyone knew, time flew on a spaceport.

"You must be on borrowed ticks by now."

"Don't know, sir." That was what all 'rats answered to that kind of question. *How'er we supposed to know age, when we all started out abandoned dockside?* No family Maura ever heard of wanted to raise-up a reject. Earliest she remembered was begging for food in the crossgenetor arena. The shops all about her stocked full and them that noticed her more like to spit than drop a single ration cube into her empty hands. That kind of thing soured a soul.

She'd started running tunnels as soon as may be, not the scythers – she'd been too young for blades – but training for scythers. Climbing, flipping, jumping – over, under, straight up walls. She'd even gone so far as to study murmels — feeding the wild ones now and again, sourcing out their litter areas. If crudratting was all rejects could do Maura intended to be best at it. Until now, she had been.

"Crudrat's all I be good for," she said, almost in a whisper. Dread sloshed in her stomach and hardened the back of her throat.

"Five cycles." Foreman frowned in thought. "I wouldn't have put you on a run if you couldn't lift a murmel. You must've been at least seven to launch."

Maura held her tongue.

He looked her up and down once more. "Time you started thinking about some other line of work."

Maura felt as though a blade had sliced right into her gut. It stuck there, lodged below her ribs. *It ends so quick as that?*

"But sir, I didn't make a mistake!" She waved her hand at the other's. Some of them had cuts from their runs. Hoike had a wide deep gash over one eye. *Yeah, he's smaller n' lighter, but he's still cut.* "I be clean as new blades!"

Maura tried not to care that Ger and a few of his pack were openly grinning.

Rees looked like he wanted to cry. His blue head was bowed, tufts of his crazy matted hair stuck up looking like one of those exotic growing things down planetside. *What're they called? Oh yeah,* pants.

The foreman backhanded Maura. He moved slower than a blade, but she hadn't known it was coming so she didn't dodge. The inside of her cheek split open against a tooth and she tasted blood.

"It's my job to see that you're stopped afore your mistakes start damaging my livelihood. Can't risk a scyther for your kind. 'Sides, it's always the best 'rats that die on the blade or bust through the walls. I don't need that kind of mess."

Maura swallowed down both blood and backtalk. Neither would turn her any profit now.

With no ceremony at all, the foreman pulled out a burn blade and melted the cord from about Maura's neck. He slid her licensing chip off of its end, large meaty fingers clutching her whole existence. The cord fell to the floor, a small sad coil of a thing.

Maura watched as he slotted the license into a pocket of his waistcoat. What little recognition she'd had from guards was gone. *Rejects that can't run. Without crudrat status I's naught more than a vagrant.* Armigers, port authority, progenetors, sequensors, enhancers, all that rode Wheel center and rank at its height, they'd be looking for any excuse to space her now. *They'll be finding it, too.* In space, non-citizens wasted air.

Tinkers only know why some citizen implants don't take, but the fact remains that once every thousand or so they don't. Love your child late or not at all, too early and you'll both suffer the loss.

~ From Claudicix's *Advice to Young Progenetors*

Foreman handed Maura the last of her pay and turned away. His big back was straight. His meaty hands clenched and released as he walked back to the scyther. No mercy there, even knowing what kind of life he'd sentenced her to. He kept to his job, and that job was keeping the scythers clean any way he could. Success was measured in the mistakes his runners *didn't* make, and spacing Maura kept him on the narrow track of good product with his superiors. Sure, now his tunnels wouldn't be quite as clean as they used to, but he'd lowered overhead risk and rid himself of bad air, that was the important thing. A new star crudrat was sure to come along eventually. Maura was no longer his problem.

Maura looked down at her pay, a handful of ration cubes. A pathetically small number on most occasions, it seemed tiny now that it made up her last food allotment for the foreseeable future. It sure was a good thing she'd been starving herself recently. She'd a bit of a stash from the last couple cycles.

Someone made a grab for her hand.

""You don't need 'em now," said Ger. He was a stocky boy, few turns younger than she, and never fast enough to get over resenting her. He'd started all red hair and freckles, but now both had gone blue. Blue freckles made him look like he'd contracted some weird alien plague.

"You ain't got more than a few months breathing without tunnel time." His eyes were calculating.

Rees kicked Ger in the shin. "Shut up, you. Maura'll last. She's best 'rat of us. That's gotta count for something."

"With no license? In whose universe would she last?"

A brief scuffle ensued. Ger and Rees were about the same height, but Rees was a good deal slimmer. He clouted Ger on the ear, but soon enough Ger got an arm wrapped tight about his neck. Rees began to go blue in a totally non-crud-induced way.

Maura tucked her rations inside her shirt and waded into the breach. She picked the two of them up and shook them like the rats they were. "That's more than enough of *that*. You two want your licenses pulled as well? You be thinking mine lacks for company?"

They looked about for foreman. He hadn't noticed the scuffle, but that wasn't to say he wouldn't do something drastic if he did. Crudrats may be licensed to work, but they were still rejects. Rejects were invisible. Rejects weren't there. If rejects got noticed, they got trouble and pain with the noticing.

"So you're fast, but how you gonna live?" asked Ger, shaking off Maura's grip and backing away. Rees, he could take easy fist to fist, but Maura? She had a mean right kick and half again his reach.

"Maura has a plan." Rees crossed his arms and glared.

"Ha!" Ger scoffed. "Ain't no place on this spaceport for a reject who's too big to run. Ain't no plan can change fact."

With that, he and the other 'rats scampered off into their various tunnels and ducts, back to whatever hole they called home.

"Don't mind them." Rees put an arm around Maura's waist, which was about all he could reach comfortably. "By going at you, they're going at their own fear."

How'd a kid with only nine turns to his credit get so smart about the brains of others?

"Do I have a plan?" she wondered.

"You'll be needing to get off the port." Rees was confident.

"And go where, exactly?" All Maura knew was portside life. She wasn't sure what planet-bound rejects did to survive, no crudratting down there, but she was relatively certain her lot until now had been at least moderately better than theirs. At least spaceports put their rejects to use for a short while, even if they rejected them in the end.

"How would I get off port anyway? Even if I'd the credit to pay, I don't have the implant to travel."

They moved across the engineering yard bay towards one of the larger air duct mains.

Air ducts were the crudrat's pathways around portside — the corridors of the unwanted. Maura swung herself in. It wasn't tall enough for them to walk upright, nowhere near the size of the scyther tunnel. Nowhere near as blue-tinted either. Of course, everything spaceside had a little blue dust on it,

couldn't keep all crud out, no mater how many filters
subgenetors rigged up. Still, air ducts were easy on the eyes,
more silver and white than blue — comfortable. But they
were only big enough to crawl in, which was hard on the
knees.

"Why not stow away?" Rees raised his voice over the
rush of air as he climbed inside the duct and crawled after
Maura.

"You spending far too much time down dockside, lead-
brain. You're needing help. This obsession with spacecrafting
be getting mighty creepy."

When he wasn't running blades, Rees haunted the air
ducts that fed into the spaceskiff docking arenas. It was
dangerous stomping ground — docks decompressed all the
nearby air ducts whenever a new skiff came in from one of
the orbiting spaceships.

Rees didn't bother to defend himself. "Some spin my
brains will be sucked straight out my ears and into space."

"What you speeching on about? They obviously already
gone there."

Rees took minor offense. "Control does a ten tick countdown over the voice amp before decompression. That's
enough time to get behind safety barriers. I be a crudrat after
all's said and done — air duct is just another kind of tunnel. I
may not be as fast as you, but I be fast enough to escape
decompression."

"Cocky and crazy. Look at you, with the living-danger-
ously." Maura whistled and rolled her head about
expansively.

"So here I be thinking, if you can't stow away on a big
ship, how about stealing a skiff?"

"Thinking and you – never a good combination." Maura
decided to humor him. "You have a specific skiff in mind?"

"Yeah, actually I do. Follow me."

Maura shrugged. She had nothing better to do at the moment, or frankly, for the rest of her life.

She let Rees squeeze past her and lead the way through the duct. She followed his scrawny backside past the larger branching tunnels leading down to port central, the slightly smaller ones to crossgenetor arenas, and the narrow clean lines leading to progenetor hotels and clubs, until she felt like they'd been crawling forever.

At a main tunnel hub, where a whole bunch of ducts met, up, down, and in at the sides, Rees paused.

Then with sudden decisiveness he dove forward over the edge. He used one of the ladder bars from an up-tunnel to swing himself over the hub-gap and slide, head first, into one of the smaller tributaries below and across. It was one of few tunnels that wasn't white or silver, but black. Maura grimaced at the color, but followed.

In the smaller tunnel the air was more compressed, making it louder and with a low whistle to it. That whistle, with its a high single tone ringing throughout the port, caused more than one planet-born sucker to go mad. Maura and Rees were born to it. Silence, now that might drive them crazy. Crawling one after the other, the noise made conversation near impossible. So they said nothing.

The black tunnel made Maura nervous. Black tunnels meant military, the steel Spoke – armigers. Not generally a Spoke of the Wheel rejects went looking for. Maura had been in lockup a couple times, caught out for vagrancy like most rejects. Licensing chip got her out, but the experience didn't endear her to armigers one iota. Now she'd no licensing chip, a catching would go ill.

Still she followed Rees to one of the armiger docking areas.

Maura looked at Rees, respect in her angled silver eyes. "You *do* like to live dangerously," she yelled over the duct whistle.

The tunnel angled downwards. The two rejects switched tactics and began to climb down its sides, like four legged spiders, using the joins and seams as foot and hand holds. Where others would have slid or fallen, the crudrats were as confident as murmels. They'd had no lessons, no learning, no family life, no professional training, naught to do since their own traitorous bodies first rejected the citizen implant. They'd had no play but what the ducts provided, no work but what they could scare up begging and crudratting. Tunnel running, crawling, climbing the metal of a spaceport's bones – that was what they did. It was what they were.

Eventually, the duct ended.

Maura and Rees crouched down on a tiny ledge that surrounded the round slatted bottom where it fed air down. It was one of a hundred other vents. Through the grated bottom they could see the armiger dock arena spread below them: a huge arched room, leveled off in areas with skiff clamps and towing machines. A few authorized civilians bustled about – subgenetor deck and maintenance crew in brown vests and trousers over white shirts, but most of the people below wore crisp military red and gold. The only major exception was a gaggle off to one side, surrounding the strangest looking spaceskiff Maura had ever clapped eyes on. That gaggle all wore white.

Involuntarily, Maura flinched. *They can't see me here. I'm far above them in one air duct among many.* Those white robes frightened the breath right out of her.

"Sequensors." She found her voice at last, but it was changed to a hiss by rushing fear. "I always thought they were like comets — traveling alone and like to destroy anything that got too close. But there's near on a half dozen or so down there. All together!"

"Sometimes they's more like asteroids, I guess." Rees wasn't as scared as he should be.

Sure is a waste of good white material, thought Maura, getting over her fear a little. She was offended by the largess of those sequensor robes – all for show. They wore the darn things over proper highstock suits – matched tails and trousers, white vest and shirt, white cravat tied high and stifling. Of course, everyone spaceside wore a suit of some kind, modesty demanded it. *'Sept us rejects. They're lucky to get a rag shirt and knickerbockers. What if the scythers stopped working? Everyone would take up all floaty-like. Those robes would be pretty darn undignified then.* Maura smiled. Those sequensors must be awful warm with all that clothing. Maybe that's why they take on more than their fair share of meanness. Maura had never seen a sequensor she didn't think would serve the universe better by being all-over dead.

"They brought in that crazy alien boat this morning," said Rees. "They ain't left off prodding it all shift."

Maura raised an eyebrow at him.

"I like to check out the docks pre-shift before hitting the scythers." He tugged on a tuft of his blue hair in embarrassment. "But it ain't the sequensors I brought you to goggle at, it's that boat they got their peepers fixated on."

Maura squinted at the odd skiff. For a small landing craft it sure was about the weirdest she'd ever clapped her silver eyes on. It looked *nothing* like the military fighters squatted around it. They were all chubby almond-shaped worker-beasts. The alien craft was almost boxy, with a flattened nose. Strangest of all, it had no visible scythers. Yet it was too skinny for a single scyther to be running down its center like in big spaceships. Not only unusual, then, but puzzling for the tech-heads. How did it get through space without scything? *No wonder the sequensors were all a'cluster.*

"How's it move with no scyther?" Maura asked.

"Look close at the hull, see all them smallish tubes? The ones like veins running along it?"

Maura squinted down through the grating and nodded. Instead of a smooth outer hull like the fighters, the skiff was corrugated, ridged with thousands of tubes running along its surface.

"I been thinking – them's baby scythers. Who knows how they keep 'em from clogging with crud. But that's the best explanation I can roster up without getting in any closer. Looking in detail seems a problem for everyone, leastways me."

As they watched, one of the sequensors tapped at the flat nose of the skiff with a tool. The spaceboat shivered, like a murmel with an itch. A crack sound echoed 'round the dock arena. The white robe caught air as the sequensor was thrown violently backwards by some invisible force.

Maura tisked. "Poor landing. He should have somersaulted to take some of the motion off his joints. What do they teach them in sequensor school these ticks?"

Rees laughed. "They be trying to get inside when I left for the tunnels."

The sequensor picked himself up. His movements were jerky with either pain or anger. Since sequensor implants were modified for enhanced abilities, including pain suppression, Maura figured it was anger. He brushed at the wrinkles in his precious robe and retrieved his cane with every sign of annoyance.

Maura's up-tilted eyes sparked in amusement as she glanced over at Rees. "That one looks mad as all get up."

Rees agreed. "If you ask me, they all are. I'm thinking they want alien tech more than most else in the universe. Always stealing what's best for the good and profit of the Wheel, you know how *that* song goes."

Maura nodded. "Almost as much as they don't want the aliens who made it to come visiting. So Rees, my whiz-type friend, if the sequensors can't get inside, how you be thinking I might?"

Rees shrugged. "I always had an overblown sense of your skills. Ain't no one never ran a scyther the way you do. There's magic to it."

"Well," Maura looked serious, reached cross the tunnel mouth, and clapped her little friend on the shoulder, "When I manage to steal it, I be certain-sure that magic of mine will augment all my vast training in pilot academy."

Rees snorted at her.

Maura had no training to speak of, let alone piloting. She couldn't fly a spaceship any more than she could breathe in the vacuum of space.

Rees knew it. "Well, *you* got any better ideas 'bout life without crudratting?"

"I was rather thinking of withering away and dying young."

"Very positive."

They watched the sequensors below them in silence for a while. Watched them try, over and over again, to crack into that alien boat. It was a real pleasure to see how frustrated this made them.

"I wonder what happened to the alien what owns that there skiff." Maura rubbed a spec of crud out of her eye.

"Nothing good. Unless it was smart enough to stay inside."

Maura nodded.

Something chittered softly above her head and Maura felt a sudden weight on one shoulder. A blue fuzzy tail wrapped itself about her neck, almost choking her.

"What you doing here?"

The murmel leaned around and twisted his head to stare meaningfully into her face out of large pale blue eyes. He twitched his whiskers back and forth coquettishly, his breath acrid with the smell of partly digested crud.

Rees looked up and grinned. "Guess when foreman chucked you out of crudratting he chucked him out too."

"We both lost our job, huh?" Maura scratched the beastie beneath his fuzzy chin.

The murmel chattered agreement.

"It's your choice, small one. There's always work for murmels. Leastways, hush up, were watching." The blue creature did as he was told. Maura bent once more over the slatted grating of the duct.

Below them one of the sequensors had pulled out a sonic gun, and was aiming it at the spaceboat. This produced a virulent argument with the sequensor who'd been thrown earlier.

White robes swished about in a seething mass for a while. It was darn scary to watch — augmented people with high-end traits and triggered for superior abilities, grappling with one another. It was all speed and muscle. Eventually, one sequensor grabbed the trumpet of another's gun and yanked it down.

The other jerked away violently, aimed the gun once more, and fired full on the ship.

The sonic whine echoed around the port dock, a higher more ear-piercing shriek than even a murmel could make.

The murmel, crouched on Maura shoulder, seemed mighty impressed by the sound.

Everyone stilled. The sequensors stopped fluttering about,

their robes settling in long drapes from shoulder to feet. Deckhands and other subgenetor lackeys paused in their various labors to turn and stare. A group of progenetor bucks, disembarking a shiny pleasure yacht, turned in a body to sneer at whomever had made such an uncouth noise. Aristocrats of the highest order, their triggered appearances explained it all – tall toppers, high cravats, shiny boots – except what they were doing in a military zone.

Maura, Rees, and the murmel hardly dared breathe. Well, Maura and Rees hardly dared breathe, the murmel found a bit of crud lodged in the pad of one paw and began nibling at it.

Nothing happened for a few ticks, and then the alien ship emitted a high keening whirr, shuddered, and released an amplified sonic wave back at the sequensors. The scream was so loud it shook the entire docking area and probably the rest of the spaceport as well. The sequensors ate deck. Canes scattered.

Maura and Rees, along with everyone else, clapped hands to ears in a defensive movement so automatic that decades of sonic gun use hadn't yet trained the pointless instinct out of them.

Rees stumbled forward slightly off his perch. One foot came down onto the duct grating. It buckled, not designed to take even his tiny weight.

Maura lunged. She slammed into him with both hands, pushing him back onto the ledge. She held him steady. With her toes still perched on her side of the ledge, she now bridged the mouth of the duct. She was only just tall enough to do it.

The whole duct swayed ominously.

Below them citizens picked themselves up from where they'd cowered down. The deckhands and other subgenetors all seemed to decide a break was on order. The high-up-mucky-mucks were getting restless with alien tech, and the low Spokes didn't want anything to do with it. They gave up all pretense of continuing with their tasks in the face of such a massive sequensor presence and exotic technology and fled the docking area. The progenetor teens, however, seemed suddenly interested, but even they were not arrogant enough to approach sequensors without out proper authorization. They paused in their disembarkation process and stood in a loose group observing the robed proceedings from a prudent distance. They leaned casually on silver canes, as though watching some sort of blood sport.

Maura looked briefly into Rees's eyes, so close to hers. He nodded to indicate he'd caught his balance. She shifted her center of gravity, rocking back to her side of the ledge. The murmel's weight on her shoulder caused her no trouble. He was a familiar presence in her balance calculations.

Both crudrats crouched back down to look through the warped grating once more. The murmel leaned his little furry-face next to Maura's.

"What in all space makes *you* interested in that there skiff, beastie?"

The alien boat was still shaking.

"It looks angry," said Rees.

The murmel squealed in agitation. Apparently, he didn't take fondly to the look of it.

The skiff began to scream again, not in human tones, or even with sonic power, but the dulcet song of metal against metal.

"Just lovely." Maura covered her ears once more.

Rees's eyes were watering.

The murmel looked ever more impressed.

What they didn't notice was the effect it was having on the fastening of the air duct cover. Already loosened by

Rees's stumble, the high-pitched noise seemed to be shaking the weakened metal links further. Without warning, the grate, including the ledge part on which they stood, gave way.

With crudrat timing, both rejects reached for handholds. Rees's small fingers found purchase, wrapping firmly about a bump of welding in the side of the tunnel. Maura might have been fine, but the murmel panicked. He hurled himself up off her shoulder with such force it threw off her grip. Her fingers missed the duct end and she fell.

The steel Spoke docking arena was certainly not the biggest the spaceport had on offer, but it was military Spoke, so designed to handle a small size battleship if necessary. That meant it wasn't a low ceilinged hanger by any means. The military always did things big, and one of their battleships, built for power not style, would probably take up most of the bay. There currently was *no* battleship in residence. Maura had a nice long way to fall.

There was a fighter docked just below Rees's duct, cutting into the distance somewhat. The military skiff was taller than the alien boat, for it had a large scyther tube riding its back, but it still barely cut her fall down by an eighth. In any event, whether she willed it or nay, Maura was heading straight for it.

Maura was not one to panic, and she'd always fancied a bit of flying. She'd just hoped it'd be in space, inside a spaceship of some kind. Gravity, even artificial gravity, was prone to complicating matters. The fall seemed to happen quite suddenly, but also took a strangely long time to occur. She flipped flat to catch as much air as possible, then upright so she was feet first. She tagged down as briefly as possible onto the hull of the spaceskiff. It jolted her knees so hard it ensured future aches. She somersaulted forwards across the top of the spaceboat using movement to channel velocity. The tumble was off so that she ended up sliding down the side of the skiff's scyther attachment, and then the rest of its hull. She kicked back with both feet near the bottom before the landing gear puffed out, launching into a forward dive. She landed on the floor of the dock in another somersault, coming out of it into a low crouch.

Why, Maura was smug, *that could almost have seemed intentional.*

Far above her, Rees whistled his appreciation in a tone only a few degrees lower than that of the air ducts. Then he vanished up the broken duct and out of sight. The murmel went after him. There was nothing neither of them could do for her now, and they all knew it.

To be a citizen is everything. Rejects are no better than aliens, both being equally contemptible in the eyes of the Wheel.

~ Excerpt from *The Wheel in Motion* by C. Venderseep

Fortunately, the sequensors hadn't noted Maura's spectacular flying descent.

Unfortunately, the group of bucks, paused to watch the antics of the alien skiff, had.

What, space curse it, are they doing docked in the steel Spoke zone instead of all proper velvet carpets and sweet smells 'round progenetor receiving arena?

Whatever the reason, their interest was piqued, and Maura found herself surrounded by tall beautiful people trussed up in some mighty expensive get-ups. It was a combination designed to irritate everyone, including each other. There they stood, the scourge of the universe, all of them eyeing Maura as though she were some new prize specimen purchased at high credit loss down planetside.

"What do we have here? Some exotic spacebird?" The voice was high rank and high tongue, nasal but melodic. *Vocal trigger trait?* Maura wondered. *Or an accident of birth left uncorrected?*

"More like space trash, brother," said a second, similar voice. *Trigger trait then.* The two voices harmonized together in a way only science could manufacture. *Expensive modification, that.*

"Reject," said the first voice, and spat.

"Crudrat. Look at its hair," said a third new voice with no melody to it.

Maura kept her eyes downcast. She risked one quick-silver glance through blue eyelashes at the third speaker. Physical trigger trait on that one – peaked eyebrows tinted bright red. She'd also been given, by accident or design, big dark eyes and long red hair cued back in a gold clasp. Nice and stylish, in a jagged way.

"I didn't know crudrats could fly." The fourth in the group had diamond shaped trigger trait beauty marks, one on each impossibly high cheekbone. He was diamond beautiful to go with it. Genetic mods all the way – those cheekbones of his were sharp enough to cut ceramic composite.

Maura straightened out of her crouch very slowly. She kept her muscles tense and knees loose — running probably her next best option. She did not rise all the way, but only uncurled into a low bow. From that position she risked a slightly longer look at the highstocks.

They seemed around her age but were fit in a way no malnourished crudrat ever could be. They carried progenetor canes, silver tops marked with genetic contract code and parliamentary alliance. They dressed like dandies but no high rank family Maura ever saw skimped on brute training. Maura figured that, standing fully upright, she'd match them in height, but in strength she didn't stand a chance – not against four at once.

Running was looking prettier and prettier.

Then a fifth toff stepped to the front of the group. There was something different about him. *Something more...* Maura stumbled in trying to suss out what it may be... *just more.* His skin had taken the brunt of the triggering. It was perfectly smooth, opalescent grey with a pearly shine.

"The real question is," he said, "what do we do with it now that we've caught it?"

"Dip it for space scabies?" suggested the redhead.

"You want it for your collection, do you?" The diamond one sounded petulant.

"It *is* very unusual." Pearly-skin cocked his head to one side and examined Maura as though she were a new pair of boots in a crossgenetor window display.

"Look at you," said one of the high range voices, "such a dilettante."

"But doll, you can't collect every little stray that falls from above." The one with the winged eyebrows kept a diffident tone. No doubt who was the power spoke of this little wheel.

Pearly-skin lifted his cane and tipped it upward until the end rested under Maura's chin. He used it to force her head up.

"Look at me," he ordered.

Maura looked.

The cane drooped. "Am Vern," he hissed.

The others all rushed around to his side and peered at
Maura's eyes. Hers were triggered, no doubt there. Maura's
eyes had nothing human, nothing *normal*, about them. They
were wide and angled up towards the outside, with extra big
pale silver irises and straight slits where round pupils should
have been. They had ability attached to them too, she
adjusted faster and could see better in the dark. The extra
peripheral vision they afforded had kept her safe from many a
blade.

"It's still a reject," said one of the triggered voices. Then
laughed. "Isn't this priceless? Even those older-spoke-then-
thou Am Verns bleed out a dud once in a while!"

"Am Vern." Pearly-skin's voice stuck on the name like
crud on a blade. He changed his grip on his cane.

Maura was seized by the horrific urge to laugh. Now *that*
was irony. *I'm to be messed about by a fist-load of triggered
toffs for belonging to progenetor stock I know naught of. Am
Vern*, she thought, savoring the name, *thanks for the weird
eyes, but why'd your ugly choices have to come after me
now?* Triggered to be sure, and a spendy one, but wasted on a
child that turned out to be reject. Maura had always known
her stock was high, unlike Rees who only wanted his to be.
Because of her eyes there must be progenetor in her past
somewhere up tall in rank and spoke. She'd just never
thought it would matter to her present. Now it seemed to be
affecting her immediate future.

Pearly-skin struck out with his cane, but not fast enough.
A cane, after all, was only an unsharpened blade. This time
Maura *had* known it was coming.

She twisted. The heavy metal whistled harmlessly
through the place her head had just been. He'd been going for
her Am Vern eyes.

He came at her again, followed by his fellows. They

were a sudden angry mass of starched fabrics and smooth movements. Progenetors didn't fight like normal folk, more like dancers. Armigers call it slippy, for it didn't have a jot of the military brute to it. But it was deadly enough in its elegant way, especially with canes all metal tipped and heavy handled. Maura dodged backwards, letting them think they were cornering her against the hull of a nearby military skiff.

The one with the red eyebrows licked her lips. Maura had thought that this progenetor might be the best of the lot, but the look on that sharp face told Maura the highstock liked violence too much.

Maura gave a little half smile, prey to predator acknowledgement.

The redhead raised her cane, the heaviest of the bunch with the most inscriptions. Maura knew what that kind of cane meant — old family, old money, and nothing to prove. Her kind knew only one thing, what *they* wanted.

But before she or any of the other highstocks had a chance to swing again, Maura jumped to the side and ran several steps along the length of the spaceskiff.

The toffs lurched after her.

Maura leapt up against the side of the fighter, far enough to elude their scrabbling hands. Tapping softly with her feet, to aide ascent, she literally ran up the side of the spaceboat. At the maximum height her small momentum allowed, she twisted, pausing for a moment well out of reach, gripping the smooth metal hull behind her. She looked down at the five progenetors, calculating distance.

Then she pushed forward with hands and feet, using her legs for spring. For a long moment she was flat out, diving over their heads. She tucked and flipped once in the air, landed, and went right into a handspring, keeping her speed up. Then, no more fancy tricks, she ran as fast as she could flat out across the bay.

They'd expect her to go for the ducts, but in situations like this, *predictable* got a girl killed. So Maura aimed for the implant-monitored standard exit instead – *citizen central*. Beyond that she could see silver-blue streamers wending off into the inky dark — beltways used by citizens to cross the spaceport, closed to rejects who had no implant to guide the belt.

Maura ran across the dock gathering speed as she went.

The implant reader was an arch of metal within an open square in the bulkhead. The arch meant there was a corner free at each side at the top, with enough space for a whip-thin girl to slip through. *Just enough.*

Before anyone could stop her, Maura shimmied up the side of the arch, and propelled herself feet first through the gap, twisting her body sideways so her shoulders could fit. She landed on the other side with a soft thud.

The two customs officials sitting watch, sprung to their feet automatically. Brown vests and coarse fabric marked them as subgenetors. It was a military arena, sure, but apparently not so risky a zone as to warrant military guards even with the alien skiff. The two customs officials weren't even armed. *Odd, that.* They looked at Maura, noticed the blue hair, and sat right back down. Crudrat wasn't worth chasing. Crudrat didn't matter. Crudrat was zero security risk, she couldn't get through any other implant-readers anyway.

Maura didn't intend to try. Before her was the opening to one of the huge long tubular coverings under which various beltways sped off. They got anybody who was anybody from where they were to where they wanted to be. Of course, rejects weren't anybody. The entirety of the well-lit plastic that covered the beltway was wired to read implants. Maura could no more use a beltway than she could pilot a spaceskiff.

Instead, she ran to one side of the belt entrance and scaled the high barricading wall there. She twisted on the dismount to grab the top of the wall and slow her momentum and then dropped down into the gutter on the other side.

Under the brightly-lit plastic next to her, the beltway sped off, whisking citizens away on their little private squares of hovering belt and then to one side or another in accordance with the choice their implants dictated. But the gullies on either side of the beltway, littered with garbage and port's end, were reject territory. There outcasts walked the length of the port, slowly, conducting the business of being invisible.

Or, in Maura's case, ran the length of it.

She zipped through that gutter as though it were a scyther tunnel only with people to dodge instead of blades. Not so many people... few crudrats, with blue hair and sullen expressions, a beggar or two not yet spaced for wasting air. *The dregs of the universe, the Wheel's unwanted.*

Maura skittered up one side of the spaceport wall, half run, half climb. She rappelled off, jumping over the gulley and a group of vagrants squabbling at its center, and landing on top of the beltway cover. She leapt up and onwards with barely a pause.

She ran full out for bit longer but then slowed, jogging along the arched top, vaulting the long beams that held the huge cover in place. She felt her body settle into its crudrat breathing pattern, not timed to blades, but timed to the spacing of the beams. Here and there she leaped high and far, bridging a gap where one section of belt ended, dumping passengers off, and another started up again. Sometimes she had to twist her leap, following a curve in the belt or split in the tunnel. Below her, citizens went about their shifts —

people with lives, and jobs, and purpose. People with implants, and clean faces, and nice clothing. And normal-colored hair.

Maura risked a glance back. Not a glimmer of followers. She allowed herself a cautious smile. Even knowing that the Wheel always sought balance and her pride would be due its penance, she was pleased with herself for getting away. *Take that, progenetor genes!* All their triggering, training, and wealth, and their kind still couldn't catch one failed crudrat. She permitted herself pleasure in each easy jump, in the strength that determination, not triggering, had put into her muscles. She had speed, nimbleness, and crudrat training on her side. *Naught can stop me! Except...*

Maura paused and looked down, a quick glance, the kind used by any crudrat, checking for the *shink* of metal. Instead of blade movement she caught a glimpse of the one thing guaranteed to throw off her pace. Below her, inside its plastic tunnel, full of sterile air, sterile life, and bright white light, the beltway had stopped.

Just up and stopped.

The beltway never stops.

All her life on board the spaceport – the entirety *of* her life – and two things were always in motion: scythers and beltways. The one that kept the port in orbit, the other that kept its citizens in motion. Like Spokes within the great Wheel, both were ever tracing their path.

Maura blinked, rubbed at her eyes. The beltway was definitely stopped.

She checked and still no one was following her. She'd like to think the highstock bucks gave up because they figured she knew the spaceport better than they. This place was just their lay-over from one pleasure jaunt to the next. It was her home. But it was more likely that young toffs like

that couldn't stand to set one crystal-cut shoe heel
gutterside.

Maura crouched down, rubbing off the fine sheen of blue
scum from the beltway cover and looked through it.

Some racket had halted the belt below her — a scrabbling
of bodies and screams. The belt squares no longer hovered.
The hum of airflow had quieted. Bright light beat mercilessly
down on a seething mass of forms.

Playing black hole to the center of this galaxy of
unWheel-like chaos was a creature. Not a citizen, not even a
person, a giant velvety-skinned being, looking almost
murmel-like only white in color, and much, much bigger.

An alien!

Maura knew they existed, course she did. After all, way
back in the turns before her body rejected the implant, the
ticks when she belonged, when she'd had stock, she'd also
had learning. About words, and numbers, and past lives, and
aliens. She'd never seen one before, and never in all her turns
expected to. *Certainly not up close and all personal-like,
under bright beltway lights, large as space.*

The alien was under guard, but the armigers weren't
much in the way of useful. The creature was writhing and
roaring — tossing aside military and civilian alike. With so
many citizens all on one place, it was clear no steel Spoke felt
it safe to use a sonic gun. The alien had reach and strength
over every other non-energy weapon.

Maura stared. *Big white ugly is holding its own downright
successful-like.* She'd seen one or two progenetors triggered
to look very strange indeed, but nothing like this. Its velvety
skin wasn't skin at all, but fur — a thick pelt. Its eyes were
fully black as dead space and it stood a head higher at least
than the tallest armiger there.

As she watched, the creature surged forward, shaking off

captors and restraints in one violent movement. It burst out of
the crowd and took off, leaping from one stopped belt square
to another, actually moving *itself* down the halted beltway. It
brushed aside occupants as if they were dust, knocking them
off the belt, to fall onto the air jets below, causing more
screams of outrage, fear, and pain.

Intrigued, Maura shadowed it from above, using easy
speed and simple leaps to keep pace. Free of the hysterical
crowd, the alien moved somewhat like a normal human but
Maura was clearly more comfortable with her run than it was
with the beltway. It made decent time jumping along, but
hadn't a crudrat's easy grace.

Maura kept her eye on the blurry white form through the
beltway cover. Perhaps pup-like? All first-run-awkward and
unsure of the bones. Bigger, of course, so its steps would
never survive blade-time, but still fluid, impressive enough.
The difference being that this creature was grounded, no flips
or wall-runs. But Wheel's Holy Spokes it sure moved fast for
such a hulking thing.

Not fast enough.

Running would do it no good come ticking time. A spaceport couldn't hide anything that size for long. No tunnel big
enough to hold it within reach of the belt, though Maura
could think of few further away. Though that supposed this
alien could escape the beltway. That didn't look to be an
option. *Why bother to run? Surely it knows? Unless, it's as
animal in smarts as it is in looks.*

On her next vault over one of the beltway support beams,
Maura saw a waiting crowd of armigers. The original captors
hadn't even bothered to chase. They'd just called reinforce-
ments while they sorted themselves out.

Poor old alien.

The creature below paused in flight.

Maura paused as well.

The alien glanced up at her, as though it had known all long she followed. A reverse shadow, cast above.

Ah, he's a he. Maura met shiny solid-black eyes through the sheen of crud scum and knew without a doubt that the alien was male. Didn't know how or why, just knew. And intelligent, there was no doubt of that.

Something in his gaze acknowledged her presence, a tiny nod. Like reject to reject, greetings between the chipless, no Spoke customs to dictate speech or social interaction. Then he sped onwards, apparently intending to break through the waiting military with sheer force.

He didn't.

They brought him down with shock batons. His thick fur protected him at first, but it wasn't enough against the number of shockers the armigers prodded into him. The smell of singing fur and the horrible hissing sound from the electric bolts reached even Maura, high above.

Maura leaned over the edge of the beltway gate and settled into watching. Sparks floated upwards in yellow twists. There seemed to be blood on everyone. The alien came fully stocked with claw and teeth as well as fur and didn't seem afraid to apply them with vigor. The shockers sizzled and hissed. The armigers yelled and swore. The creature stayed silent, even under that kind of pain. Impressive. Maura had been shocker-prod once. Once was more than enough.

Then, with a roar of rage, the alien reared away from the painful weapons. It was an animal sound, the howl of some planetside beast that Maura's instinct remembered to fear even though she herself had never been to ground. He threw himself sideways, crashing into the arch supporting the beltway gate and then to the floor. The whole front of the beltway shook violently, and Maura, perched precariously on the edge, tumbled off.

Free fall twice in one spin. Just brilliant. Perhaps foreman was right, I am losing it.

There was no time to compensate this time. Maura plummeted straight down into the crowd of armigers. They were bent over a massive crumpled heap of fallen alien so they didn't see her coming. She tried to twist mid air but hit the red and gold uniforms hard enough to throw off her landing. Almost graceless, she stumbled into a half roll coming up against someone's spit-shined boot.

I'm gonna garner bruises for that one. I'll just add to the day's collection, shall I? Fantastic.

The armigers looked at her long enough to register her blue hair – crudrat – and unimportance – reject – and then went back to the alien. The foot she rested against kicked her hard. The boots were ceramic tipped, military issue and tailored for cruelty. Maura rolled with the kick but still felt her ribs give ominously. She ended up crouched so close to the alien she almost touched him.

Ignoring her, the guards wrestled the creature upright.

Black eyes slitted open.

Eight shockers at once and he wakes three ticks later? Maura stared in amazement.

She hardly dared breathe, crouched so close to such a being. He was different than anything she'd ever known — all fur, and height, and emanating anger she could feel like air through a duct, fierce and constant. When she finally did inhale she caught smell with the anger, so fresh and clean it made her nose all tingly.

Maura sneezed.

The alien lurched in her direction, a jerky, bumbling move. The armigers responded with a surge of frantic activity. In the same instant, Maura felt a large hand grope down her arm. Her skin shivered away. *Alien touch, sure as I live and breathe.* He had a warm dry palm with the feel of felted cloth about it. He pressed something small and hard into her hand. Maura grasped it reflexively. She glanced up, all shock and confusion, into the alien's white face. Sharp black eyes looked down, and then, to her amazement, he winked at her, one white lid down and then up over one black eye.

It's not the vast reaches of nothingness that drive the spaceborn mad. It's the vast loneliness therein.

~ Proverb

Aliens wink.

Maura was momentarily grounded by shock. It seemed like such a human action – winking.

One of the guards struck out at her, in the manner of a man eliminating an inconvenient clump of crud. Maura dodged the strike and spun out of the way into the crowd. She cowered down, trying to make herself as small and uninteresting as possible. It worked. From that vantage point she watched unhindered as the armigers dragged the giant alien away. Only when they were fully out of sight did she look at the object the alien had given her.

It was nothing more than a small card, yellowed metal, thin as fabric, and punctured with a random pattern of swirls. It had a hole at one end and looked as though it was meant to go on a cord. *Jewelry, perhaps? Why so important? But then, who hands importance off to blue-haired strangers at beltway ends? I wonder what it's worth in ration cubes?* Instead of chasing after that line of thought, Maura tucked the card away in a secret fold of her ragged shirt.

She glanced around, furtively. The beltway started up again, as though nothing had happened to bring it down. As though it had never paused at all. People were getting on and off the end platform all around her. No one paid her any mind – rejects are nothing if not invisible. *Wait, that ain't right. Rejects are just nothing.* Maura never thought she'd be grateful for her lack of implant, but saddled with an alien artifact and an uneasy feeling? She took a moment to be thankful that no one thought to see her or take notice of her movements. She climbed over a side barricade, up the far side of the gulley wall, and into the mouth of a small garbage tunnel.

"Where," Maura wondered that evening, "would armigers be stashing a hostile alien critter, do ya think?"

"Aren't all aliens hostile?" Rees looked worn 'round the edges. He had engaged in a bit of a disagreement with the blades last shift. While Maura was running beltways, the blades won. The blades always won. So Rees sported a deep gash in one shoulder. The blood had slowed to a trickle but was still leaking down his arm and staining his shirt and vest. Rees was a bit over-concerned about the state of his vest, torn though it now was. Bleeding irked him something fierce.

Maura shrugged. "I rather think it tends to the other way 'round. Let me see that." She tore off an end bit of one of her own shirtsleeves with her teeth. She was never one to worry much about appearances. She spat on the rag and patted at her friend's gash.

"Purely for my own edification, why would you be needing to know such a thing?" Rees winced under her inept ministrations.

"Ran into one this spin, a few ticks ago. Well," Maura corrected herself, "fell into one, more's like."

"An armiger alien stash?"

"Nope, just the alien himself. Hold still, would you?" Maura wrapped the scrap of fabric around Rees's cut. It was the best she could do.

"Not the alien that came attached to that weird spaceskiff we were looking at earlier, when you chose to take up flying?" Rees tugged at the makeshift bandage.

"Probably. Know of any other alien ships? Stop playing with it. It'll never cure-up if you fuss."

"Brilliant! What'd the alien look like?" Rees left off fiddling with the bandage to stare at Maura intently.

"Large. White." She paused and then added, "Fuzzy."

Rees sighed. "I be all amazement. Your skills at description…unparalleled. I shudder to think how you'd verbalize me."

Maura shrugged.

"So what happened?"

"You mean after the beltway went and stopped?"

"Yes. I mean, no. I mean... the beltway *stopped*?"

Maura nodded and relayed, sparingly, what had occurred last shift. Her recitation left much to be desired. Maura was not the type of person to use two words where one would suffice. This tended to frustrate listeners.

Rees prodded her into as many specifics as possible until both of them were exhausted by his efforts.

Maura felt like she'd told him everything. Except the bit

where she ended up holding the alien's metal card thingy. It was a small secret flatness tucked into her chest band.

She ended her story with, "You're the intrepid explorer, where do you think the guns would go stashing an alien?"

"Section eight-oh-five. No thinking on it needed. That'd be high risk lockup," Rees answered, without blinking.

"Sure?"

Rees nodded. "Certain sure. 'Tis the only section I haven't been able to crack into yet."

Maura smiled. "Perfect."

Rees escorted her 'round to section eight-oh-five the very next morning.

"Sure you're wanting to be doing this?"

They were crouched at a massive duct hub. Tunnels, like rays of sunlight in space, beamed off before them in every direction.

Maura looked at him. She felt gloomy. For the first time in five cycles she wasn't heading with him to scyther level. For the first sleep shift in five turns she hadn't dreamt of blades. The universe felt all akilter, as though the spaceport wasn't spinning straight.

"What else would I be doing?"

Rees shrugged. "Trying for survival instead of risking it? This ain't no time to develop a curiosity."

Maura gave him a funny look. He was one to talk.

"Did you not hear the part about the alien? You know, here? On our spaceport." Without pausing for answer, Maura climbed down and swung herself through the hub into a tunnel across the way. Its mouth was black-tinted where the others were silvery blue.

She turned back, waved at Rees, part farewell, part dismissal.

Rees shook his tufted head and then turned to crawl back down the tunnel away from the military Spoke and toward blades and licensed work. He looked small and forlorn without her.

Maura crawled though the darkness. Usually, on a spaceport, all the ducts went blue tinged from ambient crud in the air. Crud liked metal and loved plastic static so tended to stick where it could. But military ducts were black, so there was no way to note its presence. The black also made the tunnel more than normally difficult to navigate. *Part of its purpose*, Maura supposed.

Eventually, she came up short against a thick grate, barring her way. The tunnel was so much darker than her regulars that she ran straight into it and spent a long moment rubbing at the top of her head and swearing all her most colorful swears into the indifferent blackness.

She pushed up against the grating, working her fingers through and lifting. Nothing. She pushed it downwards, pulled it toward herself, and then tried shifting it from side to side. Still nothing. With a sigh, she felt about the edges where it connected to the tunnel wall.

Then she grinned.

The steel Spoke was so predictable. When were they going to suss the fact that tunnels weren't walkways?

They'd put the barrier in as though it were a door — bolted on one side and locked, but hinged on the other. Hinges were all well and good when fastened into a nice solid bulkhead, but became something of a security risk when fastened into the thin curving metal of an air duct. And these hinges weren't even welded.

She scrabbled a bit, twisting at the hinge fasteners and

banging against the tunnel wall around them to weaken the metal. Eventually, she worked the hinge base loose enough to rip right out. She pushed hard against side of the grate, buckling it on the bolted side. It bent enough for her to squeeze through.

She wondered if that was the best security they had. True, no one worried overmuch about rejects in tunnels. *What could we possibly want or do to the all-powerful of the Wheel's finest?* In a strange way, Maura and her fellow non-citizens had more freedom portside than any real person ever did — no implant checkers, no gateways, no debit points, no credit counts. Still, technically, it was supposed to be armiger business to worry about security of *everyone*, even rejects. Of course, once every cycle or so, they noticed a plague of non-citizens slouching about sucking down air. Sometimes they swept the station for vagrancy, tossed everyone they could into lock-up, spaced the useless rejects, and let the licensed crudrats go. Crudrats, at least, served a purpose. Sometimes they went in for a kind of mass extermination program — tunnel-wide toxic gassing. The rest of the time, they forgot rejects existed.

Maura crept on, into the black. She felt the metal beneath her knees change texture from smooth to beveled. Gratings appeared in the floor. Around a sharp bend in the duct, Maura paused at a larger than normal grate. Dim light came up through the rectangular slats. She peeked through.

Below her was a tidy dispatch office. Gold and red clad armigers, all stiff-necked formality, mingled amongst subgenetor workers manning scanpads and screens. Maura cocked her head to listen through the rush of duct air, ciphering out words and conversation.

"Alien... maximum security..." A neatly clad clerk of

some kind, in a three-piece suit and bowler hat, tapping at a board covered in numerical notations.

"What *are* they thinking…?" Another clerk, less well dressed, sucking down a protein drink.

"Six-sev-oh-two… status?" A buzz through one of the audio dispatches, followed by a flicker on a screen. The image of some high-up mucky-muck armiger. There was a massive fringe of gold at the shoulders of her uniform and gold braid about her collar.

"Did what…? On my shift…?" A guard, to another guard, looking annoyed.

"Sequensors… full report." A dispatch operator, to the fringe-riddled woman on the screen.

"Tell them… clearance codes… skiff… full custody."

"What do we do with it? Won't talk…" Maura perked up at that.

"… even intelligent?"

Maura pulled the alien's small square of perforated metal out from her chest band and twirled it between her fingertips. *Intelligent?* She wondered on that point herself. *Had the alien really winked back beltside? Or did I imagine it?* She shifted around to try and spot the people talking about the alien. In one corner of the room, a group of guards crowded together looking down at a scanpad. On the pad's screen Maura could make out the image of the alien… a faint white blob pacing a small cell.

Wherever he is, one thing never fails in its portside truth — there has to be air flowing to him.

There came a loud roar and the dull thud of flesh against bulkhead. The guards with the scanpad took off down a side corridor. There was a lot of yelling and few more thuds. One of the armigers returned with a colleague draped over her shoulder, both looking a little the worse for some serious encounters with a large unyielding surface. The draped guard was lowered onto a bench while a subgenetor clerk scampered off after a med kit. She slumped to one side and had to be propped up against a large monitor screen.

"Doesn't respond any differently to females then?" said one of the high rank administrative staff.

The injured guard gave him an evil glare. "Apparently not."

"It was worth a try. Some alien cultures have gender dysmorphic treatment attitudes. Or so I've read." The progenetor, who seemed to be in nominal charge of the dispatch office, looked unrepentant.

"Well, not this one. It doesn't seem to care what sex it hits, so long as it hits." The female guard spat out blood onto a wiping cloth.

Maura noted the direction of the corridor down which they'd all run. She swung herself over the grating and crawled on through the black air duct. Behind her the dispatch maintained a high-pitched buzz of annoyed voices.

One of the side effects of being a reject was pretty good spatial orientation skills – what the crudrats called *sussing the ducts.* The tunnel Maura crawled through turned and twisted and backtracked on itself for a while before emerging into a small hub. Without qualms, Maura select a duct, one to her far right and squeezed inside. It was a tight fit. Truth be told, she really was getting too big for reject life, let alone crudratting. *What will I do when I'm too tall to handle tunnels? Join the bums gutterside scrounging in beltway muck? Fantastic future. Blast my trigger traits.* As if in response to that thought, Maura cracked one boney knee on the tunnel lip.

She inched through the smaller duct, squirming on her belly now. It was slow going, plus she had to pause every few lengths to press her ear to the floor. For a long time she heard nothing but the screaming rush of air. Then she began to hear the intermittent sounds of roaring and yelling. Eventually, both became so loud she could hear it easy all around her and didn't need to pause.

Like all air ducts, this one was fitted with multiple vents at various points. None were as large as the floor grating she'd looked through onto the dispatch room. These were no bigger than her hand — round, with small dropped caps. There was no way to look through them. But she still found the right one.

There was a pattern to imprisonment portside. Maura knew it well. Armigers weren't above pulling crudrats in for vagrancy, especially if things were slow and they wanted the sport. Maura was usually nimble enough to evade capture, even from a steel Spoke with implant-adapted reflexes. But three times she hadn't. Twice she'd been nabbed off shift, just having run the blades, all tired-tissue and sleepy-brain.

Maura knew their pattern. They locked you up, mucked you about for a few hours, and then let you alone. *That last, by far the scab end of a bad lot.* Solitary brought out the worst in the spaceborn. Places where folk could up and *live* in all the vacuumed vastness came few, far between, and tight fitting. People got accustomed to one another. A couple spins in solitary and most spaceborn would just about do anything the armigers asked. But armigers liked to a do a thing right and proper, so they generally started with torture anyway, for form's sake.

Maura listened at the vent a bit, while the latest batch of armigers tried their questions out on the alien below.

He answered them, regardless of the question, with roars and violence.

I wager solid rations that he's playing them.

Maura hung about a moment longer, while they tried

their tortures on that thick white fur. Up though the vent came the dull buzz of shockers, the beep of electrical devices, and the thud of weapon against pelt-covered flesh. The alien seemed impervious to whatever they could muster up, advanced tech or planetside basics. Not that it was at all clear that if he talked, he'd speak space-tongue, or saying anything of value.

Then a group of sequensors turned their unwelcome selves up.

Even though she couldn't see, Maura could tell from their highbrow talk and assumption of command what Spoke they sat on. She could imagine those white robes, swishing about heavy boots and hard attitudes. *White as the alien's fur. And all tied up in their own purity and righteousness.*

"What's been done here?" asked one of them, imperious and nasal.

"Just some light electroshock, and basic application of force, no permanent damage – we think." The armiger who answered sounded sullen.

"Oh, is *that* all," the response was full sarcasm.

"Why is it the military must be so perpetually lacking in subtlety?" A different sequensor wanted to know.

"Now, wait just a tick... !" That was an armiger.

"Enough. We will take over the inquiry from here."

"Enemy infiltration is our jurisdiction," a different armiger objected.

"And any clear threat to the integrity of the Wheel is ours. This creature is a danger to all we believe and hold sacred — an abomination, a chipless barbarian from heretic space. Aliens are, by the very definition of the word, sequensor provenance. Now, all of you — out."

The sound of rustling and the clang of the cell door indicated the guns had departed. Maura could imagine their expressions. But even the military bent under sequensor authority.

"There now, isn't that better? We can have a proper talk," said nasal sequensor.

The alien growled low in his throat. It was not a nice noise. It made Maura's spine cringe.

"No need to act the beast with me," said the sequensor, all kindness absent from his tone. "The Wheel has little outside contact as a general rule of spiritual mandate, but I'm from alien tech special investigations branch. We know of the outside universe. The study of aliens is sometimes necessary." The voice paused. "Disgusting, but necessary."

The alien growled again.

There was a long drawn out silence. Maura could hear a low hissing. She did not know its cause, but it resulted in the alien letting out a small, low, whimper. It was a sad tiny sound from such a large creature.

The sequensor continued. "Your kind calls itself the Kill'ki, and you're a perfectly sentient polymorph of the master genotype, entirely capable of speaking space-tongue. So talk!"

The alien said nothing.

The low hiss sounded again.

Maura shuddered as the imprisoned creature let out another baby whimper. It may be sequensors playing their game below her but it was the same pattern as that of the armigers — talk, torture, talk. The pain was just quieter.

Maura was feeling oddly disconnected. *The problem with the Wheel and its ways,* she thought – not for the first time, *is how little imagination or originality runs along its Spokes. Even torture is mundane.*

More time passed and still the alien would speak nothing more coherent than a growl or a whimper. Stubborn.

Finally, after what seemed an interminable age, the sequensors appeared to give up. Opting for isolation, they decided to leave the alien on his lonesome for a few ticks. Maura heard the door clang and quiet descend.

They'll cover over the door of the cell with blacking plastic and turn off all the lights. Leave the poor creature to rot in darkness and silence, until he thinks better on his stubbornness and makes with speech.

Maura groped about the edge of the air vent below her, feeling for how it was attached. Then she pulled out the flat metal card the alien had given her, flicking her nail against it to test its stiffness. Strong enough.

Using one sharp corner, she began to unscrew the fasteners that held the vent cover in place. It took careful precise work in the darkness, the card kept slipping, but it was ridged and thin enough for the job. As she undid the last screw, she expected the vent cap to fall down into the alien's prison with a clang.

Instead, it was lifted away by a large white paw.

The cell below was very dimly lit, but less dark than Maura's tunnel. Her vision took a tick to adjust. She found herself looking down through the small round opening, into the impossibly dark eyes of the alien. That nothingness of space without stars again. But one of them *had* winked at her. This gave Maura courage.

"Ah," said the alien with satisfaction, in perfect well rounded space-tongue, "'tis you. Good."

5

The only thing less friendly than spaceborn folk is spaceborn talk.

~ Proverb

So he speaks all ear-easy and proper-normal in the end. And he's considerable less fuzzy-then I thought.

Face to face the alien wasnt covered in a pelt of fur per say, more a fine sheen of teeny-tiny hairs. It reminded Maura of those pile cloth rugs the highstocks had outside their fancy hole-ups in the upmarket section of spaceport. 'Cept these hairs grew out skin instead of floor. Maura stared, figuring the alien wouldn't take offense at close inspection from a reject, being pretty much reject himself. She could make out that each impossibly thin hair wasn't white at all but clear. And his skin underneath was black. Strange that he looked so very white under beltway lights. She gave a little mental shrug. *Guess that's what makes him alien.*

The cell they'd put him in was small enough for Maura to

think it restrictive – and she was used to spending her ticks in *tunnels* and other tiny places. He, bigger than any citizen of the Wheel, brushed the ceiling of the cell with the top of his head. All he had to do was tilt his neck and look up, and they were eye to eye though the vent hole.

"You can talk," said Maura, inanely.

"Yes, brilliance, this one eats and sleeps, too." His voice was a deep growling rumble.

Ah, thought Maura, *that kind of alien.* She could play verbal games as well as the next outcast. After all, she had Rees as a friend.

She said, with just enough exasperation, "Whoa there, Fuzzy. We're not knowing each other well enough yet for sarcasm. First we talk, then maybe we eat, a bit of escape action, some tunnel time, then you can put on mean speech."

The alien grumbled. "This one has siblings, non-enemy. This one must stay in practice."

Maura sniffed. "It ain't a necessity for me to be helping. You are realizing that, non-human? I could be…"

The alien interrupted her, offended. "This one is as human as you, Wheel-child!"

Oh, really? Maura looked skeptically at the black eyes and fur-covered body.

"Just fuzzy?" she suggested.

The alien grinned. Or Maura *thought* he grinned, his eyes crinkled up, but that was all she could see of him.

"Ice planet seeding will do that to the genome," he explained.

"Right." Maura wasn't particularly interested in his groundside origins. "Look here, Fuzzy. I could turn myself right around, well, *squirm* myself right around, and inch on back up this here duct and get moving with my sad little life. I ain't doing this for fun, you understanding me? So you treat

me straight-up 'til I done got the spin of it, then well see
who's better at cheap talk."

Those shiny black eyes blinked at her. "Galactic common
is but one of four different languages this one speaks, non-
enemy. And it was certainly not the most difficult to learn.
This one did not mean to offend your odd blue-haired ways."

"No offense taken," Maura brushed all apologies aside,
"'tis merely causing a breach in efficiency."

The black eyes narrowed. "Ah, we are under battle
orders?"

Maura did not understand.

"You are *wari*, a professional fighter, non-enemy?" The
alien seemed to also be confused. "You move like *wari*, you
fall like *wari*. Perhaps not a *domina*, your ways are more of a
scout, all slick and stealth. This one is not so young he has
not seen your kind amongst my people."

"Wheel born blue-haired crudrats be running rampant
amongst the fuzzies down ice planet-ways?" Maura felt a
spike of hope. *Is there some refuge to be found amongst white
furred aliens?*

The alien clicked his tongue. "Not your outside look, non-
enemy, your inside feel. This one has seen your kind of
person within my own people."

Maura shook her head. "I be no warrior Spoke, what we
call *armiger*. I be reject any way you turn it. I was crudrat
until yesterday."

"These words are Wheel words?"

Maura scrabbled for a way space-tongue might convey
the right kind of rejection. "I be having no implant. I be
outcast, chipless, beneath notice... non-citizen."

"Ah. You are free."

Maura blinked. *How to get an alien to understand?* "But I
have no rights, no money, no stock, no purpose. There be no

role for me to play in the Wheel's turning. Not on any Spoke."

"It is a strange kind of freedom, but freedom nonetheless." The alien was obtuse.

Maura gave up. "You be having any kind of useable name there, Fuzzy?"

The alien reared back. "Now who is rude, asking this one his *name*!"

"Ah. Your kind don't go in for the giving out of names?"

"Yours do?"

Maura smiled. "I be Maura." Then she remembered the progenetor bucks in the armiger docking area, and added, to test the taste of it in her mouth, "Maura Am Vern." *Here I go giving out my full name for the first time in all my turns, and to an alien that don't want it. Odd way for the universe to arrange itself.*

The alien gasped. Then he closed his black eyes as though in pain. "Your trust humbles me, non-enemy."

"My name means nothing to me."

The alien looked truly troubled by that. "But what of your *gens*, your family, little blue? Now that this one knows your name, this one knows your kin, your line, your allegiances." She noticed he deliberately continued not to use her name.

"Ah, I see the source of the misunderstanding. I have no family. Those of us without the implants, we get rejected in every way from the Wheel. Including family."

The alien was flabbergasted. "But the way you move. You would make a fine fighter, perhaps a little scrawny, but good for specialty work and perhaps…" He left off that statement, whatever it was. "They turn you out simply because your body will not accept that abomination mod of sequensor making? This one begins to think there is much our anthropologists neglected to report in their studies of your culture."

The alien spoke as though he were no alien at all. As though the Wheel were all over alien instead. "We know of the rejects, of course. But we didn't know the extent to which they were rejected for not taking on that cyborg implant. What happens to you?"

"Some of us become crudrats."

The alien nodded. "Sometime you must explain that term further. This one has never before heard the word *crudrat*. And the others without kin?"

Maura shrugged. "Spaced, starved, imprisoned, left out to die. Regardless, I'll be needing to call you somewhat. Unless you be liking *Fuzzy*."

The alien paused as though he was actually entertaining this suggestion.

"It is odd to pick one's own talk-name. Especially when you have gifted your real name, little blue." A pause. "Quoin," he said at last. "It is, how you might say, a ranking. This one will respond to that, well enough."

"And do you be an armiger, quoin? A *wari*." Maura tried wrapping her tongue around the alien words.

"In training, little blue."

"Just *Maura* will do well enough. And that there training brings you floating 'round Wheel space, does it?"

The alien snorted. "There was a bit of an upset. A nasty spit of bad luck and things got out of hand. Thus this one finds himself in a muddle. One should, of course, be able to extract oneself from all difficulties. However, in this instance, a little assistance might be desirable."

"I should say so," agreed Maura. "Why you pick me for a helper?"

He looked at her as though she were insane. "Because you are free." He paused as though consciously stopping himself from saying something more. "This one saw you running above me, outside the range of those damnable implant readers. This one can pay. Mine is a strong line, with plentiful kinship ties."

Maura blinked. "Pay?"

"In the currency of my own kind or that of those outside Wheel space. This one does not have a Wheel implant nor its interlinking credit system. But there are other kinds of payment."

Maura scratched her nose thoughtfully. "What kinds in particular?" She was thinking fondly of extra ration cubes.

"Hard currency, soft currency, trade goods." He would have continued but Maura interrupted him. Rees's ideas bounced around in her brain.

"Safe passage?"

The alien cocked his head. "To where, little blue?"

Maura considered a moment. She knew nothing of the worlds outside the Wheel. So far as the sequensors were concerned, no one ever left the Wheel and no one ever joined it. It spun its solitary way through the universe. True citizens stuck to the Spokes in every way, through implant and choice and beyond. Progenetors learned somewhat of the enemies that abounded and surrounded Wheel space, and armigers learned a little more for fighting purposes, but Maura turned reject well before her teaching drone got on to those particular threats. To leave the Wheel had never before really been an option, despite Rees's overactive imagination.

"It might be nice to visit an ice planet."

The alien paused. "You want to come home with this one?"

He made it sound like she was some sort of murmel, a pet he was being forced to adopt.

Maura decided she liked this new scheme almost as much

as she disliked his tone. "You want my help, *quoin* Fuzzy, or not?"

The alien sighed. "The *domina* will have this one's pelt for supper. Very well." He gave a funny nod and then blew a puff of breath up at her. "Bonded."

Maura shrugged, and pursing her lips, blew breath back at him. "Bonded," she said, liking the sound of the word.

"Right," said the alien, "here's what this one is thinking might be the best approach."

A good while later, Maura squirmed back up the tight air duct. Her brain was a-buzz with instructions, ideas, and half formed plans. Not for the first time she wished she had the implant if only to help her mind process the excess information. She held tight to the little metal card. Fuzzy hadn't wanted it back. Much good it would do, he'd said, without freedom. A *keycard*, he called it. Now Maura knew what it was meant to do, she was determined to be even more careful with its safety. In fact, what she had to do immediately was hide it in a secure place.

She crawled into the duct hub and considered for a moment. Then with a sigh she swung herself across. She was exhausted, but the keycard was a weight of responsibility she'd as soon not carry further in space or time. So instead of heading home to her nest, she took the largest of the many silver-blue tunnels towards engineering.

It was sleep shift. Only a skeleton crew occupied the scyther bay. Back-up tunnels were whirring and four sleepy foremen ran small groups of crudrats through their paces at the far end of the long row of scythers. This kept enough scythers running to maintain orbit, which was all they need bother with during nighttime ticks.

Maura crouched at the edge of an air duct and looked down at the lay of space. She waited for the perfect moment. Like breathing along with the swish of blades, there was a pattern to the movement of people about their allocated tasks. Everyone had their route to walk, their motions to execute, their interactions with others to chart: a practiced dance. Eventually, most of the subgenetor ground crew moved towards their break area – half way through shift. At that same time, several crudrats tumbled from tunnels and carried their murmels over for weighing. The foremen followed, and the waiting 'rats looked on with interest – wondering who'd get the bonus that shift. With everyone occupied, Maura slid out of the duct and sauntered casually over to the nearest scyther. No one yelled for her to stop. No one even noticed her presence. It was hard to move around engineering without tripping over a 'rat somewhere. They lowered the caliber of the whole bay but were a necessary disfiguration.

Maura took a deep breath, measuring the weight of the air in her lungs, calming her mind of everything. Then she leapt inside the scyther.

The blades were dangerously clean. Maura took a split second to look around the blue tinged metal interior. It must of have been one of the last scythers run previous shift. Blades moved that much faster when they were clean, but they also moved more predictably.

Shink.

Maura ducked and twisted. Her body remembered what to do, like she'd stopped only yesterday.

Oh, wait, I did stop only yesterday.

The blade came in at her side, chopping toward her ribs.

Maura sprang up the opposite tunnel wall, running with her body almost parallel to the floor. She sprang away at the last, back flipping over a lower blade to land soft and silent on the opposite side of the tunnel. If only she'd run so tidy when she'd been a 'rat, things might be different. But then again, this time she was under no time constraints, and she had only her own skin to think on.

She dove under the next blade. It felt strange not to worry about a murmel on her back. Her weight and balance calculations shifted. It made the run a little easier. But for all that, she missed her little friend's chitters. She'd never run the blades without him along.

Shink. Shink. Shink.

She twisted, vaulted a side blade, tumbled under a high one, and then bounced up and spun to the left. The next blade came in low and she flipped over it, twisting at the last so she could look back the way she'd come. Her landing was gentle as spaceskiff in zero gravity. No sound from her feet and not a chance of a dent in the tunnel floor. She snaked her head up to peer back through the whirring blades. No one was following her.

Perhaps I'm not so old nor so sloppy. She twisted to face forward once more. Only to leap back away from a top down blade twirling to one side.

Shink.

Up came a blade from below, with unscooped crud behind its hinge, making it wobble slightly. Some crudrat hadn't culled this tunnel properly. *Amateur*, thought Maura, tut-tutting to herself at the failure.

Shink.

Breathe.

An upper blade cut. Maura drove herself down, sliding forward across the tunnel floor on her stomach. She popped herself up with a heave of hands into a sideways spin to avoid a blade from the left. She landed in a crouch, briefly out of harm's way and took a breather looking cautiously around. She'd never known whether it was intentional design or not, but most scythers had a wait spot halfway along their length. Under tick restraints, she'd never been able to take advantage before, but this time she did.

It was peaceful there. The light from tunnel-end throbbed as blades passed rhythmically before it, giving the impression of some living thing's throat pulse. Everything was a dim blue color, filled with whirling specks of fresh crud and no sound but the humming *shink* of deadly blades.

There.

Maura rocked forward onto the balls of her feet. Getting grip with her toes, she ran up the side of the tunnel until she was perched near the top, far above a side blade. There was a small repair in the tunnel at that point, the consequence of some now-dead crudrat's mistake. It sported a half-out screw, coated in old crud. It had jarred Maura's scraper on more than one occasion and she remembered it with loathing.

Perfect, she grinned. She took out the keycard on its long thin cord and looped it about the screw, wedging the card itself under the collected crud between screw and welded seam. It lodged there, hidden from view.

She slid back down the tunnel wall, feeling bereft. Now all she had to do was retrieve the card before the next cleaning run. Fuzzy's grand escape scheme was now on a time limit. From here on out, if they weren't spot on, all her hopes would probably end up in some murmel's belly.

She turned back the way she'd come, took a deep breath, and headed for the tunnel exit, dancing the blades.

Shink. Shink. Shink.

6

Shopping: a progenetor's last great duty to the Wheel.

~ From Claudicix's *Advice to Young Progenetors*

Maura oozed out the scyther tunnel and sauntered back towards the air ducts. Any moment she expected to be collared by a steel Spoke, but no one stopped her. Subgenetors continued about their business and some crisis with the crudrats down scyther end had everyone else's attention.

Maura headed back to her nest — a bend in two ducts near the low-market crossgenetor arena. It wasn't a bad place to kip, warmer than the tunnels that ran to private residencies, and slightly bigger, but less private. She expected to find the murmel waiting for her. He usually chose to sleep curled in her small pile of stuff, which was good as she didn't own a pillow and he didn't mind if she used him as one. She did find the murmel, but there was someone else sleeping with him. Someone the murmel didn't particularly like, as the blue beastie was sitting some distance away with his back to the interloper.

"Rees?"

No response. The lump in her turf did not bother to move.

Maura inched closer. *Too big to be Rees and with hair too long as well.*

She poked the person's side and then skittered back.

The sleeping form shifted and Ger's sharp pointed face blinked up at her. "You not dead yet?"

"Evidently not." Maura shifted her weight to her knees to better free up both hands. Covertly she looked about, no weapons handy. Small tunnels were no place to fight, but still, this was *her* nest. She wasn't gonna let it sink into anyone else's mitts, let alone Ger's.

The murmel scampered over to her. His long blue tail was lashing back and forth, a sure sign of annoyance. Maura wasn't sure if he was annoyed at her for the late return, or at Ger for messing with precedent.

The little creature leaned affectionately against her legs and patted at her knickerbockers, grooming the creases for bits of crud. *Annoyed with Ger, then.*

"Why you squatting my metal?" Maura's voice was hard with no quarter given. She was tired of Ger's little games.

"I like it here." Ger shifted up into a crouch as well. His eyes narrowed. "Ain't you heard, top run? You're out. Soon enough some other 'rat will come along faster and better than you ever were. Who knows, maybe me."

Maura looked him up and down in as scathing a manner as possible. "You're sure welcome to think that. You'd be wrong. But delusion helps some people get through life."

"How's it feel, to be useless?" Ger answered barb with barb.

"Listen, you, I may be out, but I can still kick your blade-hopping butt from one end of this spaceport to the other."

"How's that trick going to feed you?" Ger shifted slowly about and began to back off.

"Why you so worried on my health, all a sudden?"

"You know me, always after helping a fellow reject in need." Ger inched a little further away. "Just recently, for example, I helped a whole bunch of my friends."

Maura felt a sudden cold panic hit her sharp as space-ice. "Oh yeah, and what'd you help them do, jump out the nearest airlock?"

Ger smiled the kind of smile that said the real reason he was there was to watch Maura's face when he said what he was just about to say.

"More like, what'd I help them *to*." He amended her words.

Maura crossed her arms and glared.

Ger skittered away, high-tailing it down the tunnel towards his nest.

Maura contemplated chasing after, but chances were, whatever he took, he'd no longer have it on him. Besides, she hadn't the energy for more running. It wasn't like she had much worth stealing.

She rubbed her neck with one hand and patted the murmel with the other.

"Nasty piece of work, that boy."

The murmel, being a creature of discriminating taste, agreed with her. He went to snuffle about where Ger had slept, looking for crud droppings.

Maura followed, reaching down to the chink in the tunnel wall that released a little wire catch of her own devising. When pulled, it exposed a small hole where she stashed her ration cubes.

Nothing.

She scrabbled about, hardly daring to believe it. She'd been hoarding her pay for several shifts. She'd garnered much in the form of bonuses and extras, especially as she'd been trying to keep her weight down. With her runs ticking in as fastest, she put quite a number of cubes away in anticipation of the inevitable spin when she lost her license. It was one of the reasons she hadn't panicked yesterday.

Every last cube was gone.

"Why," she looked at the murmel, too shocked to yell, "that little space turd!"

The murmel, now that the immediate threat of interloping human was gone, didn't look up from his snuffling.

Maura banged about some more, cursing Ger and his ancestor's genes, whatever form they took, back to the Seeding. Eventually, she calmed down.

"I sure wish I could fuel-up on crud and bits of space dust like you," she said to the murmel, her stomach beginning to rumble.

The murmel sneezed at her.

Maura had few options. Ger was gone off to his friends, with her hoard, and there was no way she could take them all on to get back her own food. Rees would loan her a cube or two if she asked, but he hadn't much to spare and she couldn't stomach the idea of taking what little he had away. He needed to eat as much as she did. More, now that he was running blades ,and she wasn't.

So, ignoring her noisy tummy, she curled up in the spot Ger had vacated, hoping she didn't catch space scabies from his sorry carcass. The murmel arranged himself near her head and Maura burrowed against his furry stomach. She fell asleep to the soft sound of his purring. He, at least, felt that now his human was positioned correctly, all was right in the universe.

Maura awoke slowly, luxuriating in the decadence of it. Her regular routine was thrown off by a long spin and late to sleep, and no scyther shift urged her up to work.

"Don't you have crud to be eating, maybe some screaming to do?" she asked the murmel.

He yawned at her, showing double rows of small sharp teeth.

She sat up. "Well, don't go 'round expecting me to fatten you up all on my lonesome."

The creature stood and arched his back in a stretch, elongating his long blue tail, the tip quivering. He looked at her expectantly.

"Didn't you suss my meaning? No run this spin. You be wanting breakfast? Then you'll be having to go down tunnelside and let some new 'rat to take you on. Won't be the same, mind. No one else'll fatten you up as much or as fast as I did, 'spite what Ger goes 'round uttering."

The murmel sat back on his haunches and had a bit of a wash. Maura figured he'd know what to do if he got hungry enough. More than she did, in any event.

She was to go about her next task in the Great Alien Rescue Mission. And if one was going to get oneself chucked in the slammer, one might as well do it in as spectacular a manner as possible. Since she was hungry, food was going to be part of it.

She ran boney hands through her short blue hair, sliding her nails over her scalp. She then straightened out the folds in her shirt and knickerbockers as best she could, brushing at the creases and the smudges of blue dust. There was no way she could ever make herself look respectable, not in rags and bare feet. Nevertheless, she struck determinately off, dodging through the tunnels that led up-market towards crossgenetor arena where all the hobnobs and highstocks did their shopping.

Although it was early first shift, the market stall pods had all dropped down onto the floor of the amphitheater, and most were open for business already. The clear cables that connected the pods to their docks in the high arched ceiling were coiled away forming reflective nodules far above. In her more poetic moments Maura thought they looked like water droplets. In her more realistic moments, like pimples. During sleep shift, those cables dropped down in silvery ribbons. The venders would climb on top of their pods, hook the cables in, and watch their livelihoods hauled up — remote and secure. Those who came venturing into the arena during off times found it abandoned and lonely, bereft of its purpose.

First shine, with lights recently up, the arena was a thing of beauty. Maura crouched at the highest tier where stalls gave way to arched ceiling, and before her the multi-level amphitheater was littered with brightly colored displays. *No subtlety there, just spit and shine.* Some venders set up street-side with colorful inexpensive items draped about, while owners of fancier pods with inset windows took advantage of their increased security to flaunt outrageous sparkles.

The top level, in front of Maura, was mostly food vender turf. Tiny chew pods opened to form carts and more massive units, needing three or four cables, formed-up restaurants. Both offered up the best cuisine the Wheel had on hand. Next level down was clothes: high-end designer pods crammed with top-hats, bowlers, cravats, and suits nested next to cheap tin second hand stalls. Below them came munitions stores and

space skiff suppliers, some of the largest pods arenaside, then
shops selling furniture and other trinkets, and further down
venders of the mysterious and the old, objects well beyond
Maura's ken. She supposed if she'd grown up in the world,
her trigger traits dictated she'd know them all – probably own
most of what they hawked, with credits to spare.

The crossgenetor amphitheater was implant monitored
within an inch of its existence. Readers were inset all around
the perimeter, even at the edges of air ducts. New security
measures had been enacted last turn. *Lowlifes can't be
allowed to trouble progenetors at play, now can they?* Of
course, rejects weren't officially permitted *anywhere* on the
spaceport, but time was a girl could do a decent spate of
begging in the arena. Now crossgenetor zones all sported
high security, even those chipped who hadn't the credits to
afford the goods were denied entry. The Wheel took
economic exclusivity seriously.

Maura hovered at the duct-edge for a number of ticks,
contemplating what food appealed most. The murmel sat
patiently next to her, blue tail-tip a-twitch. Maura couldn't see
anyway around setting off the implant alarms, so she figured
on using the murmel's presence to her advantage. Picking the
little beastie up, she jumped down into the corridor.

A shrill, high-pitched whine rent the air, and two armigers
came immediately charging over – predictable as scyther
blades. There weren't more than a few people shopping so
early but those that were, quickly nipped into nearby chew
pods. Maura ducked down and to one side, sliding in between
two stalls, and then around the back of a pod. The murmel,
acting his usual role of deeply affronted dignitary, stood
pompous and alone in the middle of the thoroughfare.

The armigers slid to a stop, sharp and graceless
before him.

"It's only a blasted murmel."

"Spaceborn pests," agreed the second gun.

"Hassle." The first reached for the blue creature with a brawny hand.

The murmel fluffed up his tail and hissed in a very pointed manner.

Both armigers backed away right quick. It was amusing as all get out to see. The murmel, without a belly full of crud, was about the size and general weight of Maura's head. He was no match for two well-armed armigers, who, like most military folk, were triggered towards the large and bullish side of physicality. Still, there was something about the sheer number of teeth some tinker had seen fit to put inside a murmel's head that gave most people the willies.

"Stun it and chuck it into space."

"And have some engineering subgenetor scum cite us for tool damages? This one looks sassy but tame." The armiger crouched down and made a little clucking noise, offering her finger to the beast.

The murmel, feeling battle lines had been drawn, fluffed up further and minced forward in a tiptoe sashay, snapping his little teeth at that finger, in an attitude of menace.

The armiger stood up right quick.

The murmel danced in near enough to nibble at her shiny boots. He paused, tail lashing, and tilted his fuzzy face up, looking affronted. Then he leapt straight up in the air, threw his little blue head back, and screamed at the top of his not-inconsiderable lungs.

There are many sounds in the universe worse than a murmel's scream — the hiss of breathable air escaping into space, the crash of metal against metal, the slide of scyther blade through bone. But there *is* something remarkably potent to a murmel's scream, they scream it like they really mean it.

The noise was laced with terror, as though death were imminent, or the end of the world, or at least the end of the best parts of it.

Maura's murmel had a scream that won awards — little blue badges of honor and a certain heroic status amongst his fellows that amounted to "don't mess with the best." His scream was a real humdinger, hurling its way right into the brain with a deadly eardrum hit-and-run along the way.

The two armigers almost jumped right out of their military grade boots, clapping hands to ears. Maura'd been living with murmels a-screaming all spin every spin most of her life, and it still scared the crud-dust out of her when it came on unexpected. Regular-type port-goers only heard murmel screams as distant echoes at tunnel's end. Like the layering of blue dust that eventually covered all port kit, murmel screams were one more thing in a long stream of annoyances dealt out by spaceside life. But the chipped rarely got to hear a murmel up close and personal.

Maura's murmel was mighty close and getting himself pretty darn personal.

Then, just as abruptly, he stopped screaming and sat back in his heels looking embarrassed by his own outburst. He wrapped his paws about his tail and bent to wash the tip.

"Tame, you say?"

"Yes, but even the tame ones only go crazy without a handler. You stay here and watch it. I'll go get a net."

"Are you sure that's… " The gun trailed off as his partner walked briskly away, leaving him as the sole hero to safeguard the amphitheater against a vicious murmel invasion.

The blue beastie paused in his bath to give the remaining guard a disgusted look. It was a look that said much on the superiority of murmels. Then he glanced about, probably looking for Maura. Maura hoped against hope he wouldn't spot her bolt hole and come sauntering over.

Possibly sussing out her crafty plan, the little creature leaped back up into the air duct, setting off the alarm once more, and then disappeared down the tunnel. Both Maura and the guard breathed a sigh of relief.

Maura waited awhile for the female guard to trot back. When she did, her companion acquired himself a high-grade chewing-out for letting the beastie go. The two then continued patrolling about their merry way, with substantially less swagger to their shiny boots. Maura slid out from behind the chew pod and meandered in the opposite direction, all casual and unthreatening.

She was obviously a crudrat — skinny-bones, quick eyes, sporting blue hair and attitude. So the wheel citizens didn't notice her. Those few shoppers lazing about walked right past, looked straight through. She wasn't no more than a speck of crud under their high-gloss shoes.

Maura moved down the rows of small food stalls and larger restaurants, examining options from under long blue lashes. Tucked in between two larger chew pods was a stall selling drippy chunks of hot meat on sticks. It might be worth a lick and the stick might be right useful later. Across the way from the stick-meat, a vender behind a table pushed bowls full of noodles swimming in thick broth and covered in brightly colored rehydrated vegetables.

She hesitated, momentarily hindered by too many options. Choice was a rare thing and Maura savored the moment. Her stomach growled. She selected a midsized vender, not so puny that her opportunism would be an economic hit, nor so large that they would make an example of her with trumped-up charges. He sold interesting looking crispy balls stuffed inside flat bread pockets with all sorts of shredded green and red stuff sprinkled on top – adventuresome. Maura was feeling daring. She blamed it on too much contact with fuzzy aliens.

She nipped forward, snaked out a hand and pinched one of the filled pocket thingies.

The vender let out a cry of alarm and pressed a little button inside his pod. Before he could get out from behind his stall, Maura was off, jogging casually along the thoroughfare, eating as she went.

The pocket jobbie was a good choice. The foodstuff had a nice range in all things texture and flavor. It was entirely unlike ration cubes, which held the banner high for hard, chewy, and dense – never a thought to variation. Maura's nibble was all soft chewy bread, crunchy saltiness from the round things stuffed inside – *are they meat?* – and a tangy flavor that seemed to come partly from a white sauce drizzled about and partly from the shredded stuff on top. *They must be fruit.* Fruit *is a more satisfying word than* vegetable. *These yummies are fruit.*

Right about the time she crammed the last of it into her mouth a whole herd of armigers glommed onto her tail.

Intruders were one thing, and murmels were a bother to be sure, but stealing was a sin against the Wheel. Such a serious business required numbers. At a glance Maura estimated the group after her as over half a dozen guns. *All for little old me? Must be a slow shift.*

Maura was never one to be taken quietly. She was a bit of a kicker, though not much of a screamer – best leave that to the professionals like her murmel. She applied speed to her casual jog, and dodged easily away from their clumsy graspings.

They came right on after, of course.

Maura licked off the last of the tangy white sauce from

her fingertips, *mighty tasty meal to go out on*, then settled into her knees, loosening up her muscles, glad to not be distracted by her stomach anymore. Balancing all her weight forwarded onto the balls of her feet, she began to really run. She looked about, taking in levels and pods, people and things, all of them shifting, becoming obstacles. If nothing else, this was sure going to be a fun one.

She slid, thin and lithe, in between two of the larger chew pods and dove forward. She placed both hands shoulder width apart on the roof of a clothing stall of the next ring down and swung herself forward. Tucking knees to chest she vaulted over its roof, swung her feet to the front so that it looked like they were traveling right through her hands. In fact, she'd lifted her hands up at the last second. It was a flash move. Maura was sad Rees weren't there to see it shine. She landed in a crouch in the street of the next level down and took off in a sprint, nipping around shoppers until she spotted the pack armigers closing in on her once more.

Maura zigzagged to one side, crashing into a display of brightly colored silks. The rack, an arm of metal sticking out from the pod, swung spilling fabric into a kaleidoscope puddle in the middle of the street. The vender swore.

Maura ran on.

Leaping up, she grabbed a short beam sticking out the side of a stall roof. She swung up, stepping against the pod with her feet. She let go at the last moment, flying forward into the air and twisting to the side so that she soared through the narrow divide between the pod and its neighbor to land on a roof the next level down.

Still the armigers followed – in a slightly less spectacular manner.

That is until one of them drew his weapon.

7

When enhancers triggered their first trait, the progene-
tors knew they'd found the way to track their own, for
the great families have always appreciated a proper
accounting of what rightfully belongs to them, and now
they could mark the generations that followed, forever
and ever.

~ Excerpt from *The Wheel in Motion* by C.
Venderseep

Maura ducked.

The sonic gun's screech brain-rumbled its way around the
shopping arena. The resulting point-wave hit a still dangling
cable across the way from where Maura had been standing.
The force of the shot tore through that cable and buckled the
side of a pod behind it. The armigers clearly weren't joshing.

Maura didn't wait to see if the next guard would have
better aim. She took off to the left, staying low, running the
amphitheater ring by leaping from one rooftop to the next,

weaving erratically to stay out of direct line-of-sound. Some pods were taller than others, which threw a challenge into the pattern. She side vaulted any obstacle she could, one of her more efficient jumps, placing one hand down and swing both legs to the side. For those leaps when the next pod was further away or higher up, she jumped the gap and then climbed part the way, hand-springing over the top.

Perhaps she was having too much fun. She'd left the armigers trailing behind, less agile and causing more harm than good in their attempts to catch her. Most of the shoppers stopped and gawked, and a goodly number of venders had wandered into the thoroughfare to watch her progress. She was now traversing the third level pods, big muscle and corporate business — munitions, ship supplies, that kind of bric-a-brac.

She was contemplating a long-leap across the thorough-fare, so she could shunt herself down to the fourth level and keep up the festivities, when a very calm voice stopped her dead. The voice oozed hard-end steel Spoke training of the bruise-and-blood variety. No cushy low-muscle of the kind to spend his life portside on piddling guard detail. His tone bespoke some serious military campaign, planet-grounded and brutal. Here was one of those armigers who'd worn full armor and caught regular battle time on contested worlds — who served the Wheel at its fringes, discharging honor and glory.

"I'd halt that scurrying, little 'rat, if I were you."

Maura halted. She turned around all slow and careful, on one heel, like a dancer, and looked down into the street below.

A large angry man with an augmented arm stood, loose-limbs and wide-stance, glaring up at her. His good arm was so muscled it was about twice as wide around as Maura's waist.

What little hair he had was worn close-cropped and practical, and, so far as Maura could see, aside from height and muscle, he didn't have many major trigger traits. She'd lay good odds there wasn't a single progenetor phenotype in that man's body. He stank of military all the way back to the setting of the Spokes.

The most interesting thing about him wasn't his appearance, nor his stock, but the fact that he was sporting the largest gun Maura had ever met, resting all casual and comfortable on one beefy shoulder. It was trained on her. It bore about as much resemblance to a sonic pistol as a meteor did to space dust. It was the kind of gun that progenetors bought when they had somewhat to prove and someone to prove it to, probably in front of parliament. It was the kind of gun that settled differences – once and for all, or all at once, it mattered not. It was old, deadly, and unsafe spaceside — a planetborn weapon that could tear a hole through a person one moment and a main bulkhead the next.

"Sure you wanna risk vacuum with that thing?" Maura asked, all conversational and cozy.

"I don't miss," the hard-liner replied, the muzzle of that massive gun not shifting one jot.

"I move right quick."

"I still don't miss." A man of few words. Maura could respect that.

The armigers came running up, having finally jumped down from pod roofs themselves and tracked Maura in a more respectable manner through the streets. They skittered to a stop in a broiling mass of red and gold uniforms around the large man with the large gun. They drew their sonic pistols and pointed them at Maura.

Their pistols looked like children's toys next to that mammoth bullet slinger.

"Lucivian, careful what you do with that there boulder-hurler," said one of the guards to the big man.

"It's licensed," the vender replied tersely, not lowering the gun and not bothering to look at any of the military folk who now surrounded him.

"Licensed to sell, not to use."

The beefy man snorted and shifted his gaze, at last, away from Maura and onto the crowd of guards. He found them wanting. His expression was not unlike that which the murmel had issued the two armigers only a few ticks earlier. "Caught you a 'rat with it, didn't I?"

"Yes, well."

"She was giving you some slick." He swiveled his gaze back to Maura.

Silence greeted that statement. No spoke in the Wheel ever admitted to a flaw.

Maura winked at the big vender, giving him the benefit of blue lashes and silver eyes.

He spat out the side of his mouth. Cleanliness violation, but nobody seemed interested in pointing out that little fact.

Everything was still for a long tick.

The big man curled his lip and lowered his hulking weapon. Then he swung himself 'round, cutting a swath through the armigers like a scyther blade, and marched off into one of the larger munitions shops without a single backward glance.

Well, he certainly knows his business. That'd be where I'd buy, if'n I were chipped-up, credit-rich, and gun-happy.

Several of the watching shoppers appeared to agree. They gave over staring at Maura and the multiple sonic guns stuck on her air space, to follow the man into his pod. A couple of cane-carrying progenetors with pinched faces and furtive looks, seemed like they might be in the market for particularly large guns of just such a fashionable style.

Maura switched her attention back to the guards. *Ought I make them climb up and get me? They might be annoyed at fetching someone as insignificant as me or they might be annoyed if I give in too crudding easy.*

Maura gave up trying to figure on the thinkings of the military. She could no more comprehend the workings of a Wheel mind than they could understand a reject's feelings. She was in for a bum time no matter what step she took. So she flipped over the edge of the roof and landed with a soft thud in the street below. She stood up ever-so slowly, to find herself surrounded by armigers, all of whom seemed much larger than they had when viewed from topside.

They reacted as quick as good air turns bad.

Maura was only a little thing by weight standards and it took them mere ticks to truss her up and cart her off to the military end of spaceport. They clicked a prisoner collar 'round her scrawny neck. The plastic was cold and tight against her skin, making it difficult to swallow. The blasted thing came complete with temporary implant, so she'd not set off alarms wherever they dragged her.

They used the beltway to transport her.

It was disorientating to be on a little square of floor, with it moving under her and she not doing any of the moving herself. Unsettling to the stomach, making hers do all manner of strange things, flipping about and wobbling side-to-side. The lights under that long archway that she'd run the top of so many times were much brighter than when viewed through a blue film of crud dust. They made her feel hot and scrutinized by too many eyes. How did citizens bear up under this feeling of being inspected every tick of spin?

The beltway sped along.

Maura shared her square with two burly guns, one holding each of her arms in a grip docking clamps couldn't rival. Everything seemed to be proceeding according to plan until someone yodeled at them from a square of belt zipping in the opposite direction.

Both belts slowed and veered towards each other as the guards notified their implants and the yodeler notified his, and all three implants did whatever it was that they were supposed to do to control belt and speed and communication.

Maura was horrified to find out that the yodeler was a certain progenetor buck with smooth opalescent skin and an overdose of posturing.

Apparently not responding fast enough for him, the progenetor jumped belts onto the square in front of Maura and her little party, drifting in the same direction.

He turned to face them, staring fixed and firm at Maura's silver eyes.

"What do you want?" Asked one of the armigers with all the rudeness of one Spoke about his proper duties being interfered with by another.

The highstock looked offended, but, unlike most progenetors, didn't knee-jerk respond with superiority or anger.

He's one, Maura felt her stomach shift about more at the realization, *who's smart as well as dangerous.*

He leaned on his cane in a parody of casual, one foot crossed over the other, eyes heavy-lidded. Those eyes only looked lazy — climb on through the lowered lashes and they were all sharpness and calculation. He seemed to be weighing his options. Here he was, full progenetor, with all the money and power that Spoke entailed, but there were two armigers opposite him, both older and marching on official business. Hard to determine who actually held higher stock in this particular situation.

Put off by his silence one of the armigers pushed, "Well?"

Pearly-skin dipped his head down as though dozing right where he stood. His top hat tilted forward.

He made them wait.

Then he said, "That one is Am Vern genotype."

Maura wondered where all his many friends were. No other belt squares slowed or moved in their direction. The universe was upside-down — sequensors were slithering about as a herd and progenetors traveled alone.

"Oh yeah?" One of the guns grabbed Maura's chin and yanked it, looking into her face.

Maura blinked angled eyes at him, her pupil small as a bulkhead crack under the bright beltway lights, almost invisible. Like she was blind.

"Better say that she started out Am Vern. She's crudrat now." The guard actually corrected the progenetor... confident type of fool.

The other steel Spoke snorted. "Even Am Verns can breed a washout? Just like everyone else. Must have rubbed the family raw to spend all that money on the most expensive trigger traits going, and then lose her 'cause she couldn't take the implant. Wait 'til captain sees her. He don't like Am Vern politics."

The first nudged him, gesturing to the progenetor buck on the beltway in front of them. "Doesn't do to go on about these things on a public beltway."

The know-it-all guard laughed. "I follow trigger traits. You ought to get more involved, Grodin, or you ain't gonna make it very far. Armiger and progenetor walk hand in had whether Wheel admits it or not. It's never a bad idea to memorize the geno-traits of the Great Families. That boy there," he pointed to the pearly-skinned buck, "has Am Xinyn patents all over him, unless I miss my guess."

The toff in question grinned.

"So?"

"So Am Xinyn and Am Vern been gene feuding six generations or more now. I'm thinking those eyes of hers might be the reason he stopped us."

"Good," praised the progenetor. "So, how much?"

"How much what?"

"How many credits do you want for that Am Vern chip-less wonder you got idling between you? You can't be holding her for anything all that important. What she going to lockup for? Disrupting the peace? Vagrancy? Which garners what punishment this cycle, solitary confinement and eventual death by spacing? She'll only suck down air in the clink, not to mention wasting your valuable time. I could think on any number of ways to put her to good use."

"A reject?"

"Ah, perhaps I should say — any number of ways to put those eyes of hers to good use."

Maura went cold. She'd thought the beltway lights hot and over-powering mere ticks before, now they felt a freezing and icy white. She swallowed hard and really looked at the buck across from her. He was about her age, yes, and still round in the face with youth. But he did look like he might enjoy removing someone's eyes, particularly hers. She wondered if he'd make sure she was dead first. Probably not.

The two armigers laughed at his wit.

"We'll need to know for certain if the vender intends to press charges," said one of the muscle-men, cautiously, feeling out his comrade's willingness to take a bribe.

The other seemed eager enough. "She's on record so we must book her into the system."

"And after that?" wheedled the progenetor.

The two looked at each other.

"We may be able to come to some kind of arrangement."
The first was all affability.

"It won't be easy, to get her back out to you," added the
second, so as not to appear overly keen.

"So it won't come cheap, you realize?" agreed the first,
licking his lips, seeing an easy mark.

Maura was mildly unsurprised at becoming a main
bribing token in the ongoing corruption of the military.

The progenetor buck grinned. His face sliced almost in
two by a vast set of perfectly white teeth. This kind of talk
was his comfort zone, highstocks lived to buy and sell —
things, people, stations, countries, worlds. He straightened
from his relaxed stance, opened his eyes a little wider, and
swung his cane back-and-forth against one foot.

"Three hundred," he said, opening negotiations.

Tap, tap, tap went the cane.

"Seven," countered one armiger, widening his stance and
looking bullish.

"Five, and you deliver her directly to my yacht. It's
docked in your bay anyway," countered the progenetor.

Tap, tap, tap.

"And why is that?" The armiger sounded a bit huffy.
After all, military section was meant for military use, not to
be wasted on the rich and idle.

"Am Xinyn, remember?" hissed his companion.

"So?" Armigers sure did go in for bullish.

"So, Am Xinyn's serving on the parliament as nomarch of
military spending this cycle," replied his companion. Maura
wondered if he had delusions of Spoke hopping.

"Ah, well, in that case — six hundred and you haul your
crystal-white self 'round our end of the port to pick her up
end of next shift. See how real people live."

The progenetor nodded. "Done." He stopped tapping his cane against his foot.

The armiger not making the deal said, "My implant has notarized and recorded this transaction."

Maura gaped. Six hundred credits was a veritable fortune. It'd feed a crudrat belly-full for a whole cycle long. Two crudrats if they ate sparingly and were trying to keep the weight down.

The highstock reached across the gap separating their still drifting belt squares and tapped the top of Maura's blue head with his cane. The silver tip glinted in the harsh lights, momentarily blinding her. He kept his gene marks polished to a high shine.

"You're mine, little nobody. Oh, the delicious things I am going to do with those eyes." Once again the grimace split his face — a beautiful pearly face that never thought to wrinkle, or show humor, or show humanity.

Then he signaled the beltway monitor with his implant. A toss of his head to one side and his belt veered off to midway, at which point he leaped across belts to the faster, high cost, express route, and continued the way he'd been going origi-nally towards the crossgenetor arena.

Maura twisted in the grip of the two guards to watch him. Jealous of the relief she felt in his leaving. Knowing it wouldn't last. For a long time after he'd vanished 'round a bend in the beltway, she thought she could see his cane and his pearly skin glinting under the lights.

Maura's two escorts spent the remainder of the journey discussing what they were going to do with such an unex-pected influx of funds.

8

And the first Tinkers took themselves unto space to grapple with the void. There they found pathways between the stars. They also found a nothingness filled with something. *Then they made the greatest discovery of them all — that* something *could be used.*

~ Introduction to *The Application of Dark Matter Theory, A Primer* by T.L. Prozzer

The dispatch area was still a-buzz with guns and too many sequensors for anyone's comfort. Everyone ignored Maura, except the two guards who now handled her carefully. A prized investment opportunity, her eyes had become. Maura was surprised no one noted the care they took of her.

They booked her in personally, pushing subgenetor clerks out the way, and then made sure they were the only ones with keys to her cell. They patted her down for kit, of which she had none since she'd hidden the key-card and lost her license, and saw her into the clink with real concern.

"Now you sit pretty there a while," said one as he bolted her in.

"We'll be back for you shortly, just got some data to tweak, and a vender to pay, make sure he don't push to see you spaced," added the other.

They swaggered away, leaving Maura looking about her narrow cell and wondering about taking a nap. Next part of the plan wouldn't kick in until scyther shifts rotated. She had a good number of ticks to waste.

She checked over her cell, top to tail. The only opening, besides the bars, was the vent centered above. She checked to make sure she could climb up and reach it. Her cell was narrow enough so that with her legs braced between the two walls she could get high with relative ease. From what she'd learned of the layout, the alien in solitary was probably two or three cells down and across the way from her. Things would have been best if he were closer, but it shouldn't be too much a bother, assuming those two guards didn't come back first.

Nothing happened for a long time. The cells all about her were empty, so there was no one to talk with. Armigers paraded by, mostly trying to catch sight of the alien. But rules were rules and they were supposed to leave that end of the alone, so they poked at Maura instead, prodding through the bars with shock sticks and nasty words. She avoided the shockers easy, and ignored the words easier. Most words, when they came upon rejects at all, were of the needling variety. A girl got used to name calling right quick if she lived gutterside. It came with the territory.

Things got interesting again near the end of that shift. Apparently the sequensors had decided to interrupt the alien's solitary. All that alone time should have worked, but hadn't. Maura suspected this spoke more on the alien having been raised planetside, where solitary came all too easy, than on a failure in technique. But the sequensors seemed to like blaming each other, or accusing the armigers of sneaking looks. There were recriminations and even some physical threats taking place right there in the hall near her cell. Maura watched the show with interest.

Finally they opted for continued torture and pain. Maura hope they wouldn't go damaging her alien beyond repair.

Then two sequensors returned with some sort of large bubble computer. It looked to fit over the head, with tiny needles and screws poking into the brain and one or two long ones meant for the eyes. Sure wasn't a pretty bit of kit. Maura shuddered to see it. Poor old alien. But then again, she'd lay on some good credit that it wouldn't work on Fuzzy anyhow. *Alien's alien, brains got to be different.* Not that she knew what that kit was meant to do, but it seemed to her the alien might beat even it.

Turns out she was dead wrong. A few ticks later and Fuzzy started up howling again. Only, this time there was extra pain edging the tone of it.

Maura shuddered and huddled down in the far corner of her cell. She drew up her legs and wrapped her arms about them, burying her face in her knees. Nothing left to do but hope Rees got out of his shift, collected their secret weapon, and got himself over fast enough to stop the torture. Not to mention stop her being taken away by the two bribed guns.

Next thing she heard, through the alien screaming, was the sound of a sim-key in her cell lock.

She looked up.

Seems my ticks are all beat out.

There stood the two armigers, and behind them the Am Xinyn progenetor, all smug and pearly. There was a look of too much satisfaction on that highstock's perfect face. Maura stood, slow and careful. Sudden moves could be used as an excuse for pain.

One of the guards began coughing. He sucked in on his breath, scrabbling at his throat. Just as the door to her cell unlocked and started to slide open, the other one started coughing as well.

"What in Wheel's name is going on?" asked the high-stock, starting to cough now also. He shifted his grip on his cane, as though some tangible enemy were bound to appear.

Maura caught a whiff of a sharp chemical smell punching through the dryness of the spaceport air. It was acrid and hit the back of the throat. She knew the scent well, though it was usually carried on a slight exhalation of murmel breath. It was hundreds of times worse now, clawing and toxic.

She ignored the partly open door to her cell. Instead she shimmed up the sides, placing her mouth against the air vent in the ceiling. She tried to breathe as calm and regular as possible. Behind her the two armigers and the progenetor collapsed to the floor, limp as dead beltway.

"Rees?" Maura hissed through the vent, when she felt it was safe.

"Sure is," came Rees's voice.

"You suss out which vent belongs to the alien's solitary?"

"No problem there, you left it all twisted off, and wide wide open. I checked and he's breathing right pretty. Sure is a weird looking beastie. Hey, you think... ?"

Maura cut him off. "I reckon we got about ten ticks before the alarms sound and we got cleaners swarming up the place. Best we get moving. No need to lift the keys. They opened my cell right up, all convenient like."

"Now, why would they go and do such?"

"No time to waste on explaining."

"Right, meet you at crossgenetor south major hub?"

"Done." Maura took a deep breath and holding it, jumped down from her propped position between the two walls.

She moved with quickness and economy, no air to waste, no time to wander. She wormed out the cell door. Both guards and progenetor lay still on the floor outside. She prodded one guard with a foot. He didn't move. She moved onto the buck, and poked at his stomach with a toe.

Quick as a flash he grabbed her ankle with both hands. Despite herself, Maura let out a little squeak, losing some of her precious air.

The Am Xinyn looked up at her, eyes watery, struggling to breathe. Beads of sweat popped out on his pearly face, like water on plastic.

"What'd you do, Am Vern?"

Maura yanked at her foot.

His grip held sure.

She was running out of air. The acrid smell was creeping in. Panicked, Maura reached down and clawed at his hands with her fingernails. They barely made a mark on the high-mod shiny surface of his flesh.

"Never trust Am Verns," he wheezed, not seeming to notice her scratching. "Always got some plot or another, Am Verns do. I should have known that you would, too. Chipless makes no diff…" His speech faded into coughing and his grip slackened.

Maura pulled her foot free and skittered back into her cell and up the wall. She placed her mouth up close to the vent, one of the only two that Rees hadn't clogged, and breathed deeply in relief. Her heart was loud as a scyther pulse in her chest.

It took her a few too many ticks to convince herself to try again.

She was running out of time.

This second try she moved fast and sure, jumping down, and running over to pat down both guards. She fleeced them for anything that might be useful yet not implant coded — ration cubes, kit tools, sparkles. She even kept one of the sonic guns. A body needed a chip to fire the nasty, but sometimes a girl didn't have to fire to get what she needed.

After a quick climb back up her cell walls to take another breather, the air fresh and sweet, Maura did the same to the fallen progenetor. He was littered with interesting kit. She also took his cane. She wasn't quite sure how it might be useful but he'd regret the loss and that was a good enough reason for her. She made a bundle using his cravat and tied her loot to the cane to carry, leaving it propped in the hall.

Then it was back for more air.

Once more down this time she lifted the guard's sim key and went to the alien's cell.

He was standing all calm, solid as a bulkhead, mouth to the open vent above. At his feet lay the crumpled forms of four sequensors. In the corner of the cell, all mangled and scrunched up, was the bubble contraption they'd been using on his head. *Guess he didn't like that.* Blood leaked out through his white fur at various points about his skull. He seemed to have just ripped the thing straight off his noggin.

Maura fumbled various keys at the lock. Sliding one bit of metal in after another. She was starting to really worry on time, since alarms would have sounded at the first measure of toxins in the air. Right now it was only a matter of how fast the cleaners could get across spaceport from dockside to deal with Rees's little mess.

Wrong key.

What if she ran out of air? She'd have to go back for another breather. That'd waste even more ticks.

Wrong key.

By now the alarm would surely have brought the cleaners. Subgenetors would be crewing all over the place. She had to get it right.

Wrong key.

Not that that Maura could do much good at all if they'd keyed his cell to implant instead of using mechanicals. She began to smell the acrid sent and knew she'd have return to her own cell soon, get more air.

Wrong key.

Maura glanced desperately about.

The alien sensed her plight, for all of a sudden there he was, a looming mass of white. He motioned her towards his cell bars with one massive paw. Maura bent, still fiddling with the lock.

And then his strange furry mouth was over hers and Maura breathed in. Shocking intimacy. He smelled warm and exotic, like sun on growing things she'd never seen. His breath was warm as well, and not unpleasant. There wasn't much oxygen in it, but it was enough to get her through the last of the sim keys on the guard's chain.

The fated click. Right key.

Maura pushed the cell door aside. She had no ticks to glory in her success. Yet again, she was almost out of air. The alien offered her a wide furry hand and a bent knee. No time to flinch away from contact with foreign fur, she simply climbed right up him, as though he were a wall or a tunnel. He braced her, and they spent a long moment together like that, mouths to the vent.

Sweet air sung through Maura's lungs.

"Quoin Fuzzy," she said softly, "you sure that ice planet of yours is worth all this bother?"

He looked at her. Right close his black eyes were even more like the void of space. "You seen the sun rise over a glacier, little blue?"

Maura shook her head.

"It is worth it."

"Right then. Let's get you out of here. Just give me a tick." Maura jumped down, stripped the four sequensors of their robes, and then clambered back up for one last gasp.

"Follow me." She dashed out of the cell, the alien following after, his long stride eating up three of hers. Maura grabbed her bundle and progenetor cane. That plus the sequensor robes made for quite a load. She hoped she'd not have to do any *real* running - she'd have to drop the loot.

She'd give Fuzzy credits, if she had any, for he followed her with only slight hesitation when she veered into the duct tube. It was barely big enough for him. Anything smaller than a main tunnel and he'd get stuck like a foam in a blast-hole. Still, he crawled gamely after. His pelt made a whispering noise on the metal. She wondered if he were cleaning it of dust. They moved as quickly as possible from one major line to the next until they came out into one of the biggest hubs.

The alien still took up most of it and looked uncomfortable besides. There was more room here than his cell, but not by enough to make him happy with it.

Rees's tufted blue head poked 'round a tunnel corner soon as they settled. He swung himself to a soft landing next to Maura, looking with wide eyes at the alien.

"You stink," stated Maura, by way of greeting.

Rees waggled his hands at her. They were stained dark blue. "Don't come off easy. Guess that's why subgenetor cleaners always wear gloves."

The alien said, "You clogged the vents up? This one is indebted to you, small stranger."

Rees puffed himself up at the moniker. He'd always been

sensitive about his size. Except that it stood him in good stead with scyther work.

Maura recollected the alien's obsession with handles. Figuring on introductions, she said, "Quoin Fuzzy, this is Rees. Rees, this is *quoin* Fuzzy. He's a bit odd about names. Won't give his real one out all easy and quick the way we do."

The alien could not seem to help a little gasp when Maura said Rees's name aloud.

"Oh yeah?" Rees looked with interest at the alien.

Fuzzy was staring at Maura. "You are as free with the names of others as you are with your own? What a strange alien place this Wheel is where such liberties are taken with *gens*."

Rees grinned. "Rees ain't a very tip-top name."

The alien turned back to him. "You also have no *gens*?"

Rees looked at Maura to translate.

"I'm thinking he's meaning something like progenetor families." She gave a one-shoulder shrug.

"Well," Rees looked a little militant, "I do have kin, they just lost me is all."

"Rees has delusions of being chipped. He keeps on thinking someone made a mistake not giving him the implant."

"You are — how do you say — *crudrat* as well?" The alien eyed Rees's blue hair.

Rees nodded.

Fuzzy cocked his head to the side. "If this one may ask — how did you manage it? What did you use for the vent clogging? This one was favorably impressed by your successful execution of the plan."

Rees and Maura looked at each other.

"I'm thinking you probably don't want to know *what*," said Rees finally.

"It's a substance," said Maura right about the same time. "Subgenetors make good use of it 'round portside. Very sticky, holds nice and sure even in a vacuum. Scuttles use for repairs mainly. The handlers always keep a back-store. We lifted a bit of it from tunnel sites they don't rightly know about. Smells somewhat awful, of course, but us crudrats have found it most handy in the past, so we like to know where-abouts it might be at any given tick."

"So long as we avoid thinking where it came from on the get-go," added Rees, sporting an evil smile.

The alien looked mighty curious, for a fuzzy-faced beastie. "So, what is it?"

Maura sighed, crossed her arms and glared at Rees.

"Murmel plop," said Rees proudly, hoping for a rise out the alien. He did like to shock people.

The alien didn't look shocked, just more confused. "What's a murmel?"

Right on cue, because he always did have perfect timing, Maura's murmel stuck his blue head 'round a side tunnel and squeaked at them all, imperiously.

Maura gestured. "That's a murmel. Don't you have them on your skiffs or ships?"

"No."

"Gosh," Rees was now the one shocked, "how'd you control crud?"

"What's crud?"

"We speaking the same tongue?" Rees asked Maura.

"He's a funny accent but yes." Maura gestured all about, at the blue dust permeating everything and explained to the alien. "You know, the blue death, plaguing scythers and stopping air. You must have crud. Everything afloat in space has crud."

Something bumped into Maura's heel and chittered at her.

"Ah!" The alien nodded. "Residual dark matter particulate. DMP my people call it. Most certainly we have it. We use a flushing mechanism to clean the harvesters. Doesn't the Wheel do the same?"

"Nope. Wheel uses murmels and crudrats most of the time."

"This one does not understand, small one." The alien looked like he didn't want to understand.

Rees rolled his eyes. "We climb inside the scythers and clean out the crud and the murmels eat it."

Maura could tell Rees was putting things as simply as he knew how. She supposed there were just too many Wheel words the poor alien hadn't happened on before, they spoke a variation on the same language but it wasn't *exactly* the same.

The alien shifted in the tight confines of the hub. He seemed to have finally realized that, for the moment, no one was following them. "You mean your harvesters are big enough for humans to go *inside*? While they are *moving*? With animals to help? This is too weird, you must be making a funny." The alien was shaking his head in astonishment.

"Naw, what's weird is that you aliens don't do the same."

Fuzzy looked to Maura to help. "You run around inside harvesters, feeding DMP to little blue animals, and then call *me* alien?"

"That's crudratting." Maura bent and offered her shoulder to the murmel. The beastie jumped up, wrapping his long tail bout her neck.

"So then what was it you used to clog the vents? It can not have been DMP. It does not smell like it."

Maura flushed. "Well, you see, the murmel's eat the crud

and then, uh…" The alien was so high class in his speaking, such things were probably beneath him. She gestured ineffectually.

The murmel peered up at the alien with fascinated blue eyes.

Fuzzy finally put all the parts together. "Excrement. You used animal dung to rescue me, small one?" His lip curled up in disgust or a smile, Maura didn't rightly know the difference. It was black underneath.

Rees hooted with laughter at the alien's expression either way. He'd finally got some kind of reaction, that was all he was after.

Maura smiled. Her old friend had just lost all his fear of her new one.

"This Wheel space of yours," the alien said with a funny sigh rumble, "keeps getting more and more peculiar." Then he seemed to settle on acceptance. "As the universe wills it, and as *gens* bid, so it be done. So, what is next?"

"We sussed out your skiff," said Maura.

Rees glared at her. "We?"

"Fine, Rees sussed out your skiff."

"Swarming with subgenetors and in steel Spoke docks. Ain't pretty, that's for certain sure." Reese crossed his arms.

"It's going to take something *like* to get you cross station, not to mention dockside, skiffside, and into space." Maura nibbled her lower lip.

"Right, then," said the alien, whose plan didn't continue much past escaping lock up, "where do we go from here, non-enemies?"

9

There is truth in open space.
~ Proverb

"Don't you two find it unbearably warm on this floating berg?" Fuzzy looked curiously at the two crudrats.

They were squeezing through various tunnels, heading in the general direction of the armiger zone. The murmel trailed behind them, all curiosity. Slow going seemed the run of it and too many backtracks when they came across a duct overly narrow for alien bones.

Rees looked back at Fuzzy, genuinely startled by the question. "Temp controls be all kinds of standard for a portside. Been the same feel all my life."

Maura nodded. She assessed the big white alien. It was hard to tell through the fur but he was looking a mite peaky. Perhaps the torture had taken more out of him than she'd thought. She asked, all concern, "You sure you feeling up to snuff there, Quoin?"

The alien sighed. "Ice planet," he reminded her.

"Ah, of course," said Maura. "Your kind been triggered to run on the hot side?"

"Exactly so, non-enemy." Fuzzy looked about as tuckered as a crudrat after six runs in a row.

"Is non-enemy meaning somewhat like *friend*?" Rees asked.

"Not precisely, but it's not a bad name to be granted either, small one."

Rees sighed. "I wish you'd not call me that."

The alien actually smiled, his teeth were too sharp and pointed for anyone's comfort. "We must all labor under the names we are given."

"So, non-enemy," Rees wheedled, "you taking Maura with you when you leave portside, ain't ya?"

"We have a bond on it." The alien spoke without a hint of emotion.

"Could I maybe come with?"

"This one does indeed owe you, small one, but such a number would tax the limits of my whale. She is only meant to transport *one*. Already we stretch the air with two of us on board. You could require it. This one acknowledges debt for your assistance with the," he paused looking down at the murmel dogging his heals, "plop. But it would risk us all."

The murmel took the look as an invitation. Lashing his tail, he approached the alien and tugged on a bit of Fuzzy's leg fur with his paw.

"Ouch!" The alien glared down at the beastie in a most offended way. "Stop that."

The murmel chittered at him.

"I think he's in a mystery about that fuzz of yours. Fur's usually only on murmels. Even the progenetors don't trigger to that extreme. Not this side of the Wheel anyways." Maura bent and grabbed the murmel up, draping him into work-style on her back. The murmel turned all business faster than a tick, holding still, wrapping his tail about her waist, and waiting to be fed. *Poor little thing, he'll never garner another scoop out of me.*

Rees shrugged, trying not to look too disappointed. "It's all good."

The alien seemed struck by his sad face.

"This one might be able to manage you on board as well, if we take the greatest of care."

Rees brightened up. "Hot dust!"

They crawled out into another major duct hub.

"Well," said Maura, "I'm off to get your key back, Fuzzy. I'll catch you two near armiger dockside tunnel main. Good on?"

Rees nodded. "Go. Have yourself all the fun, leaving me with pup detail."

The alien was confused. "What's a *pup*?"

"You are, though with size like yours we could be off a tad with the name," said Rees.

"Pup means a crudrat afore tunnel time turns the hair blue the brain wise to the blades." Maura fluttered her hand about her own head.

The alien nodded once.

Maura extracted herself from the murmel. "You stay here." She backed away.

Surprisingly enough, he stayed.

"Right then, see you three in a couple of ticks, or not at all." Maura dipped off into a side tunnel toward engineering.

It was high traffic and busy this shift which gave Maura pause. She looked down from her perch at the assembled masses. Sure seemed like there were more subgenetors hauling about than normal. But she figured that must be her jitters tweaking the look of things. Now that Maura wasn't licensed, it felt like all eyes were fixed on her anywhere she went. There was nothing for it but to act like she was still meant to be crudratting.

Maura dropped softly out the air duct.

The tunnel she'd used as a hidey-hole for Fuzzy's keycard was up for cleaning in a few ticks. Both crudrat and foreman attention was focused a few tunnels down. So she sauntered, casual and away from notice, toward that special scyther.

Not quite believing how easy it was, she slid inside.

Dodging the blades went easier this tick-time for some reason. It was as though there wasn't a single risk anymore to running. There was only Maura's body flipping, and climbing, and breathing with the slide of metal, no fear to sour the dance. No concerns, no cares, no worries. It was almost fun, doing something so dangerous so well. It never had been fun before. Maura thought, for one shocked moment, that she might actually miss it – the blue dust in the air, the pulsing light, and sharpness of bladeside. Then she realized *that* was why she was enjoying it so much. Soon she'd never have to run blades again. She'd be done with tunnel-ticks forever. Big Fuzzy had said there'd be no scythers, not as she knew them, in his part of space.

The keycard was where she'd left it, tucked in behind the loose weld. Crud had built up over the ticks since she'd stashed it there, coating the blades in thick sludge. They moved slower and more erratically. Soon they'd have to clean this scyther or it'd simply stop. Portside progenetors couldn't allow that, now could they? Too many scythers crudded down would breed all manner of problems spaceside.

Maura tucked the keycard into her chest band, patting it once for surety's sake. Then she back flipped away from the hidey-hole. She slid, smooth and easy, under the next blade coming in from the top, and somersaulted into a crouch.

A couple of vaults, two wall runs and a few flips and she was out the tunnel entrance once more.

"Check in!" barked a voice at her soon as she landed.

Maura gasped, wondering at the familiarity of that yelling. For one instant she was terribly afraid it had all been a dream brought on by blade rhythm and inhaling too much crud: the alien, the rescue, everything. She was right back where she started — running scythers for ration cubes with no break to the pattern of her being.

"Four-four-five, sir!" Maura said automatically.

"Weigh out then, crudrat, don't waste my ticks." The foreman didn't even look up from his scanpad to see who Maura was.

Automatically, Maura reached around for the murmel on her back. He wasn't there, and there was no scoop spoon in her hand to feed him with either.

Not a dream. The only thing Maura had was the keycard to an alien skiff, hidden in her rags.

"Did you not hear me, reject?" Still not a glance up from the pad.

Maura turned towards the weigh station. Around her, crudrats she'd never met, not her shift and not her crowd, stared in confusion and this stranger in their midst. Maura hardly dared look up, willing the foreman to keep his head down.

Step. Step. Step.

The voice came at her, hard and sharp. "Hold it a blasted tick there space scum, where's your murmel got itself to?"

Maura didn't wait for anything more than that. She ran.

Voices yelled. Hands grabbed at her. Her shirt, already torn for bandages and all over frayed, ripped. She secured it as best as possible over the embarrassing bits, as she ran, trying not to worry on modesty overly much. She ignored the hands and the voices and pushed forward.

She nipped down an air duct, soon enough and fast enough to bruise her knees. No one followed. So an unlicensed reject was dodging blades during shift? Who much cared? So long as the tunnel remained un-dented her reasons didn't matter. Reject business couldn't possibly mean anything to real people. Not in the long haul.

To her relief, Maura saw the foremen put his crew of blue-haired nobodies back to their traces.

Maura made her way tunnel by tunnel towards steel Spoke dockside. She followed the path she and Rees had taken the spin before, silvery blue metal changing to black. She found her little tuft-headed friend and the big white alien waiting in the last duct hub big enough to hold quoin Fuzzy.

Maura swung herself down and handed the alien his keycard.

He wrinkled his nose and rubbed away at the blue crud coating the key's surface.

Maura took it back from him, spat on it, then rubbed it rough and fast against her much abused knickerbockers. It came away still blue, but less so than it had been, and generally cleaner. She shrugged off the alien's obvious disgust. "Safest place I knew to stash it was inside a scyther. No one but a crudrat would ever encounter it or get it out. You might as well get used to crud. Gets onto everything."

She turned to Rees. "So, did ya get a look-through at the

stuff?" She gestured to the pile of things she'd salvaged from the passed-out armigers and sequensors back in lock-up.

Rees nodded, grinning wide.

"Anything useful?"

Rees proffered a handful of steel Spoke tools — strange little laser devices, small skin shockers, and other mysterious metal tackle.

"Excellent. You keep those, for your help in the break-out."

Rees looked surprised, but pleased. "Why?"

"Never know what might come in useful 'round about an ice planet, do we?" She looked to the alien for support. "We're gonna need some kind of goods to sell where we're going, right?"

"Sometimes this one thinks he has a fix on your weird way around Galactic Common talk, sometimes not so much."

Maura sighed. "Can we bring this stuff with us?" she asked, clear as could be.

"Certainly, why not? Never know what might come in handy."

"There," said Maura to Rees, "ya see? Here, take these as well." She handed him half the ration cubes and kept the rest for herself.

Rees shrugged and pocketed the items 'round and about, inside his vest and knickerbockers.

Maura tore open a ration cube and bit into it. Chewing thoughtfully she looked at the small pile of objects still littering the tunnel floor.

Absentmindedly, she handed the alien a ration cube. He unwrapped and sniffed at it dubiously. It presented itself as a dense square of dark brown foodstuff tinged slightly blue.

"Won't bite, won't scream." Rees was amused by the alien's distrust.

"That's more than you can say 'bout half that weird prog-enetor real-type food," added Maura.

The alien took a bite. "Ah, field provision ration cubes."

Maura and Rees ignored his strange words, but he inhaled the rest of the bar so quickly, Maura handed him a second one.

Then she reached into the pile and gave Rees the guards' sim keys as well. "You're more likely to need these than we are in the next bit."

Rees nodded and took them without comment.

Maura riffled about in the remaining pile, looking for anything interesting or valuable. The murmel, who'd been pretending disinterest off to one side, swaggered over and sniffed at the objects. He nibbled wistfully on a plastic water tube, spat it out and wandered away. Maura fished out the sonic gun.

"What good will that do you?" Rees wanted to know.

"It is a weapon, is it not, small one?" The alien was confused.

"Yeah, but it won't fire 'sept under orders from the chip it's registered to. And Maura, I'm sure you are all surprises about this, ain't got that chip. Whatcha want it for, Maura, decoration?"

"Why Rees, don't you know all the progenetor toffs are wearing them this turn?" said Maura, and then seriously, "Sometimes it's enough to wave it about." She tucked it into a pocket in her knickerbockers as well, but left the handle out, so it'd be easy to draw.

"Now this one sees why you have garb with multiple pockets."

"We be wearing knickerbockers," replied Maura bitterly, "'cause we were never given anything more adult. We ain't never got past the age when we should've taken the chip.

Even if a reject managed over a hundred turns, we always wear children's duds. No hat, no coat, no proper trousers."

The alien finished his ration cube and nodded. "This one will fix that."

Maura blinked at him. He didn't wear any clothing at all, she couldn't quite imagine what his icy world might come up with for her.

"Right," Rees looked ready for anything. "What's next?"

"Simple really," said Maura. "Me and big Fuzzy, we break into the armiger dockside. You activate the docking sequence. Then once you set that, you slide on out and join us just afore lift-off. Sound?"

"Oh so simple." Rees was all sarcasm, but he looked like he was about to sit pretty with extra cubes for a month — pleased with himself and his immediate future. *Sure is a danger-monger, this one.* Maura shook her head at his joy in risk. She'd have hung it on youthful folly, but she'd a notion Rees would always be a bit wiggly in the head about peril.

Fuzzy looked suitably upset at Maura's summation. "That is cutting things a little thin, non-enemies. Any mistake in the timing and this one could end up leaving the small-one behind."

Rees shrugged. "So I safety-make it so that things don't get off tick. All will be well. Don't you be concerning your-self with my troubles. You're the two taking all the real risk."

Maura didn't say anything, just handed two of the sequensor robes wordlessly to the alien. She pulled on one herself, flipping up the hood, it fit well enough.

Rees gave her a suspicious once up and down. "You know, without the blue hair, those eyes and that robe be looking far too comfortable together."

Maura turned to quoin Fuzzy. "Now you."

The alien tied one robe about his waist and put the other

on, pulling the hood well over his face. It looked a little off, but at least he was mostly covered top to bottom. He also looked more miserable, as the weight of the cloth added to the heat only he felt.

Maura couldn't quite keep down a grin at his appearance. He seemed to be made up of one sequensor sitting on the shoulders of a second. The absurdity of it appealed to her quirky humor.

Rees put on the last white robe. It was a good hand-breadth too long on him. It would trail something awful when he walked.

Maura snickered. "I'm sure hoping they don't look much past that robe there, short stuff."

Rees kicked her in the shin. It didn't work too well through the excess fabric. He stumbled slightly over the hem.

Maura hid a broad grin and picked up the Am Xinyn's silver-topped cane. It would lend truth to her role, if no one looked too closely at the genetic contract code and parliament alliance symbols etched into its top.

"No offense intended, non-enemy, but this one would be better off with that weapon there."

Maura tipped her head at the alien. "Why you be thinking that?"

"You know how to wield the staff in combat, do you non-enemy?"

"And you do?"

"Of course."

"Why, of course?"

"Kill'ki are warriors from the bones out, and this one is quoin rank." His tone was gentle and reasonable.

Maura looked at him a long moment. Strange, but she didn't want to give the cane up. Some wrongness kept it hooked into her hand. It made sense, though, his talk. With a sigh she passed it over.

The alien weighed it in his hand, testing the balance and the heaviness of the silver end. He looked like he wanted to take a swing or two, but there was barely room for him in the hub let alone him plus a weapon. It would have to wait.

Maura turned to the murmel still lurking about them and their ever more entertaining activities. "Go on, you, go home. Settle." She gave him the *return home* command. It was phrase that after weigh-out usually sent the fat beasties back to their dens, resting up for next shift.

The blue creature crouched still on the tunnel floor and watched her with a suspicious expression in his limpid eyes.

Maura felt like crying. She wouldn't of course, none of that feebleness for her. But her eyes felt hot and itchy and wanted to spill over. Long turns they'd spent together, she and that fat murmel. But she was going to a place without crud. Not just the ice planet, because from what the alien had said even Kill'ki skiffs and spaceports had little crud hanging about. Murmels were made for crud, tinkered from the get-go to deal with the Wheel's biggest space-made problem. There would be no purpose for him where she was going, and he'd likely starve to death from the lack.

She scratched the top of his head one last time and then turned resolutely away. She jumped, grabbing tunnel top and swinging herself into an exit tunnel, motioning Fuzzy to fall in behind.

Before the alien could do so, the murmel made to follow, as though he thought Maura's gesture were meant for him.

"You," Maura said in her non-quarter tone, "you stay. Settle."

The blue beastie gave a little sigh and sat back, ears twitching in annoyance. Then he reached about and pulled his tail 'round with his little paws and bent to wash the tip. As if to say, what did he care? It was clearly bath-time.

Maura and the alien crawled away. Rees took one last look at the remnants of the loot. He sighed regretfully but left it there. Tying up his sequensor robe in a little knot at the hem to keep it out of his way, he too crawled off through one of the black metal ducts toward military Spoke.

Behind them, the murmel sniffed at the leftover plunder with interest. He nibbled once more on the bit of plastic tubing as though to reevaluate his first assessment. Then, after great deliberation and a few more nibbles, he curled up to sleep in the center of the pile.

Maura and quoin Fuzzy jumped down out one of the ducts of the armiger dock zone behind a military skiff. They straightened as quickly as possible and walked out from around the spaceboat as though they were there on a particular mission. They headed directly for the alien skiff. *What had Fuzzy called it? Oh yes, a whale.* None of the armigers milling about tried to stop them. Maura timed their entrance with shift change, so that it looked as though they'd just entered the bay along side a new group of dockhands.

They walked shoulders back, heavy footed, all arrogance and confidence. The alien kept his robe's hood pulled down far and his head dipped low so it was near impossible to see his face. Maura's only concern was her hair, so she kept her hood tight, but she wanted them to see her face. For once, she intended to put her weird silver eyes to good use.

The group around the skiff was smaller than it had been, clearly some of them, gone off to question the alien prisoner, had not yet returned. Maura wondered if they still lay on the floor of the lockup, struggling to breathe. Cleaners had probably caught them up by now, robeless but alive.

There were four still prodding at the alien's spaceboat,

and they seemed to have settled into a more scientific approach to cracking the casing. They had an array of tools, from laser saws to plasma torches to old-fashioned rotary mechanical metal drivers, which they were applying one after another to the body of the whale.

The skiff seemed not to care what was attempted, nothing would get through its protective guard.

As Maura and Fuzzy drew closer, one of the sequensors broke off his fussing and came towards them, hand raised in greeting.

He looked to Maura first, apparently not put off by the alien's immense stature. *There must be more extreme triggering going on amongst progenetors than I thought, if the uppers see no need to question such massive height and obviously cloaked face.*

"How do you do?" He bowed all politeness.

"How do you do?" Maura imitated his accent and bowed in turn. The alien followed her lead in silence.

"Who's introducing?" the sequensor asked, unsure of who held higher rank.

"Maura Am Vern," she said, no reason to lie. She hoped they couldn't see the way her hands trembled. "This is my, uh, cousin." Dismissed and unnamed, Maura had implied the alien was of much lower status.

Thus better knowing everyone's relationships, the sequensor ignored Fuzzy and took a careful look at Maura's face. She forced herself not to check to make sure her hood hadn't slid.

"Am Vern, of course." He sounded none too pleased at her appearance. "We should have known you'd turn your creepy eyes up as soon as word go out about this little gem. Well, come put those triggered organs of yours to good use and take a look."

Maura and Fuzzy followed him over to the other group.

"Am Verns have come," barked the man, as soon as they were within talking distance of the other sequensors.

One of the others looked up sharp. "Of course they have." She sounded even less pleased than her compatriots with this turn of events. Maura noted, without much surprise, that her eyebrows were red and winged out. She was older than pearly-skin's friend, but the same stock. She too would also lean anti-Am Vern by family politics. Maura wondered if there was anyone allied with Am Vern stock amongst this lot, or if her family members simply preferred to make enemies of every highstock in the Wheel.

So far no one had yet been pleased to see Maura's eyes. Except old pearly skin and that only because he wanted to turn them into earrings. Maura pretended all business, narrowing her triggered eyes in a way she hoped came off as menacing. She used foreman's tone and foreman's words. "Report!"

"Ain't that typical Vern? All they got is formality and regulations, no class," grumbled the third sequensor, not looking up from the diamond edged saw he was testing on the hull of the whale.

"Report," barked Maura again. She and quoin Fuzzy shifted subtlety 'round so that they were as close as possible to the side of the alien skiff. Maura had no idea where the door would be located, but she figured she could follow Fuzzy's lead.

"We can't get inside this blasted thing," explained one of the sequensors, sounding more that a tad annoyed.

"Have you tried sonic guns?" Maura pulled the one she tucked into her rags out from inside her robe. The gun would never fire for her, but the sequensors didn't know that.

All four reached to stop her. "No!"

In that same instant, while all attention was on Maura, the alien reached over and did something to the skiff with three quick movements. A small drawer slid out from the space-boat's side. He placed his key-card into it. Instantly, it slid back away.

The skiff shuddered once. That got the sequensors' attention away from Maura and her pistol. As they all watched in amazement, a door fell downwards from the hull's side, exposing a set of stairs and a tall opening.

Quoin Fuzzy threw off his two robes and leapt for that opening. Maura broke towards it as well. Two of the sequensors grabbed at Maura, pulling the white robe from about her head, so that her blue hair shone under the dock lights. One drew his sonic pistol and seemed torn between whether to shoot at Maura or her too-tall accomplice. The fourth sequensor went after Fuzzy, already partly inside his whale.

That fourth sequensor, for all his chip-improved skill and strength, was no match for the alien. Fuzzy twirled the silver-topped progenetor cane about in his hand, almost faster than eyes could follow. It hit the sequensor square in his stomach and sent him flying backwards.

That decided the one with the sonic gun. As the two holding Maura shoved her struggling form down onto the deck, she saw him shift his aim onto the alien.

"Watch out!"

Quoin Fuzzy ducked to one side.

"Go!" Maura called, struggling to get loose from the sequensors and their triggered strength.

The sequensor fired his sonic gun missing Fuzzy but hitting the ship.

The alien skiff vibrated, letting off that impossibly loud screeching noise. Apparently, opening the entranceway didn't turn off the spaceboat's defensive mechanisms. The two sequensors holding Maura and the one with the gun all fell backwards.

Their grip loosened, Maura kicked one in the head, and clawed at the fingers of the other, managing to writhe free. She crawled away, clawed her way to her feet, and dashed towards the opening.

The skiff started to emit a humming noise that Maura took to be the engines revving up.

A sequensor caught her foot, bringing her back down sharply to her knees on the deck. It was the kind of fall dented a tunnel and cost a 'rat her license. Maura gasped at the pain.

Fuzzy's white head appeared in the shadowed darkness of his skiff's entrance.

"No good," yelled Maura, "go without me."

The alien didn't seem to hear. He leaped back out of the skiff, onto the floor of the docking bay.

A voice came over the loud speaker, an automated computer voice. "Decompression in ten ticks," it said, and then, "Nine…" It continued to count down with perfect measured time, dispassionate as only a computer could be.

Rees had managed his end of the business.

All around them, dockworkers and armigers scrambled for decompression safety points. The sequensors didn't seem to notice. They hung onto Maura, no matter how much she jerked and kicked. Even her running muscles weren't strong enough to combat their chip-enhanced grips.

"Eight… Seven…"

Then there came a new noise, the sad wet crunch of breaking bone. Fuzzy was there, whipping about with his cane as though it were an extension of his already impossibly long arms. Sequensors went soaring.

"Six… Five…"

Maura had never seen such physical combat. Sequensors were supposed to be the best of the Wheel's best, triggered to be faster and smarter than even other progenetors, chipped to be strongest and most able. Yet that big white fuzzy alien felled them like they were the rejects. Like they were *nothing*. The cane nipped out to the side, then whirling to the front, a spinning wheel all of its own and just as deadly. When all four sequensors were eating deck and not looking likely to get up any time soon, Fuzzy offered Maura a massive paw and hoisted her up. Only then did he turn back to his skiff.

"Four…"

Maura regained use of her feet. Her knees were screaming but she worked well enough to follow him.

The alien was inside, Maura was still a handbreadth behind, scrabbling to reach the entrance in time. She wasn't yet in as the door began to raise against take-off.

Out of the corner of one eye, Maura thought she saw a flash of blue streak across the docking bay floor and leap into the alien's boat, tail lashing.

"Three…"

"Stop," yelled the last of the sequensors, the one with the sonic gun. "I'll fire on you, crudrat, not the skiff. You, at least, will stay behind and answer to the Wheel."

Maura froze, the entrance just one leap away.

"Two…"

10

As soon as humans entered space they determined how best to fight in it.
~ Proverb

Maura had nothing to lose. What kind of life portside would she have in a sequensor embrace? No, there was an ice planet in her future. With a glance over her shoulder at the mouth of that deadly gun, Maura dove. Crudrat's reflexes kicked her up into a flip. She came out of it into a vault over the rapidly closing door, sliding through the narrow space left, and into the open body of the alien skiff. The door clanged shut just missing her foot. Behind her a sonic gun sounded and the whale shook, screaming its objection into the docking bay.

Maura's murmel sashayed over to her and placed one paw on her ankle.

"What do you think *you're* doing here?"

The murmel looked up at her, wide blue eyes all innocence. Not even a chitter of apology.

"And how am I gong to fill that fat belly of yours?"

The murmel turned away. Clearly Maura was not going to be reasonable about this. He went to investigate this new alien world he'd leaped into.

The skiff shook, and Maura decided she best follow the murmel's example.

She looked around at the interior, but she wasn't looking exactly at *it*, not yet. She was hoping that Rees had made it inside, perhaps while she had been lying flat to the deck while Fuzzy bashed sequensors with a cane.

No such luck.

"Where's Rees?" Maura asked. "We got us a murmel but no Rees?"

Fuzzy had made his way to the front cockpit of the spaceboat and sat down in what must be a steering seat. It was a strange kind of interior, all round and molded, no sharp edges or corners anywhere.

"Sorry, non-enemy, it would appear that he didn't make it in time."

Maura damped down a great well of sorry, knowing they couldn't afford to wait and see if he would. She pinched her ear to stop the tears and looked around at her new nest. It seemed almost tunnel-like. Maura felt hugged by close rounded walls and darkness. It was alien-odd to see no blue floating through the air. Upon closer inspection, the skiff's inside was beamed with rib-like curves of white. They seemed to form a boned skeleton upon which the black skin of the hull was stretched.

Maura shuddered, for that thought made the whole set-up uncomfortable, like she was riding inside the belly of some beast. She climbed to the forward part of the ship.

"So why'd you come back out for me?"

The alien glanced up at her like she was crazy to ask, then

quickly looked back down at a complex sequence of sliding knobs he seemed to be moving about within a three dimensional sphere.

"We are bonded," he said, as though that was all the explanation needed.

Maura nodded, understanding. "Rees was not."

"Exactly."

At the twist of a dial, the skiff shuddered again and lifted up off the bay floor. Maura stumbled slightly, and after a quick glance about, wedged herself into a curve of the cockpit. It looked a fit area to brace against and mostly out of Fuzzy's way.

The decompression alarm sounded, loud enough to hear, even inside the skiff. The countdown had ended.

"Air is still going to be tight. We got a murmel but no Rees."

"What?" The alien glanced up.

"Stowaway, hopefully it'll all work out," said Maura, hoping not to distract him from important work. Like saving their collective asses.

The skiff hovered, swinging about, as the bay doors began to open. A screen in front of Fuzzy lit up, showing the huge dockside walls and multiple military skiffs, and the illuminated control rooms of the vacuum-safe area around the top side of the bay.

"There!" Maura pointed to Rees's small blue head.

He was the center of a hive of subgenetor activity in one of the control rooms. It was a broiling mass of citizenship milling around her friend's small white-robed form. As they watched, Rees shook both his attackers and the robe off, and crawled like a murmel up the wallside of the room. He popped the cap off of an air duct there and disappeared inside. It was a tight fit even for Rees and none of the subgenetors were able to follow him. Last thing Maura saw of him was the underside of one dirty foot.

The alien skiff screamed and shook violently.

A couple armigers had clearly run to their spaceboats right before decompression and were now taking it upon themselves to bring down the alien ship the hard way. Pot shots inside a spaceport were considered big stupid, but these were desperate ticks for the military. No Spoke would be happy if the alien got away. Everyone would feel the burn of sequensor vengeance regardless of rank. Battle regulations were spaced easy under such circumstances. The alien skiff was under an onslaught of gravity fire.

Behind them, the decompression doors were beginning to slide shut.

"We must leave the small one behind, non-enemy."

Maura's face felt prickly and stretched. "Ain't right, he did more than his fair share." Then, after a pause, "I'm thinking maybe he knew all long that he might get left behind."

The alien nodded in one jerky motion. Sliding his controls about he brought the skiff around and dove it out under the closing bay doors without a dust's worth of room to spare.

"We will come back for him," the alien said, no doubt noting Maura's stricken expression.

Maura, knowing the significance now, replied simply, "Your bond on it?"

The alien swallowed. "There is no bond to action, only to a person. But here is a promise, little blue — there is a debt, a barter in play, help for help. And this one sees now what a world it is that your friend is left to. Balance requires reciprocate aide in equal measure to what your Rees did this day."

"Good enough," Maura replied, but she hadn't much faith

in a simple promise. She herself made a vow, with or without
Fuzzy's help.

Just then she felt her whole body, organs on out,
commence a floating expansion.

"Woah!" Her every little skin hair took on life of its own.

Next to her Fuzzy looked even fuzzier as all his fur puffed
out, no gravity to weight it down. She realized this must be
space's free float. There weren't a speck of gravity spun to
life in a skiff, not even an alien skiff – too small. She'd heard
about this, dire warnings doled out to keep the crudrats cleaning. It's what happened when a spaceport halted spin. But
she'd never thought to feel it.

Fuzzy maneuvered his ship around, unperturbed, while
Maura floated off to the side and bumped into the hull, like
dust in an air duct. Only then did she realize he was
completely strapped in.

She squeaked, surprised and unusually clumsy for a
crudrat.

The alien glanced over at her and grinned. Maura
wondered if she would ever get used to seeing that furry face
come over suddenly human looking like that. His head was
now a perfect sphere of fur, no matter that he grinned, his
expression was one of perpetual surprise. That halo of white
somehow looking like the high arched eyebrows of shock
would on a human.

Turning back to his controls, the alien gestured to one
side of the cockpit where a bunch of cloth straps were tied-
off, their ends floating. Maura, whose feet seemed to have
drifted upwards of their own choice, pushed herself over, all
ungainly and bumbling, and untied a couple of them. Then
she swam back to her original niche and used them to lash
herself to the hull. The white bones that made up the ship's
chubby frame were not attached completely to the outer skin

but were fixed point-by-point with synthetic coils. This meant that the unattached parts in between were ideal handholds for steering a wayward body around in free float. Maura used one of them as a mooring point for her weightless self, lashing the cords about stomach and shoulders and affixing them best as possible behind her.

Only after she'd secured herself did she hear a rapid-fire chittering of annoyance emanate from the main cabin of the skiff. She craned her head around in time to see a tumbling blue puffball of lashing tail and affronted dignity go rolling past.

Fuzzy glanced at her but was too busy with his piloting to take ticks to see to the cause of her laughter.

Maura faced forward in time to watch the spaceport enter the screen as the alien flipped his ship about in a quick twisting maneuver.

She'd never seen her spaceport from the outside before. There it floated, her whole world right up to until now. It looked like some huge sphere of wound-up metal cords and plastic chunks. The metal cords would be the harvesters wrapping around the habitation center in coils and twists. Their funnel mouths open every which way to space, breathing in the fuel that scythers would eventually cull to usefulness. That whole mess of a spaceport spun, creating the artificial gravity within. It was ugly. A piece of kit that if Maura saw lying gutterside she'd not bother to scavenge. She was not sorry to see it twist out of view as the alien brought his pudgy skiff around, pointing it away from Wheel space, towards soem far distant ice planet.

The skiff shook again, not so bad now that it was out of gravity, but still reacting to more shooting. Some of the military boats had mobilized to follow them out of dock — a small swarm of almond shaped space beetles trailed them through the blackness.

Untroubled, the alien seemed more comfortable now than Maura had yet seen him. His thoughts and movements floated easily in three dimensions, his skiff dipping and swaying not just side-to-side but up and down as well, relaxed as could be. It made for a hard target and a harder mark, but it also made Maura's stomach take new interest in bile production. Sure she could flip and dip herself – any time, any tunnel, any blade – but having the ship do it for her took a certain toll on her internal organs.

"How many hits can this ship of yours take?" She swallowed down nausea.

"Not many more. This one may have to put you to returning the fire. You ever shot a ship's cannon before, little blue?"

Maura looked at him like he was crazy. "I've never even been on a ship."

He goggled at her, black eyes wide. "You were *born* in space?"

"Near as I can tell. Don't have much memory before crudrat life, but that would look to be the truth of it. Can hardly see why my ex-family'd fly me up from planetside just to dump me."

The alien tossed his head in amazement. "Ah well, now would be the time to learn. See that screen there, flip it up."

Maura found a small flat screen in front of her and flipped it into place, horizontal like a table. It generated a three dimensional spherical image, at the center of which was their floating boat, a snub-nosed blip of green. Always at the center, a cone of red emanated up from its top, taking a wedge out of the display sphere. Zooming into and out of the display area, bobbing towards and then away from Maura, were various blobs of yellow light.

"Those bits of yellow are enemy fighters," the alien explained. "The red is dead space, since the guns are mounted underneath us, and my whale won't fire through herself. A smart enemy will try to say inside the cone, but you Wheel rarely fight smart."

One of the yellow blobs spit out a little beam of light which arrowed towards their green blob at the center of the display. Fuzzy nosed his whale down and to one side, and the shot missed. All the enemy blobs of light moved up and to the opposite side in front of Maura.

Maura's stomach took up occupation somewhere near her right ear. The three dimensional image was making her even more queasy.

"Now what?" she asked.

"See those two coils? Put one each around the front part of your finger and thumb. Should be on your head-hand, not your heart-hand."

Maura found two ring-like metallic coils on wire tethers attached to the base of projection screen. She slid them on, as directed, pulling them tight 'round the tips of her forefinger and thumb. She assumed by head-hand he'd meant the hand she used most, for eating and dressing and the like, which in Maura's case was the left.

"That is your firing solution, little blue, when you clasp the two rings together."

"Really?" Maura was all interest. Experimentally, she pinched the air in front of her nose, the rings made a faint tink.

Fuzzy gave her a withering look. Despite that fact that there were other ships around, and that he was focused on flying, he was very nonchalant about explaining things to

Maura. "It will not work until it is turned on and your hand is inside shooting space. Also it won't work inside the red cone." He was speaking quite quickly.

"Right." Maura carefully pushed her tethered left hand into the bottom sector of the display image in front of her. Nothing happened. The blobs of light still buzzed around, some going straight through her hand.

The alien made a quick course correction, spinning his ship nose over tail. The stars whirled.

Maura swallowed hard.

Then he reached over with one furry white paw, and tapped some kind of code into the edge of her projection screen.

Maura's hand began to tingle and it was suddenly hard to move it though the image, as though there were extra gravity just there. A slight metallic smell sifted through the weight-less air, like fresh blood or shaved metal.

"Magnetic drivers," Fuzzy explained. "Now all you need to do, little blue, is get your fingers around an enemy fighter. Don't miss, the whale doesn't have ammunition to spare." With that terse admonishment, he went back to his woozy piloting.

Maura bit her lip. Her brow creased, bringing blue eyebrows together.

It was harder than it looked. The Wheel ships, blobs of light, moved very fast into and out of the spherical tracking space, following not only their own trajectory but also shifting whenever Fuzzy steered his whale one way or the other. Maura quickly realized she *had* to glean the tune of her companion's movements, sense where Fuzzy might be going next, watch his shoulder muscles out the corner of her eye. Otherwise she lost all grasp on the blobs. It was a tad like reading blade movement. Once she'd got him down, she'd could space one variable.

But catching the blobs between thumb and forefinger was mighty hard. The first time she missed, clinking the metal rings together sharply on emptiness. The metallic smell spiked and the skiff shook once around them. She caught a flash of something off to one side of the view screen and the shot waffled harmlessly into space.

"Sorry."

Quoin Fuzzy ignored her.

More determined, Maura tried again. This time she managed it, catching a blob of light right between the metal rings on her fingers. She didn't get to see the shot actually occur on the view screen, but something significant happened as the alien skiff shook and the blob she'd pinched blinked out of existence.

Fuzzy gave her a look of surprise. Second attempt and a successful outcome was apparently impressive.

Maura, concentrating hard, went after another blob of yellow. This one skittered off screen with slippery speed before she could pinch it. She dove in again, hand tingling and sluggish. It was like trying to catch crud dust in a multi-fold air tunnel, particles spinning this way and that, air blasting several directions at once.

A blob streaked down in front of the nose of the whale. On Fuzzy's viewing screen an almond shaped armiger skiff appeared, scyther riding its back like some tubular parasite, guns mounted just below. Fuzzy dived their skiff. The Wheel ship followed. Maura reached over, through the read cone on her display, into firing space and caught the yellow blob neatly. Her coiled rings chimed. The metallic smell wafted forth. The whale shook, and right before their eyes a Wheel fighter silently exploded in a flash of blue flame.

Quoin Fuzzy zipped them through the spinning wreckage.

"Very pretty," he commented.

Maura tried not to think about the fact that she was actually killing people. "How much longer before they give up the chase?" Her hand was back in motion, hunting down the next pinch.

"Your guess is as good as mine."

"How long 'til we get out of Wheel space?"

"About ten more ticks." He jerked the skiff to the left sharply.

In front of Maura all her yellow blobs zoomed to the right. "Then it will be eleven ticks before they give up," she replied, confident.

A flash came from one of Maura's blobs. "Enemy fire," said Maura, because it seemed the right thing to say.

Fuzzy twisted their skiff again, but not soon enough. The whale shuddered and whined.

"How come we can take the hits and they can't?"

Fuzzy gave her a look suggesting she best not ask again about his people's defensive tech. *Still not entirely trusting? I can suss to that. I'd be making a good Wheel spy, except sequensors don't have that kind of imagination.*

She voiced his unspoken order: "Shut your trap Maura and kill things."

She went for another shot. Only four blobs of light still remained in and out of her display image. One seemed to have sussed the red cone trick, and was shadowing them from safe space directly in that zone. Must be a pretty good pilot, for he was sticking close to Fuzzy's rapid course changes. Ironically, this meant he couldn't shoot at them. Steel Spoke fighters had gun mounts on their forward tips only, not underneath like the alien's skiff.

Maura pinched at a different blob, but the target slid out from between her fingers. Another wasted shot.

"Sorry."

"This next is your last shot," was his only reply.

Maura snapped her mouth shut and concentrated.

Pinch. Another silent blue explosion out of sight-line and only three blobs were left.

Maura relaxed slightly. She was surprised to find her stomach seemed to be back in its normal location. *Fancy that.* She slid the metal rings off of her fingers leaving them to dangle until she was told what to do next.

Something chittered at her. The murmel had managed to float his way into the cockpit. He was lashing his tail about as a kind of propeller using it to steer as best possible through the weightlessness. He bumped into her ankle. At which point he wrapped all four paws and tail, solid as crud-glue, around her foot. Maura let him.

She watched the alien as he piloted. Fuzzy's hands moved and danced as they steered, jumping between four levers, and the ship slid about in response. There was a liquid beauty to it, and Maura, who until then would never have called the alien graceful, was impressed.

Then the yellow blip shadowing them in the safe cone of space above dropped back and took one last spitting shot.

Quoin Fuzzy rolled the skiff over and the shot missed by a speck.

Then all the yellow blobs disappeared off of Maura's display. Some invisible barrier had been crossed, they were out of Wheel space.

"Are we now in *your* people's territory?" Maura watched the alien's dancing hands slow and his shoulders relax a tad.

"No, little blue. This is Cotyla space, but at least they

aren't Wheel. So long as we pursue our own business and not theirs, we will be left to our own devices."

Space flight was overly calm without fighters blobbing about or the whale shaking itself something fierce. They followed a smooth steady course, and it felt almost like not moving at all.

Quoin Fuzzy checked some of what Maura assumed were read-out instruments. They were mostly circular shapes, showing degrees of colored fullness.

At Maura's obvious interest he tapped at one. "Flush capacity and fluid levels, tells us about how many times the scythers need to be cleaned, before a refuel."

That'd be the alien skiff's main limiter on space travel time.

Fuzzy pointed to a collection of about fifty smaller circles all half full of blue. "DMP for ship's scythers, tells when flush is required. We'll probably have to flush before we hit enough void to fold, all that maneuvering through real space means a high amount of build up."

Maura translated DMP to crud in her head, but had no idea what *fold* meant.

Fuzzy tapped a different readout. "Average fuel levels inside the harvesters." That one was nearly full. While they'd been maneuvering and shooting at Wheel fighters, the whale had been hard at work collecting dark matter and processing it. "Looks like we have enough to fold." The alien sounded pleased.

"What's *fold*?"

He looked at her, head cocked to one side. "The quick way to get around."

Isn't that what they had been doing? Getting around quickly?

"You do know that the distance between stars is too vast

to cross in a lifetime? We need a way that's faster than light. This one doesn't know Wheel tech, but Kill'ki use dimensional folding. It is," he paused, "uncomfortable, but efficient." He pointed to another dial which seemed only to flash either red, blue, or white and not indicate a percentage of any kind. "We cannot be in proximity to other matter when we fold, even dark matter. It," he paused hunting down the right word for it in space-tongue, "wrinkles things. We must find void, truly empty space, to fold."

The dial in question suddenly went from blue to flashing white.

"Ah." Fuzzy yanked the ship into a tight spin to keep it fixed at that one point. The dial continued flashing.

"Excellent." He looked back at the DMP build-up dial. It was about three quarters full. "Best flush first." He looked at Maura and her murmel, "Ready?"

Maura had no idea what she was readying herself for so she simply nodded.

"Flushing." He flipped a switch.

The hull walls of the ship, which Maura had thought stiff and solid, shimmered, and then went to a semi-transparent liquid state. Suddenly, there she sat, surround by a frame of white bone and the absolute nothingness of a watery space peopled by watery stars. Through those liquid walls, from nose to tail, ran multiple blue veins. The part of Maura's brain that wasn't terrified figured there must be about fifty or more, mini-scythers used to both steer the whale and fuel it. As she watched, the blue began to slowly disappear, starting at the front of the ship, until there were no veins visible at all. Maura had the feeling that she could reach out a hand and punch straight through that thin veil of liquid wall and out into the vacuum.

It was downright petrifying.

The murmel appeared to agree with her assessment. He screeched high and distressed, clutching her foot even tighter and burrowing his little face into the nook between her ankle-bone and heel.

Maura choked on her own breath.

Then the alien flicked the switch back up and the walls around them became solid black and fabric-like again. Maura stopped herself from retching. She felt she would never trust in the solidity of walls again.

Fuzzy, utterly unruffled, was looking at his read-outs. "Good." The DMP was at empty, the fuel was almost full, and the void detector still blinked white.

He flashed Maura a grin of pure delight. It was getting easier to cope with those bursts of human on his alien face. "Let's bend us some dimensions, shall we?"

Maura, after the whole flushing debacle, could only stare at him, knowing that her pupil would have dilated fully from looking *through walls* into the dark nothingness.

He did not wait for a reply. An apparently blank part of the control panel slid away to reveal an innocent looking pad of numbers. He tapped in a sequence. The pad spun about, presenting a single large button on its backside.

Fuzzy pushed the button down hard.

And Maura's whole universe ate itself alive.

11

With the harvesting of dark matter came the under-standing of light and its purpose. From there it was only a short time before humans determined how to hurl matter across space. It has yet to be determined if this was a good idea.

~ Introduction to *The Application of Dark Matter Theory, A Primer* by T.L. Prozzer

---

Until the moment the stars took her to rest, Maura would never forget her first fold. It was like having her brain removed out of her skull, twirled about on the end of a piece of string, stretched a bit, then reinstalled, backwards.

It began with a sensation of space-stuff moving all about her, not air, but actual reality-crux. It seemed to want to collapse, trying to cram itself against other parts of itself, and in so doing drag the Maura-being, from skin to blood to bone, with it. She became the tiniest thing in the universe, a fraction of fractions, closing inwards until she was nothing more than a pinpoint, one single dimension, a speck adrift in space. She was divided down to a square root of herself – negative matter.

Then she was back, almost simultaneously, and herself was everywhere, flattened and drawn, stretched beyond all limits out over the entirety of the universe.

That was not the worst of it.

That same fold – the one that buckled of dimensions, that bent three through four and shortened distance – it also shortened ticks. At the moment that she was a single point in space, she was also a single point in time, with no history and no predictions, the non-inertia of stopped nothingness her very thoughts bent into circularity.

Then with reentry, with the unfold and extension, Maura became all times, her own future and her own past and all the moments in between. Her brain balked — trying to comprehend travel beyond the physical limitations of three dimensions.

As the world patiently reconfigured itself, Maura found herself staring blankly into emptiness. Fuzzy would tell her later that her pupils had gone totally Am Vern, almost pure silver with only a slit of fine black, as though she'd been staring into a bright white light. They looked solid silver while she saw nothing but blurry blackness.

Maura wondered, stomach crumpled with panic and brain rutted by shock, if she had gone blind.

Then, slowly, she began to make out shapes. A blurring back and forth of whiteness became a large furry paw waving in front of her fixed gaze.

"Where did you go, just then, little blue?"

Maura hesitated, not sure she could trust her voice. "I think," she croaked, cleared her throat. "I think I went everywhere and nowhere at all."

Quoin Fuzzy nodded gravely. "Fold takes some folk like that." He appeared genuinely sympathetic. "They say some gens can see the atoms of dimensional reality."

Maura blinked again, finally beginning to focus, and her brain smoothed out into thinking of other things – like the murmel. Worried, she looked down to find the beastie's wide blue peepers staring up at her. His little face was a picture of concern over her strange behavior. Clearly murmels weathered fold unruffled. *Rees always said they ain't got the brains of a pea-hen. Whatever a pea-hen is. Probably not enough noggin to stretch over space and time. Lucky critter.* Maura scratched him about the ears and they both felt better.

"I think, I could be happy in life, never having to jump that noggin-twist ever again."

"Unfortunately, non-enemy. This is not likely to be the case. Thus, you are doomed to unhappiness."

Maura took stock. Her brain still all cut and torn, as though it had run scyther blades on its lonesome, from outside her skull, and been slashed by every single one. But her stomach had finally settled into weightlessness so perhaps things weren't so bad.

"Fold was on point," Fuzzy announced, "look there." He gestured at the view screen before them, an abyss of black speckled with stars. Not much different from the space they'd just left, only there weren't armiger skiffs gunning at them.

"What am I looking at?"

"Kill'ki space." Fuzzy puffed up his chest.

"I don't mean to come over all rude, but it looks like any other squat of space to me — black with stars a-speckling."

The alien actually laughed, his mouth an open maw of blue black in his white face. "Shows what you know." He turned back to his panel of dials. "Now, to see how simple it will be to get home without any of the gens having noticed that this one has been cavorting about in forbidden space."

"So you weren't supposed to visit us? I'm sure the sequensors are crushed. You do realize I'll be skulking about next to you — a shining example of your blundering? 'Tis not like I'll just be fitting in all secret and stealth among fuzzy white giants, now is it?"

He looked her up and down. "Point taken. We must come up with a good story to explain your presence and our bond."

"As opposed to what actually happened since I tumbled down on top of your big-boned carcass from beltway lid?" Maura was thinking that made for a pretty decent spate of telling, if telling was what he was after. Apparently not, for he was shaking that fuzzy head of his.

"Can't have that. Wouldn't do for *them* to know this one was imprisoned amongst the enemy, you see?"

Maura didn't, but figured it was another one of those alien culture things so she went along easy enough.

"You tell me what you want me speech-making, Fuzzy, and I'll speech it."

"Without wanting to know why you are being asked to perjure yourself?" The alien was impressed by her loyalty.

Maura looked at him from under blue eyelashes. "How many turns do you have under your skin, white oversized?"

"How old is this one?"

Maura nodded.

"Fourteen," then adding all defensive, "Nearly fifteen."

"Then I be knowing why you need me coloring truths for ya. Your age, mucking about Wheelside, plus you having family to go accounting to? I seen how it works with them progenetor highstocks 'round the arena. All fun until ticks turn and they got some explanation to make to the parentals." Maura nodded to herself.

Fuzzy looked as though he'd like to take offense, but there was too much truth in what Maura said. So he countered with, "So, how old are you, little blue?"

Maura shrugged, shivering slightly. In all the excitement she hadn't realized how cold the skiff was. She wasn't used to this much cold. "I'm guessing I be something on the order of twelve or thirteen turns. Hard to know for certain sure." She flashed him a grin of camaraderie. "Leastways, I know how to lie. So what's our story gonna be?"

Quoin Fuzzy considered for a moment. "This one found you stranded in an old skiff. You had floated away from your local space city…"

"Spaceport."

He continued as though she hadn't corrected him. "By accident and drifted into Cotyla space. You were running out of air and this one happened upon you while practicing maneuvers. Since you have no gens, you requested sanctuary in Kill'ki territory. Let us keep the details of what it means to be a reject, and the fact that we are bonded, dark for now."

"You just picked me up out the goodness of your big heart?" Maura looked skeptical.

Now it was Fuzzy's turn to shrug.

Maura was untroubled. "Ain't plausible from the Wheel side of things, but we ain't touting this to Wheel folk. If'n you think it'll fly with your kin, I'll glean to it." It was no blade cutting her if they were found out. She bent to pry the murmel off her ankle and wrap him around her neck like a cravat, for warmth. The blue creature huffed at the indignity, but let her do it.

"All right, that is settled." Fuzzy looked relieved. He scratched behind one ear with a paw. "Here's hoping the wari track us down soon." He pointed to yet another of his circle dial reader things, this one was near empty. "That is our breathable air. This one told you his whale was only meant to carry one at any distance. For skirmish it's designed for two. But folding with you, plus your little blue pal, and now we've not got much air left."

Goose bumps pricked her skin and Maura felt, if possible, colder. She tried to breath more shallowly. All it did was make her cough.

"Is there naught we can do?"

Fuzzy shrugged. "Believe in any godlings in that Wheel world of yours? Prayer is always an option."

Maura shook her head.

"Then no, not a lot to be done." The alien settled back comfortably into his curved cradle of a seat and crossed both arms over his wide white chest.

Maura shifted the murmel 'round her neck to maximize warmth. He murmured sleepily at her and nibbled a bit of her hair. She found herself staring, fixed, at the air registry dial.

Quoin Fuzzy spent several ticks looking out the view screen and several more frowning at the little flashing void light. He seemed to be purposefully not interested in watching the air diminish.

They sat for a while in silence while the dial slowly sunk.

Then the void alert flashed red, proximity alarm.

Fuzzy smiled and swung the skiff around. And there it was in their view screen — a massive ship, getting bigger by the ticks. Fuzzy enabled all of the whale's scythers and they sped to meet it.

Maura wasn't sure what she was expecting. Something like a big version of the whale perhaps, or one of the huge armiger battle ships, or a Wheel-style spaceport – now that she knew what one of those looked like.

This thing wasn't near to looking like any of them.

"Wow."

It glittered white, reflecting the light of a nearby star. The white was irregularly shaped and organic looking, curved and dull in places, sharp and angular and crystalline in others, plane and sphere in random mineral forms. Riding the white and spiking out of it were blocks of dulled silver and black. These were ribbed with faint lines that, even from a distance, Maura guessed meant more of the mini scythers with which Fuzzy's people covered their skiffs.

After a spate of mental processing, she asked, "What's it made of?"

Quoin Fuzzy looked at her like she was crazy. "Mostly ice, of course. Ice planet, remember? What else would it be made of?"

"A ship of ice?" Maura was incredulous. What about metal and plastic and silica all them sensible type things? Was ice safe? The blasted thing had no apparent front nor back either. How'd it move? It looked aimless and blind floating there, lost and adrift. Maura found herself losing confidence in Fuzzy and his people.

"Not a spaceship," the alien corrected her. "It can't really get about or maneuver much on its own. We have tugs for that, when needed. No, she is designed to provide a lay-over point for whales of all sizes, more like your spaceport idea, only only not fixed around any planet, just orbiting free around the star."

"Like an asteroid?"

He shrugged. "Basically, what you're looking at is a Kill'ki city."

Maura had heard of cities. Planetside build-ups, bigger than spaceports, millions of people living together. She'd always found them difficult to imagine. She looked again at the great floating ice thing getting rapidly closer to them. *That's really what cities look like?*

Fuzzy was frowning at it. "Wonder which one she is."

"You have more than one of those things?" Maura was impressed. It seemed like such a feat of construction. As they neared, she was beginning to understand the scope, for it nearly tripled the size of the spaceport. And she had thought that pretty darn huge.

Fuzzy cocked his head. "Most of the major gens have at least two or three cities. This one's gens line boasts five." He looked proud. "Plus a fleet of Blues as well as countless Greys. This little whale here, she's a Grey."

Maura reared away from him. Suddenly fear was boiling her blood. She was no longer cold. She was no longer caring about the lack of air. Had the alien been deceiving her all these ticks? His family *owned* spaceports, and fleets of spaceskiffs? In Wheel terms that meant only one thing. Her face crumpled with the realization. "You're progenetor stock!"

He looked at her, not understanding.

"Property monger, landed gentry, highstock, credit rich and morals poor," she explained further, nearly spitting the words in her horror.

He shook his head. "Kill'ki are not Wheel. That is not how we socialize. This one's gens has cities and ships to command, certainly, but ownership is by the gens entire. And this one's gens numbers in the thousands. We are a warrior people, so most of us climb the grades, to become wari and possibly domin, but many choose other journeys once they've completed service. We are not rich and idle like your Wheel progenitors, nor as cruel as your sequensors." He touched his head as though remembering the pain of that cranial drilling machine.

Maura wasn't reassured. To own, even as one among thousands, a share in a whole entire city? *He must be rich.*

And rich means progenetor. And progenetor means body-risk.
No matter that big Fuzzy fought like armiger and claimed no
progenetor tampering. Maura's defenses went all the way up.

Not knowing what else he could say to soothe her, Fuzzy
turned back to stare more closely at the ice city, now filling
most of the whale's view screen.

This time he noted something familiar about its makeup.
"Well, great floating frozen blue bollix."

Maura was impressed, she had never thought to hear a
bad word, never mind a string of them, exit that pretty-talking
mouth.

"It *would* have to be her, wouldn't it?"

"Her? Her who?"

Fuzzy closed his eyes and shook his head back and forth
in the wasted denial of the doomed. "Oh just you wait, little
blue non-enemy. This is going to be an *experience*. Make no
mistake about that."

"Fuzzy, I hate to be breaking this to ya so late into our
association, but, so far, all you been giving me is a long string
of odd-style experiences. I'm coming 'round to expecting
them."

"Good, at least one of us is prepared."

They set down, going through a kind of invisible atmosphere
shield, which appeared to keep breathable air in, and still seal
tightly about the whale as it passed through. It was tech well
beyond anything Maura had ever seen around Wheelside.
Sequensors would give up their own implant chips to get their
grubby mitts on it. The strangest part of the proceeding was
that they grounded the whale with *people* milling about the
dock area. No need to flee in fear from decompression. It was

like setting down a skiff in the midst of a shopping arena – surreal.

Quoin Fuzzy brought his whale in nimble and smooth, clearly gravity didn't trouble him. There certainly was gravity, the magical bubble that kept out space and all its vacuum, also kept out the weightlessness. Fuzzy's hair flattened back down as did the murmel's. Both of them looked much less ridiculous as a result.

Maura had never before been so happy as when she felt herself actually sitting fully onto the floor of the cockpit. *Ah, wonderful gravity.* The murmel seemed to agree with her, for the moment they entered through the barrier he let out a trill of delight.

Once the ship had docked, Maura wrapped the murmel close about her neck and shoulders like a coat collar, and followed Fuzzy out into an alien city.

It sure was the strangest docking area she'd had ever clapped eyes on. *And here was I thinking the progenetor dock zone down the old spaceport haunts were at the odd end of things, but this is alien in ways there's no way I can suss.*

The floor was icy white, but when Maura put bare feet to the surface she found that while it was *very* cold it was dry and seemed to be some kind of plaster or packed earth like in the gardening zones on the spaceport. Possibly set down on top of the ice? The far distant walls, enclosing the parked ships, appeared to be made of stone, some plastered over, some not. The place smelled of plaster too, that dusty-musty-smell Maura once sniffed down crossgenetor way, when a shipment of clay came in and busted all over the hallway floor. Weirdest of all, there was no roof, just that invisible barrier with the stars beyond. Much as when Fuzzy had flushed the whale, turning the walls transparent and watery, the feel of exposure to empty space gave Maura the screaming willies. When she looked up there was this sense of looking down, and she was pretty darn certain her feet were about to let go and she'd drift away. She hurriedly resolved to never tilt her back again.

Which meant she had to look down at her feet or around at her surroundings. In addition to a number of ships, mostly shaped like Fuzzy's whale — although there appeared to be a second bigger size — there were also people mucking about. Maura was taken aback to find they weren't all-over white fur like her companion. Instead, they appeared to be trying to cover all manner of genotypes, well beyond the Wheel standard of acceptability. She was utterly fascinated by a dark red individual, sporting red eyes and red hair too. *Why would anyone need that kind of tinker?* Red alien was dressed head to toe in some nice warm looking gear. Maura was envious.

"They aren't all like you." Maura's tone suggested Fuzzy had been intentionally deluding her.

"Of course not. Some are non-warriors, and very few are quoin. Quoin don't tend to work the docks, they are busy running other errands."

"No," Maura interrupted him when he would have gone on. "I'm meaning by way of looks." She waved her fingers up and down.

"Oh." Fuzzy looked about him as if he had never noticed before. He seemed at a bit of a loss. "You know we Kill'ki are not genetic xenophobes like the Wheel? Some of the ones that aren't Kill'ki by birth have spousal contracts, some have hired on to work, and a few are gens adopted. We like to think of ourselves as being open to all possibilities. The Kill'ki built a coalition after all."

"Yet they are staring at us a mite more than polite," commented Maura. As odd as the aliens were around them, it was Maura and Fuzzy who were garnering some pretty peculiar looks not to mention long stares.

Fuzzy went ominously silent.

Maura went on without his help. "So they ain't staring 'cause I'm Wheel born, blue haired, and packing a Murmel 'round my neck?"

Fuzzy was clearly embarrassed. "Nope. It is this one they are staring at." He pointed a big paw at himself and hung his head slightly.

Maura was about to ask why, when a ripple in the bustle of alien life spoke to the reason she and her companion hadn't moved from their stance next to the grounded whale. They were being *approached*.

The three jogging towards them mostly looked like Fuzzy, all over white. But when they halted right close, it turned out there were ranging kinds and styles of fuzz amongst the Kill'ki. Two had much longer fur than her Fuzzy, one shorter, and all had shaved parts around face and shoulders, exposing black skin underneath.

"Those patterns meaningful?"

"Kill markings," Fuzzy explained. It wasn't much of an explanation but it did inform Maura as to what these three were – armigers. But instead of a red and gold military uniform they wore a kind of wrapped cloth about waist and legs. *Improvised knickerbockers?* Only these were shorter, and weren't the same cut or style. They were red and gold, but also blue and silver, embroidered all over in complex patterns. They wore jewelry as well. Maura'd seen progenetors with more and better sparkle, but there was still enough on the three to leave her impressed. It was mostly gold and copper — strands of necklaces, earrings, and bits hanging from other piercings around and about the rest of the face.

However, once she got over the twinkle and looked

closer, she did see the warrior in them – for all three had multiple weapons tucked about belts and into the wrapped knickerbockers. Right unfriendly type weapons.

The smallest one of the three looked Fuzzy up-and-down and then said in heavily accented space-tongue, "Quy, what you showing your scrawny arse up here for? Aren't you supposed to be journeyman floating out Okechukio way?"

Now *that* was familiar talk to Maura. All guns, alien or not, spoke in the same bold crass way.

One of the others said, "We know things are a bit more casual in other branches of the gens but this is Manzanilla's city. You do realize we wear *clothing* here on Pillkiacta?" That was all sarcasm.

Maura grinned, understanding why people had been staring, and why her companion had gone over all embarrassed once they came to ground. Old Fuzzy was *naked*. She gave him an assessing look. Somehow no breeding bits were showing, but still. He'd been so comfortable with her, she'd never guessed it wasn't normal for his alien kind to be without clothing. But now, looking 'round, she realized that even the fuzzy-types wore some nod in the garment way.

Fuzzy ignored them all and said to Maura. "Non-enemy, these are my semi-cousins. This one will not trouble you with their talk-names. This one, in case you had not surmised, is called Quy on this city." He frowned, realizing he had best explain further. "That is not this one's true-name, of course, merely a talk-name among this branch of the gens."

The three warriors formed a loose semi-circle about Maura and Fuzzy.

Maura asked, "What should I be called?"

"That, you have to *earn*, little blue stranger," explained the shortest.

Maura was intrigued. "Oh really? So the talk-names have meaning? What does *Quy* mean?"

Fuzzy held up a paw.

His semi-cousins spoke over his hopes of stopping the explanation. "Guinea pig."

Apparently, this was somewhat bad, for Fuzzy bared his teeth in annoyance. "Pah, family."

Maura, shoeless feet on ice-cold floor, began shivering. This was all interesting, but despite alien surroundings, she was getting more concerned with finding warmth than anything else.

Fuzzy seemed to agree with that sentiment. "Are we going stand here chatting or do you three have orders? If not, this one is going around to the storehouse to get some clothes."

The middle-sized of the three warriors snorted in amusement. "Best you get that little furless friend of yours some clothing right quick too. She looks to be turning about as blue as her hair. She is all skin, and doesn't have more than a stitch on her, except that blue ruff thing."

The blue ruff thing, with his usual impeccable timing, chose that precise moment to reveal that he was not, in fact, a garment at all. He shifted around Maura's neck, placed two little paws a top her noggin and hoisted himself up to rest his chin on the crown of her head. He looked with mild interest at the three furry warriors. He was either worn ragged by the shock of the journey, or too hungry to care, for he stayed somber and silent. Neither a chitter nor screech rent the air.

"Great frozen frog teats!" said the smallest of the semi-cousins, a knife sprouting in his hand. "What in space is that thing?"

Maura frowned. "My murmel."

"And what, precisely, is a murmel?"

Maura shrugged, odd question. "This is, of course."

The short one narrowed his gaze on her. "Now we see why you and Quy are so friendly. You are a smart-arse just like him, aren't you?"

Maura felt she ought to take offense, but was too cold to act on the idea. Besides, it was true.

"Clothing will have to wait," said the largest of the three. That warrior had not spoken yet, but she seemed to be less in the mood to tease than the other two. She also appeared older and, to Maura's wild guess, more responsible.

"Will it?" Quoin Fuzzy was both unsurprised and resigned.

"*She* wants to see you." The explanation was flat – welded tight with no wiggle room.

"Of course *she* does." Fuzzy sighed.

The three warriors turned to lead the way. The smallest, shorter than Fuzzy but still taller than Maura by a head or more, tucked his knife back into his belt.

Fuzzy gestured at their backs in a manner Maura took to be rude. She memorized the hand movement for future needs. He looked down at her. "Are you warm enough for the moment?"

Maura could no longer actually feel her feet. "Sure."

Together they walked across the wide expanse of dock, and into an open doorway. The doorway and the wall in which it sat was made of shaped stone.

Maura smiled. No chip readers or beltways.

Every alien they passed looked right at her. Not necessarily with interest, but at least they *looked*. They did not see through her. Maura was just another alien among many. But she was real. She existed. Perhaps things wouldn't be so bad.

As it turned out, of course, they were worse.

12

*They say the first Tinkers got everything right, all the
aliens and all the pure bloods, right up and down from
the time of Manufacture to Seeding. But those who like
to contradict, claim that they really messed up with the
Kill'ki.*

~ *On the Civilizing of Worlds* by J. Kilsen Slliurp

Maura wished she knew what to expect. Still she'd gone and
thrown herself into this, might was well see it through to the
exit. The hallway she now walked though felt a tad more
spaceborn than others so far, but not by much. It was appropri-
ately narrow and tight fitting, but it was still made of stone not
metal or plastic. It was many stories high, with plaster above,
and plaster below, painted white. The stones were fit tight to
each other, but pillowed out slightly in their middles. Despite
the fact that there appeared to be not a bit of space between
them, a soft white light shone from the cracks, illuminating
the hallway. Oddest, to Maura's eyes, was the absence of crud

dust in the air. The light stayed white with no blue edge to it at all. So far as she could tell, there didn't seem to be air ducts either. Which meant no tunnels. This last made her nervous twice over. *How are we breathing? And where do I hide?*

The hallway was ever so slightly warmer than the landing area had been. Not enough, mind. Maura had never before been this cold in her well-regulated Wheel life. *A right unpleasant sensation.* Her teeth were rattling up against each other and she couldn't seem to stop them.

The hallway kept on going for quite some ways. There were little lead-offs to more hallways, and here and there fabric covered doorways that she supposed were private residences. It was all very illogically set up. *Why mix residence with working areas? How was one to determine Spoke? Who outranked whom?* Periodically, two little walls would poke out into the hallway from the sides, forcing them to single file. These bits would be dangerous if the ice city had to be evacuated. Maura's mind teemed with questions, but as the three warriors held silence and led them a brisk pace, she kept her peace.

Eventually, they deviated into a smaller even narrower hallway, up a set of three stairways, down another little hall, and through a curtained entrance into a large empty room.

"We will leave you to her," said the smallest warrior.

"Sooner you than us," said the middle one.

The large female said nothing only nodding to them once and marching the others back out of the room.

Maura looked at quoin Fuzzy.

Quoin Fuzzy looked at Maura.

"Can I call you Quy, too?"

"You might as well, everyone else here does." His tone was resigned.

"What are the... " Maura started to ask the next in her long stored-up string of questions.

"Hush, listen." Quy shook his fuzzy head, interrupting her.

Maura hushed and listened.

A voice echoed down the hallway outside. "...squeeze like a rotten melon after spring festival!" it was saying and then, "Where in the arse end of space is that little floating fish turd of a nibling of mine? I'll use his entrails for earrings, you see if I don't!" The voice was loud, but not as angry in tone as the words it uttered would make a person think it should be. It was as though the voice were speaking trash as a matter of course, rather than a matter of insult.

Quy's shoulders sagged. "And she couldn't be too busy running an entire city or something useful, could she? Oh no, she has to come down here right now, in person, larger than life and twice as frustrating." He looked to Maura. "Prepare yourself, non-enemy. Now comes the real battle."

Next thing Maura knew, the most splendid creature whipped aside the curtain across the doorway and came striding into the room.

She was just as white and as fuzzy as Fuzzy, but a good deal taller, and two times as wide. A giantess. She wore an elaborate crescent headdress with gold tassels and red fringe that added to her height. She wore something a little like a sequensor robe, only without sleeves or hood and belted at her waist. It was made out of a material stiffer than anything Maura had seen Wheelside. It was littered with decoration and embroidery within an inch of its existence, silvers and golds and reds and yellows, sparkling and bright. The giantess also wore multiple metal chains about her neck, and a veritable plethora of weaponry tucked into her wide belt. It made for a most remarkable sight. Maura lost all her vaunted crudrat cool and gaped openly.

"There you are, you disastrous little flotsam," said the vision to Quy almost affectionately. "Where have you been? You think the gens wouldn't notice your absence? Your poor father, worried sick, you thoughtless little remnant." She appeared prepared to continue in this vein indefinitely.

Maura would have enjoyed it, such an awesome sight with such impressive volume in every direction — like some massive angry work of art.

But Quy interrupted the giantess by turning pointedly to Maura and saying, "Non-enemy, might this one present, gens Aunt, called Manzanilla, Patrona of Pikillacta."

The giantess stopped mid rant, appearing to see Maura for the very first time. "A *guest*?" she practically roared. "You disappear for days and return with a *guest*! Are you mad or just mildly insane, nibling mine?"

A pause. No one said a whit.

"Does the little furless sapien speak?" the Patrona finally asked.

Quy sniffed. "Only when strictly necessary or entirely unhelpful."

Maura poked him in the ribs. Then mustered enough courage to talk – mouth all clogged with chattering teeth and nervousness. She said to the Patrona, in a weak imitation of highstock greeting, "How do you do?"

The hugeness turned all kindly, eyes a-twinkle. "Welcome to Pikillacta, my dear." She looked at Quy. "What do we call her?"

Quy shrugged.

"M…" Maura started to say her name, but stopped when Quy squeezed her arm. Hard. "I'm called, um, Crudrat?" she offered finally. She'd responded to it often enough so far in her life.

Quy said, like it was his idea, "We may call her Crudrat here at Pikillacta."

"You are adult in your craft, young Crudrat, to be using the personal?" The Patrona's necklaces-of-plenty clinked about as she peered down at Maura, squinting liked she couldn't quite see the outline of the girl.

Maura had no idea what she meant. She looked to Quy for help.

"She is Wheel made," explained her friend, as though to satisfy all possible questions.

"Barbarian culture. You may explain to her the proper protocol." Necklaces and bracelets jingled as the Patrona crossed wide arms over massive chest, and rocked back on her heals.

Quy chewed his fuzzy bottom lip. "Until a Kill'ki is adult in skill there is no selfhood." He was struggling, for the first time in Maura's presence, with space-tongue. So far it seemed to be the preferred mode of speech-making on this great floating ice city, but now it seemed to be failing him. "At this one's age, there are many choices," he glared as his aunt, "even if preference has been registered. The elders see the soul as unsettled." He looked back at Maura, frustrated. "This one cannot say 'I' until adulthood. My aunt here is shocked at your use of the word, being as you are still young. Younger than *this one*."

Maura mulled it about. "Am I," she paused, then rephrased, "Is *this one* expected to do the same?"

Manzanilla looked at her with an air of surprise, "If you would like to try, such an attempt would be encouraged."

Maura shrugged. "This one will give it her best run." She would have smiled but her teeth *would* persist in chattering.

Quy's aunt whirled back to him, suddenly fierce and angry again. "You thoughtless scab."

"Now what?" wondered Quy, rather too casually.

"Your furless friend here is shivering nigh unto death. Go fetch her some warmth, and get yourself decent in the meantime."

"But…"

"Now!"

Quy shuffled off, all reluctance. Maura, truth be told, was a little nervous herself. They both knew Manzanilla's ploy, to get Maura alone without Quy's guiding tongue. It worked, quoin Fuzzy disappeared out the curtained doorway, and Maura found herself alone with the giantess. Ruler of a whole space city!

"Well?"

Maura swallowed. What tunnel to pick? There was kindness to those black eyes, perhaps a plea?

"Might this one beg sanctuary in your space, Patrona?" She hesitated over the words. *What kind of debt will this wrap me up in?*

Manzanilla looked her up and down, sharp and assessing, as progenetors might review a new purchase. "A petition? Very well, ten days granted, then proof of usefulness will be required, barring other legitimate claims."

Maura didn't quite follow, but figured ten spins – *days must mean spins* – was better than a spacing. She'd many ticks to figure things all out, or find a place to disappear. She winced. There was someone else to consider in this bargaining.

"And for this one's murmel?" *If he lasts without crud.*

At the mention, the little creature raised his sad blue head. He was lackluster with shock, cold, and hunger.

The Patrona started violently. "Are you wearing a *snack*, young crudrat?"

Maura frowned. "I'm wearing a friend," she said sharply, forgetting her polite speak.

"Looks like he'd go well with hot coca, a tasty blue biscuit."

Maura hadn't heard the word before. "Biskweet?"

The murmel cheeped at that, either in disgust or approval, hard to tell.

"Well," said Manzanilla, "that would appear to be its talk-name, at least."

Maura sighed, now she had an entirely useless pet named after a snack food. "He eats crud. This may be an issue."

"Crud?"

What had Fuzzy called it?

Quy came back just at the moment. "She means DMP, the Wheel calls it crud."

He was wearing one of the brightly colored embroidered cloth wraps about his lower body, and carrying a large white fur pelt with black lining. He draped the pelt around Maura's shoulders and the murmel. Maura immediately felt better. The murmel didn't object either.

"That creature consumes DMP? Is that why it's so blue?" The Patrona was clearly intrigued. She peered, all myopic once more, at the murmel.

"Would you believe they have scythers hundreds of times the size of ours, and clean them manually using child labour and those murmel creatures?" said Fuzzy, as though this were the strangest idea in the universe.

"No, I wouldn't," replied his aunt, without blinking.

"Well they do."

Manzanilla looked to Maura for support.

"This one was just such a runner-type. Biskweet here was my partner. He be needing DMP to live."

Quy looked thoughtful. "Do you think he might be able to drink it? We could give him dirty flush, and see if that'd work for sustenance. When did he get a name, anyway?"

"Your Aunt just up and gave it to him, thought he might be some kind of snack food. This flush stuff might suit. Could we get mitts on some, you think?"

Quy looked to his Aunt sharply.

The giantess tilted her head, fringe waggling thoughtfully. "Once I have finished with you three here, I'll have someone see to it."

Maura had finally stopped shivering. The fur pelt was soft, cozy, and familiar feeling. Biskweet seemed to enjoy it too. He perked up, turning into a restless little lump under the weighty fabric.

"This is lovely warm."

"Mmm, whose is it, anyway?" Manzanilla asked her nibling.

"Great Uncle Raqchi."

Maura felt queasy, the familiar feel of the fur now explained. It was, in fact, *exactly* like Quy's.

"You mean that this is the pelt of a dead Kill'ki?"

The Patrona nodded. "High quality too, he died young."

"It is a guest compliment," hissed Fuzzy at Maura's appalled look, "to wear a member of the gens."

Maura tried not to be sick. An unsettled stomach, she was finding, was the sum average of her experience amongst these Kill'ki types.

The Patrona turned her attention back to the task at hand by forcibly rerouting the conversation. "So, Quy, where have you been, and how did you meet Crudrat here?"

Quy relayed the story they'd concocted.

"That is the biggest load of space dross this side of the galaxy," his aunt said eloquently when he'd finished.

Maura issued Fuzzy an I-told-you-so look.

"Really, nibling mine, you might have come up with a better fib."

Fuzzy wrinkled his nose. "We didn't have much time to get creative. Give us a day or two and we'll invent something better."

All sarcasm ended then, and Quy's aunt finally got genuinely angry, rather than just an imitation of it. She went from bumbling to scary. Looming up to her full height, she glowered down at them, all narrow eyes and sharp teeth. Maura backed away and angled towards the door. Not that there were tunnels to take too, but she was a runner right and proper, instinct wasn't something that changed with environment.

The Patrona's voice went low and quiet and lost all expletives – all the more dangerous for its honest smoothness.

"Listen to me carefully, child of my brother, this is a serious matter. Your previous transgressions have involved larks and forays, but this time you went into *Wheel* space. Hostilities could result. People could come looking for her. Important people. The Wheel does not take kindly to outside interference. Does not take kindly to outsiders at all. Truth in this matter is not optional. We Kill'ki cannot just *keep* a Wheel civilian as if she were a pet intended for our entertainment."

Braver than Maura, Fuzzy ignored the menace, remaining silent.

Maura said timidly, "No one is coming from the Wheel after me. I ain't a civilian." She remembered her speech protocol too late but slogged on. "This one is *reject*." Then struggling for terms Kill'ki might garner. "Without *gens.* Alone."

The Patrona blinked. Her wrath seemed to increase. "You bring us one of their rejects, Quy! What good to us is some young sprocket without an implant chip? She affords us no opportunity to study nor understand their technology. What worth could she bring to the *gens*? You are mad."

That made Quy angry. "And what kind of words are those from a Kill'ki? You have not seen her move. You know nothing of her value or skill. Save your judgments until you witness worth, or you are no better than they."

"Watch that keen tongue, nibling. I am still your superior and Patrona of this city. I could turn you both back out into the vacuum, no better than we found you."

Maura's silver eyes glanced back and forth between the two. *Sharp as blades this speaking, with no affection or mockery left to it.* And herself, the source of the cutting. The murmel, sensing antagonism, buried his face in the side of Maura's neck, and wrapped his tail, tight and desperate, about her arm.

"And how would you explain *that* to this one's father, Aunt?" Quy only stood taller, unafraid.

"You have been a blight of the first order since you first found tongue. He'd not cull me for action within my right and power."

Quy crossed his arms in an imitation of her stance. "So, do it."

"You refuse to tell me the truth in this matter? How did you find her? Why did you bring her with you?"

Quy held his tongue.

Maura, nervous, held hers as well. She'd picked her side the moment she fell upon Quy from the beltway top. He'd seen her solid so far – no changing now. It was a shame because she liked the Patrona.

"Very well, we shall bring in the big claws then, shall we?" Manzanilla strode over, stuck her head out the curtained doorway and hollered down the hallway. The loud echoing against stone made the words unintelligible to Maura. But Fuzzy chittered nervously, strait-away worried by this turn in the proceedings.

Manzanilla came back to stand facing them, silent and glaring, which was more unsettling than any other act she'd committed so far.

About a thousand ticks later, the curtain was pushed aside and a whole new kind of alien glided into the room.

"You summoned me, my beloved anchovy button?" said the man, in a deep buttery soft voice. He was less tall than the Patrona, but still taller than most Maura had seen. He had skin instead of fur, but such skin. It was pure starless purple-black, and he wore, in stark contrast to all those around him, a kind of long frock coat, without the pleating, in simple undec-orated blue over plain warm-looking shirt and trousers. He held some sort of scanpad that he was poking at with a fat-tipped finger, only half interested in the world about him.

"Husband, we have a family problem."

Maura started to hear the title. Who'd have thought? Aliens, married across the species divide? Weird that.

The man said reproachfully, without looking up, "I had assumed as much, my golden turtle shell, or you would have left me to my work. One would hardly suppose you require me all the way down this end of the city for mere piddling politics. What has happened?"

The Patrona gestured with her head at Maura and Quy. Her husband did not see the movement, focused on his pad.

"Oh, really, Sillous, pay attention for once."

The man looked up, scratching the side of his nose. There was something funny about his hands.

"Oh, hello Quy," he said, with a little half smile. Then went back to his pad.

Quoin Fuzzy said, "Uncle Sillous, this is Crudrat. Crudrat, this is Dr Sillous, Pikillacta's head surgeon."

"A medic?" Maura was duly impressed.

That comment forced the man look up for longer than a tick. "Certainly not! I am a *surgeon*."

"He thinks it better than a medic, because surgeon requires a good deal more training," Quy explained to Maura in an aside.

Only one thing in Maura's world was better trained than a medic. The realization hit hard. Regardless of cold floors, fur pelt, and a squirming murmel, she sank to her knees, head bowed in full reverence.

"Interesting response." Dr Sillous's attention was now fully caught by the slight alien girl kneeling before him.

"She did not do that for *me*," huffed Manzanilla.

"What are you doing?" Quy, tugged on Maura's arm. "Don't be daft."

"But," Maura glanced about from under lowered lids, "If he's hyped better than a medic, he must be an *enhancer*."

"She is Wheel born?" The enhancer crouched down in front of Maura. He placed a cool smooth hand under her chin and tilted it up. His eyes were blue-black too, and the bits that should have been white were red. Nevertheless, they were kindly. "No, my dear, Kill'ki Coalition doesn't tinker with the genome, not since first seeding. We prefer to interbreed as we are. I do not deal in genetics, just ordinary slicing and dicing."

He slid his hand softly about the back of Maura's neck, feeling for the tiny bump that wasn't there. There was something very odd about the size and width of his fingertips.

"No implant." He glanced up at Quy. "You brought us one of their rejects, nibling. Why?"

Quy opened his mouth and trotted out his tall tale once more.

Dr Sillous listened impassively, helping Maura to stand and straighten the pelt about her neck and arms. His eyes continued to assess — thin shoulders under the fur, corded muscles on her legs, bare feet, blue hair. Nothing escaped him.

When Quy was finished, Manzanilla said mildly, "Lying little sack of rotted pus."

"Be fair, my sweet pickled herring, he is only staying true to the course of his nature." Dr Sillous turned a sharp look onto his nibling and began systematically picking apart Quy's story from start to finish. He used short choppy words but his tone remained mild throughout, an effective technique. By the end, Quy was looking limp, Manzanilla victorious, and Maura was pretty certain they'd be telling the whole truth, and nothing but it, shortly.

"Fine!" Quy said finally, "This one got curious, okay? This one had the whale out for a bit of spin, and Wheel space was just right there, and this big spaceport came drifting by, and this one thought — it can't be all that *bad*, just to take a little peek. We have all heard the stories, this one just wanted to see truth behind them."

"And did you?" Dr Sillous's red eyes we intent on his nibling's face.

Quoin Fuzzy shuffled his feet a bit. "It is worse than the stories. They sent eight fighters out and muscled this one in – no talk, no treaty offered up, no protocol at all. This one was thinking they wanted an in-person parlay, but they just trussed this one up and dumped him in the slammer. This one only just managed to lock down the whale against interference."

"And goodness did that give the sequensors a bother," interject Maura, grinning wide at the memory.

"And how do you fit into this?" Dr Sillous asked her, all casual-like.

"Oh." Maura shrugged. "I fell on top of him. Oops, sorry, *this one* fell on top of that one. This one was tracking him cross the beltway, never having seen a real live alien afore. He popped his key at me and this one was suddenly in the mix and suckered into rescuing him."

Quy took back over. "She got this one out. Well, she and another blue haired friend of hers." Then he went on to explain the entirety of the prison break. He seemed almost proud now that he was onto truthful detailing.

"Why did she help you, nibling?" Manzanilla asked the important question. "What was in it for her?"

Maura smiled. "This one ain't got no purpose, no gens back riding the Wheel." She looked to the surgeon thinking he might suss her truths best. "I'm reject. Been chucked out of crudratting as overgrown, and anything's better than starving to death or being spaced for vagrancy. Thought a visit 'round your starside might suit me a tick or two."

"Oh, you did, did you? Taking advantage of *my* kin while he was in need? That is *not* civilized behavior." Manzanilla, not so jovial, loomed toward Maura.

Quy stepped between them. Flinching he said, "Aunt, we are bonded." He shuffled his feet nervously.

The Patrona reared away, jewelry tinkling in outrage. "*What!*"

"This *is* an interesting development."

"Oh, Sillous, really!" said his wife in exasperation. "This

is a catastrophe! Household bond to an alien girl we know nothing about, except that she is Wheel. Of all things. *Wheel* indeed! Her lack of upbringing alone!"

"And no implant chip," added the surgeon, who couldn't seem to let that fact go. *At least he realizes it's import.* But Maura wasn't sure that was necessarily a good thing.

"So we test her," the doctor made a face of deep though. "We can always find a use for an able pair of hands even with low scores. She is half starved, but clearly fit enough."

"And how will that help? They are bonded, of all things. I mean really, Quy, could you get yourself into worse trouble?"

Quy looked thoroughly ashamed of himself. "Very probably."

The Patrona backed down quick as blades. "That was *not* a suggestion."

"Test, what test?" Maura clutched the murmel for reassurance. *This is not good.*

"Test to figure out where you train, what field you would be good at." Sillous spread his strange chubby-ended fingers expressively.

"You mean Spokes? None," replied Maura, "This one fell off the Wheel. I can't take a chip."

"Neither can we."

"What?" Now it was Maura's turn to be in shock.

Sillous turned and showed her the back of his neck. No scar. No bump. Too amazed for modesty, Maura reached up and brushed it with her hand. Smooth.

In that moment, Maura had to change her whole view of the universe. *Why does this keep happening? How many shocks is a girl expected to take in one turn?*

Sure these were aliens, but she'd figured on them being chipped. Everyone who was anyone was chipped. How did Manzanilla rule an entire space city, or Sillous medic about without an implant? Where'd they get knowledge skills? How'd they buy and sell, travel and live? How'd they communicate across station? It was utterly confusing.

Maura smiled to herself. *Clearly, if the Patrona was anything go by, they just yelled a considerable lot.*

Maura could learn to yell.

"So, we test?" Dr Sillous looked to his wife.

Patrona sighed loudly, and sucked her teeth in clear annoyance. "We test."

13

When the Tinkers came to the end of all things and
went - for just that moment - entirely mad, only then
was it possible to dream-up the Jakaa Nova.
  ~ On the Civilizing of Worlds by J. Kilsen Slliurp

Maura had never taken any kind of test before. Not one that she could recall. There might have been some before she was declared reject and chucked, but that was many turns ago. Still, this alien testing was looking to be not at all like what she might have expected, had she had any idea of what to expect.

"They want me to do *what*?" She glared at Fuzzy, narrowing her eyes in annoyance. This could all be construed as his fault.

Sitting on top of a block of stone, that appeared to be the only furniture the Kill'ki went in for, the murmel lapped at a bowl of flush. He seemed pleased with the blue liquid. At least someone was happy. *Guess he might live a while longer after all.* Which was good, Maura was a might fond of the beastie, not that she'd tell him that.

"They want you to work in the big kitchen."

"What be a quitch-em when it's itself?" Maura was dubious.

"You know, the place where people cook, keep food, that sort of thing."

"They want me to go about prepping ration cubes?" That was fully strange. What kind of test would wrapping cubes in sealant tape make a girl into? *Don't they have machines for that action 'round this side of space?* "Work a food stall?"

Quy grinned. "In a space city like Pikillacta we eat communally. All of our food is prepared and served in one large centralized location."

It was the most amazing thing Maura had heard. Well, since the last amazing thing, which admittedly was only a few ticks ago. Why, there must near hundreds of aliens roaming about this icy star floater. Imagine them all chewing away together, like they were progenetors at a fancy table-feast. The quantities must be enormous, not to mention the noise of the chewing, if they all bit down on fresh foodstuffs at once.

Still, Maura could see nothing wrong with work shifts spent mucking about in massive amounts of food. Could be worse fates for a reject. Ain't that the truth of it? So she found herself inclined to be pleased with the idea.

"We, most of us, test first in food production and preparation."

Maura shrugged. "Well it seems all over odd to me, but I'll run it straight if that's what they're wanting. When do I start?"

"This one will take you down directly."

Maura pulled the fur more firmly about her, she was getting used to the idea of wearing an alien's skin. *Former*

alien, as was. Makes it, well, sort of used? At least it kept her
warm, not much else seemed likely to. This floating city
might be made of stone by appearances, but she'd swear it
was all ice from the feel of it.

Quy had said she'd be rooming with him until they
figured out what was to be done with her. Another alien crazy
idea, just two of them in that whole room. Why, four or five
crudrats could fit curled across the floor alone, not including
the stone blocks against each wall.

But two sleeping mats on the floor seemed so suggest no
other purpose intended but their nesting. The walls had niches
to hold objects, which Maura didn't own, and pegs for clothing, of which she didn't have extra. Imagine having more
than one set of clothing. Why would a girl need more for?
Can only wear one at a time.

Not to mention that there was a second tiny room attached
at the far end, for excrement. A whole *other* room just for
hygiene! Amazing.

They left the murmel behind in that room, slurping away
in total happiness. He barely looked up as they wandered off.
Maura figured as all doorways seemed blocked with nothing
more than a drape or two, he could come and find her later if
he wished. His roving about might be construed as a problem,
except that these folks seemed used to all matter of alien life.
Of course, there *was* the Patrona's snack food comment, but
murmels could take care of themselves. Maura figured on his
screaming being enough of a shocker for him to get away,
should anyone actually try to eat him.

Quy led Maura through a whole new set of tunnels. All
were made with those pillowy stones, cracks of light sneaking
in around the edge. But these were bigger in size than before
– almost twice as wide, and different in color – reddish
instead of grey.

"Think you can find your way back to the room, Crudrat, from where we are going?" Fuzzy asked as they walked along.

Maura's head swayed about, like an angry murmel tail, as she tried to take everything in. It wasn't that she was lost, these hallways may be made of rock, but that didn't mess with her sense of space. No trouble there. It was the other scenery that caused her to come over all curious.

Aliens crowded past, mostly Kill'ki but a goodly number looking like Dr Sillous, and a few ranging over other geno-types far beyond anything even the most exotic of the prog-enetor families triggered to. *Full on total aliens, the lot of them.* There were so many, and the hallway so long, that by the end of it Maura felt she might be getting used to all the weird formation of life in the universe. She could not, however, manage to get used to the way they looked at her. Some seemed friendly, some indifferent, and some inquiring – for even in Pikillacta blue hair was rare.

But that wasn't what gave her the shivers, it was that they all looked right straight at her. One or two even nodded politely.

A few greeted old Fuzzy with a, "Quy, what you doing back here?"

The treatment, though unobtrusive, made Maura feel naked. The novelty had worn well away. She was being *seen*, all the time, by *everyone*. Gazes stopped on her face and did not slide past the blue. She curled down into the white pelt and tried to avoid the looks – *harder to dodge than blades*.

"This one is not supposed to help you test," admitted Quy, oblivious to her discomfort, "but some knowledge you lack through fault of birth, not innate ability. So this one will warn you now to be *most* wary of the Jakaa Nova as you cook and serve."

Maura gave him an enquiring glance.

"Those who look like my Uncle Sillous, furless and dark purple to red. We Kill'ki are an open cheerful folk, but the Jakaa Nova lean towards moody, and are quick to anger. And, of course, they are far more dangerous than most."

Maura would not have thought this, given her ticks 'round the surgeon's calmness, and compared to the obvious size and strength of the Kill'ki. But she nodded her acceptance and kept her opinions to herself.

Quy answered to her doubts anyway, though she hadn't given them voice. "Do not take this one's uncle as a model, Crudrat. He is, after all, married to my aunt. It would take the calmest of any gens to take on such a role."

Maura realized, with dizzy horror, the reason behind his giving advice. She became, if possible, more nervous. "So you will not be with me in the quitch-em?"

"The kitchen," he corrected her. "And no. This one already did his test and his time."

The plaster floor began to angle downwards and, after rounding a sharp corner, they were suddenly birthed into a wide gathering place.

"Welcome to Pikillacta's assembly plaza," said Quy with a grand sweep of an arm.

Maura looked around, and quickly directed her gaze downwards as much as allowed. Once more there was no ceiling above – no apparent barrier to the stars.

The plaza was large and its floor white, a surface of all sparkling plaster. Like the stones of the walls, it seemed lit from within, only this time the whole surface glowed faintly. It was not as big as the docking area they'd sunk the whale down onto, but still large enough to impress. Two long sides were lined with stone benches upon which lay a spread of food so vast it hit Maura right upside the head and knocked

her silly. Of all the strange things she'd glommed on so far –
ships with disappearing walls, furry aliens, ceilings into the
starry void, and rooms solely for sleeping – it was the food
before her that surprised most.

"What's it all doing a seated right out there like that?" She
spoke hushed and serious-like, as though in the presence of
something sacred.

"When we are hungry, we come here and eat. It is really a
very simple premise."

"You help yourself?" Maura's silver eyes were so wide,
they were as like to split her face open under the forehead.

Quy looked at her, head to one side. Troubled by her awe.
"Well, yes actually."

As though testing his truth, Maura skittered over to one of
the stone platforms and grabbed at an interesting looking bit
of some protein kind of thing. Could be real dead animal. She
crammed it into her mouth afore anyone could stop her.

No one tried to. No one even blinked or spoke at her
action. No one did nothing.

Maura reached for a round goby sort of putty object and
tucked it away in a pocket of her knickerbockers, under cover
of the fur pelt.

Quy shrugged at that. "Technically, you are not supposed
to take the food away with you. It is provided communally
in order to build community spirit — everyone eating
together. Since there is always something here to snack on,
even outside major meal times, there is no need to hoard.
But I don't see that anyone would mind you keeping a
bread-roll about your person, if it makes you feel more
comfortable."

This was simply too much for Maura to believe.

So she didn't.

Quy dragged her away from the mounds of food, for she

would have gone on nibling and hiding bits inside her clothing forever, if allowed.

"Really," he said in annoyance, when she darted after a piece of actual fresh fruit, "there is no need to take on so. It's the only good thing about kitchen detail, you get to snack as you work."

Maura thought that she might be in for the bestest job she'd ever heard talk of in all her spins. Who wanted to be a progenetor or a sequensor? Even they had to *wait* before they could get about eating. "This is going to be *amazing*," she said fervently.

"Glad you think so," said a gangly Kill'ki coming up behind them. Then she said to Fuzzy, "What you doing back on our ice, Quy? Thought we shook free of you a full three years ago."

"There you go, have I not said before? Thinking is not your strong point," replied Fuzzy, all mild and soft. Then he reached forward and pulled the other alien into a bone-crunching hug.

They drew apart, both grinning. It was a fearsome kind of sight – all those teeth at once.

Quy slapped the other Kill'ki's shoulder. "Got yourself that whale yet, Korakay?"

"This one," replied Korakay, "ain't got herself a powerful gens with too much barter owed for certain people's own good."

"Ha, this one bartered for that beautiful little ship all alone, no gens needed, thank you very much!"

Korakay sniffed. "Well, you going to introduce me?"

"Crudrat," said Quy, "this here genius is called *Korakay*. She is this one's age mate. Korakay, this is *Crudrat*. New recruit, brought in for testing."

"Ah, you will be this one's drudge then." The Kill'ki gave

Maura a friendly nod. She wore the usually colorful cloth wrapped about her legs and waist, but over it she had on a robe-like striped garment covered in various stains.

"What did you do to get yourself grounded as kitchen supervisor?" Quy wanted to know.

Korakay cast her hands up to the void of space. "What else? Angered the Patrona."

Quy nodded sympathetically. "This one entirely understands."

"Thought you might. You be helping here as well?"

"Not as such. But trust my aunt, this one will pay up somewhere." Quy rolled his eyes to the stars.

"Ouch. Well, good luck with that. Speaking of, we had better get back to it. Drudge, come this way."

With that, Quy wandered off towards the docks of food and Maura was left to follow Korakay the rest of the way across the plaza, through a huge doorway, and into *the kitchen*.

Maura had thought she was getting accustomed to things like stone rooms and places that didn't look much like anything else she'd ever seen in her life. But the kitchen put all abnormalities trotted out before it to shame.

The whole area, and it was a big one, seemed solely and entirely committed to the cultivation, storage, and preparation of foodstuffs. Korakay pointed and explained about the banks of heating devices, sanitation machines, dehydration and rehydration units, walls of growing things with sunlamps, and the two super-cooling boxes. Though, those last weren't likely to be overly used, given that the whole city was freezing. There were stone blocks high enough for cutting and preparing, huge bowls for mixing, and, at one end near the grow walls, rows of cages with small fuzzy animals locked inside. The beasties made a strange watery warbling sound, punctuated by occasional squeaks. They were furry, brown and cream colored, and scuttled about without much apparent smarts in the noggin to draw upon. They also lent an odor to that end of the kitchen that was rather unpleasant. Maura wrinkled her nose.

"Those are animals!" She was impressed despite the smell.

"Do you not have them around your part of space?" Korakay looked at Maura, confused by her surprise.

"We have murmels but they don't much count. They're part of the machinery. They're used for, you know, work-type action."

Korakay raised her furry white eyebrows in her furry white face – or at least Maura thought that was what she was doing, hard to tell in all that furry whiteness.

"Well, elsewhere we farm chickens for eggs and to eat. And there are goats for milk and meat. They're both too big to keep in a kitchen. But those are quy, and they are used mainly for eating, and small enough to keep on hand."

Maura swallowed. "Eating live?"

Korakay grinned. "And still wriggling, so when you bite in the blood goes trickling down your chin."

Maura gagged slightly.

"Whoah there Cruds, you are going a bit green under that blue tinge. Sure you feeling quite the thing?"

Maura took a deep breath and reminded herself these were aliens, things were bound to be mighty deferent all 'round – food, smell, sound. The little caged beasties warbled sympathetically.

Another Kill'ki made his way through the busy activity of the kitchen towards them. "Whatcha got there, Korakay?"

"New drudge."

"And she is all kinds of useful just standing around like that?"

"You object so much to her doing so, you just got yourself a partner." With that Korakay abruptly turned away, yelling, to someone off to the side, "No, Tambo, not in there!"

The new Kill'ki seemed on the younger end of things, more Maura's age, and on the smaller side, which Maura was beginning to realize usually meant male.

He glared at her, clearly annoyed at being stuck with a newbie. "Very well, come on."

Shifts seemed to run about the same time span for Kill'ki as they did Wheelside, so Maura spent the next two trotting about, doing anything she was told, and learning fast as she could given the utter strangeness of that crazy place. One of the things she learned was that both Korakay and her new partner, she never did figure on what to call him, were as liberal with their slaps as foreman had been. If she messed up, she got a right walloping upside the head. She tried not to mess up, but mostly she didn't know the right path, so she couldn't help doing things wrong. She'd no idea prepping food was such a chore. She was strong enough, and able and willing, but didn't have the know-how, and everyone seemed frustrated that she needed every tiny thing explained.

"I don't think I did so well," she admitted to Quy when she was finally free to go back to their room.

"Saying 'I' all the time can't have helped."

Maura sighed, lying back on her floor mat and staring up at the stone ceiling. "They whacked me every time I missed the littlest thing."

"Did you hit them back?"

"Don't they both outrank me?"

"Rank? That is what the fighting is for. You must stand up for yourself, little blue, or no one will respect you." Quy spread his white paws expansively. He was sitting cross-legged on his own floor mat next to her.

"Ah," Maura understood, "like with other crudrats?"

Quy grinned. "Exactly like. You know, you will never have any public standing at all if you don't get into a full on fight."

"It's a lot to get brain-in, all sudden and sharp-like." Maura rubbed her blue head with both hands as though testing her skull for leak-holes. "You people are very strange."

Quy shrugged.

"Do you really eat those little brown squeaky beasties alive?"

"Korakay tell you that?"

Maura nodded.

"And you believed her?"

Maura nodded again.

"Her kind of humor. Of course we don't. Kill'ki are perfectly civilized. Up to a point. Cooking is a fine way to handle meat. Especially quy. Did you end up encountering any Jakaa Nova?"

Maura shook her head.

"Well, that's something to be grateful for."

The murmel, who seemed to have adapted fine and dandy to both the ever-present cold and his new surroundings, now that he'd been given food, shuffled over to worm himself under Maura's head in his customary pillow placement. Maura fluffed him slightly into a better position.

"I can straight up to do the work asked of me, easier than

blade running," said Maura after a short silence. "But I'm not sure about the rest of it."

"This one suspects: that would the point of you being there."

"I just don't know anything!" Maura wailed, frustrated. Her murmel pillow, disturbed, chittered and she softened her tone. "If I'm this bad off already, what about these tests thingies that are coming down the tunnel next?"

"This one has seen you in action," reassured Quy. "You'll be fine."

But Maura was beginning to learn all about reading the truths in her fuzzy alien's words. *The Patrona was right. Quy is a terrible liar.*

She drifted off into sleep. Her dreams were troubled by the quiet of the floating city with no murmels screaming in the background and no whistle of air in ducts. Somewhere though, far away, the quy warbled softly.

14

Galactic Common is the amoeba of languages,
subsuming the useful bits of all others it encounters. It
hasn't a unique bone in its body. To be fair, it hasn't
any bones or any body to contain them, either.
  ~ On the Civilizing of Worlds by J. Kilsen Slliurp

It turned out, however, that Quy had given Maura some decent advice. For the very next early shift, when Korakay went in to whack at her, Maura dodged the hit and kicked the Kill'ki hard in the shin. This yielded some surprisingly good results.

Rather than being upset, Korakay smiled appreciatively, all the while rubbing at her leg. "Well, someone picked up a little pluck last night."

"In my part of space," said Maura, annoyed, "we only hit when strictly necessary."

"So do we. Speaking of which: use of personal," said Korakay, hitting her again.

Maura blocked the strike and kicked the Kill'ki higher up this time in the side. Rejects may be chipless but they weren't stupid — kicking would always be Maura's best option. Kill'ki had reach on her, but turns running bladeside and scrapping regular with the other 'rats and Maura may not have much technique but she sure had some serious leg muscles.

Korakay let out a woof noise and issued up a much less approving expression. "No need to get tetchy."

"You *just* said…"

Korakay waved a large paw about her head dismissively, as though Maura were an annoying speck of crud dust afloat in the air.

After that, matters improved. The work was dull and hard, lots of heavy lifting onto surfaces all slightly too tall, but manageable. Maura was paired with a different partner that shift and every shift thereafter. Seemed kitchen detail was usually a punishment in Pikillacta, with a core set of personnel taking on the important, and fun, work, and drudges eating up the slack and the scraps. Drudges mostly carried things about, mixed things with other things, and cleaned. A punishment rotation clearly didn't last long, for Maura had to learn new faces most every spin.

Seemed that even if the alien wasn't Kill'ki to look at, Kill'ki types of behavior were the standard. Maura learned to answer insult with violence no matter what, and those about her learned she had a mean right kick. Everyone but Maura seemed eminently pleased with this arrangement.

"You people are weird," she finally mustered the courage to complain to Korakay, during shift break about six spins into her kitchen workings. They were sitting together outside the entrance, watching the endless array of alien life that wandered into the plaza for the fetching of food. The murmel, now a regular fixture around the plaza, shuffled about exploring. Biskweet had learned that if he was actually *in* the kitchen, more than a few of the cooks really did think he might make a good snack. So while Maura worked, he stayed in the plaza. The direct result of this was that most the of aliens in the city were getting pretty familiar with his blue fuzzy self, even if they'd no idea who Maura was. He caused far more of a stir than she ever could anyway.

"Weird, says who?"

Maura munched on a bit of fried starchy vegetable, which she'd learned was called a poe-tay-toe. This particular starch was popular in the floating city, and there seemed to be about a thousand different kinds. The Kill'ki collected tribute from a number of their allied words in shipments of the round multi-colored things. Maura thought they tasted a mite like dirt, which she'd tried once around the bioponics end of portside. Still, they weren't bad as such. She nibbled on a fat bean. She liked beans better, a food with a bit more personality. She was finding herself with quite the palate now that her diet wasn't solely gel cubes and ration bars. Quy was right, the best thing about kitchen life was all the sample scraps.

"All that hitting and kicking all the time, just to get a grip on rank. My side of space we assign rank, then you don't have to waste ticks during a shift trying to sort it all out for yourself."

"That sounds boring," replied Korakay. "Fighting is what Kill'ki do best, so we do it a lot."

Maura looked her up and down. "You sure of that?"

"Is that a challenge, little furless one?"

Quy had said Maura needed a public fight. In fact, he'd been getting more and more insistent on the subject. As though he had a vested interest in her getting beaten up for all to see. Which he might — difficult to tell with aliens. Maura looked around, wondering if this was public enough. The plaza was packed with mid shift visitors, some come down for the food, some for the company. They called the break between first and second shift *lunchtime* this end of space. The assembled made up a raucous bunch, the Kill'ki in particular, but other aliens of their Coalition took to the talking and jostling as well. It was odd to Maura to see them joshing about, like a great pack of multicolored murmels, all chittering and grumbling – less screaming, though.

Maura stood up, brushing off the seat of her knickerbockers. They'd never given her local dress, nor directions on how she might make or get some for herself, nor any indication that she ought. Which, given that local dress seemed to consist of long strips of fabric wrapped around the body according to some mysterious method, Maura was cautiously pleased to ignore. Still, as she'd been in Pikillacta a number of spins so her brushing off the knickerbockers didn't do much for their general state of cleanliness. Not, of course, that she'd had opportunity to clean them much in her past life but, even without ambient crud dust, Pikillacta was proving itself a much dirtier place than the Wheel spaceport.

"I could do with a little light exercise." Korakay stood as well.

They faced each other, taking measure. Korakay had height on Maura and much longer reach. But Maura was willing to bet good ration bars that her reflexes were better and faster.

"Now what?" All Maura's past fights had been started by Ger-type repulsives. There'd been insult and nastiness to spawn the occurrence. Korakay was nowhere near as bad as Ger. This left Maura with a strong inclination not to hurt her.

Korakay had no such compunction. As was the apparent

rule with Kill'ki, she dove in with a fist to Maura's head right to start. No warning.

Maura ducked the strike easy and kicked out.

Prepared for that response, now, Korakay blocked Maura's leg with one forearm and kicked back.

Maura used a blade dodging back flip to get out the way. She leaped right out of her flip and forwards into a wall hop, using Korakay as the wall to run up.

The Kill'ki seemed confused by this. Clearly she'd never had to fight against Maura's kind of moving before. She grabbed at Maura's foot as she ran up her body but missed. Maura, merely for the sake of amusement finished the run, and then leaped up high and used the Kill'ki's head to vault over landing behind her opponent.

She spun about fast enough to catch Korakay still facing the wrong direction and drove her fist, hard as she could, into the alien's kidney area. Or where she thought a kidney might be located. Korakay didn't even flinch, merely spun to face her.

Maura scuttled out of range and paused warily. She wondered if she could really hurt this alien race they seemed denser than a real human. A run up like that, designed to hold hard against a tunnel wall would have knocked any crudrat flat backwards. Not to mention the kidney hit.

And here was Korakay, just looking confused.

No time to think on these problems too much, the Kill'ki got over her disorientation and charged Maura.

Maura twisted to the side to avoid her. Dense and invulnerable those alien forms may be, but Korakay was still slower than a scyther blade. Maura turned her dodging twist into a spin, striking out with her leg. She'd no technique to it, never having learned to fight as a progenetor or armiger might. So when her heel connected hard with Korakay's hip it hurt Maura more than it did the Kill'ki.

"Ouch," said Maura, vexed with herself.

Korakay stepped back slightly and cocked her head to one side. "Crudrat, you have got some very large gaps in your fighting technique."

Maura was belligerent enough to forget her proper use of personal again. "I'm still standing!"

"Agreed. But this one should not be. You had all the advantage from the moment you took to tossing yourself through the air in that floaty way. Yet you have not taken one single opportunity to its end. Whatever your people do, it's not *real* fighting."

Maura relaxed slightly at that. "'Course it isn't. This one was crudrat through and though. We ain't taught to fight. All us 'rats know to do is run."

Korakay bit her lip. "No impertinence intended, Crudrat, but what *are* you doing still down here in the kitchen? Shouldn't you have moved on by now? This is not the right place for you. A little training on how to strike proper and with that jumpy style you would be better than many at fighting, despite your size. You ought to go in for wari. Even with all your ignorance and blundering, did you really manage to upset the Patrona that badly? Kill'ki are always looking for new wari. For the good of the Coalition and all."

The murmel, who'd been sniffing a nearby wall without particular interest in their mock fight, came wandering over. Now that Maura came to think on it, no one else had shown any interest in the fight either. Their battle seemed merely another regular occurrence in the busy plaza, not worth a pause in conversation or consumption.

"This one is happy to stay where told," replied Maura.

"There's food here, and standard shifts, why would this one want aught else than kitchen duty?"

"What about wanting to do what you're good at?"

Maura just blinked at her. The very idea. What she was good at was running blades. This strange icy place had no blades to run and no scythers to run inside. She wasn't trained for the least little bit of anything else. *Who cares what I do with myself? Leastways, here I'm still alive and eating.* Better than what could be said were she still skulking about Wheel space.

Maura turned the talk back on Korakay. "What about you? You be belonging in this here kitchen all turns, do ya?"

Korakay grinned. "This one is back to the quoin ranks tomorrow – my food service done for this rotation, thank the stars."

Maura was crushed. Perhaps she and Korakay weren't exactly friends, but at least she'd had someone to sit with during shift breaks. Korakay had been nice enough once they got the whole hitting thing sorted. Now who would be her supervisor? *I'll have to wander around hitting someone new.*

The murmel plucked hopeful at the corner of Maura's torn hem. With a sigh she crouched down and offered him her shoulder. He climbed up and wrapped himself about her neck.

Korakay's gaze shifted from looking at Maura inquiringly, to fixing on a point just behind Maura's shoulder. Maura thought at first the Kill'ki was looking at the murmel. Until Korakay said, "Uh oh, Jakaa Nova. Quick let's get back in and…"

But the warning came just that much too late.

A voice behind Maura said, "How much you want for it?"

Maura turned, slowly so as not to startle anyone. The murmel made a little rumble noise of prudence in her left ear. Like she needed the hint.

"Well?" Three Jakaa Nova faced her.

They all looked much like Dr Sillous, tall and dark with those black and red eyes. But these three were younger, perhaps Quy's age, and with mouths that had eaten something sour. Ever since Quy's warning, Maura had taken care to avoid these aliens as much as possible. There weren't any on duty in the kitchen, not even as drudges, so they obviously didn't get into trouble all that much. Maura simply maneuvered out of their vicinity the rest of the time.

Now, forced into confrontation, Maura tried the politest way to speech-make she knew. "May this one be of assistance to you gentles?"

Apparently, this was not the right thing to say. The three Jakaa Nova in front of her looked, if possible, even more surly.

"How much you want for that furry piece of food you are wearing around your neck?"

Maura narrowed her eyes. "A murmel is not food." She did not see Korakay's frantic motioning her to be quiet.

"It looks like prey to us, little blue haired sapien. We like them alive and we are tired of quy. Quy do not run away fast enough."

Maura was pretty sure that this time the aliens were not making fun of her ignorance. They looked like they really would prefer to eat the murmel alive.

"He is not for sale."

"How about you? Maybe we hunt you, little sapien girl."

Maura gave a small half smile and evaluated them. It was hard to tell for certain under all the layers they wore. Here at least was a species that found it as cold in Kill'ki climes as she. She'd guess them as fit, all three, but she wouldn't give them her odds on nimbleness. Not with that bulky clothing and too much height. Plus she was pretty sure that she'd enough ticks spent on this floating city now to have a general lay of the place. She could get away easily.

"You'd be welcome try," she said, perhaps a bit too cocky. For Maura this came out as the ending line in a list of frustrations. Normally, she was not so brash with her tongue, but six spins stuck fast in this alien culture and her temper was frayed. No one ever behaved logically 'round these parts. They never explain anything. And it was always too cold.

That was when she found out why the Jakaa Nova were avoided by most everyone on Pikillacta.

The apparent leader of the three, the one that wanted Biskweet for lunch, raised those strange wide-ended hands of his and proceeded to extend a full set of claws. While some small corner of Maura's brain made the connection to Dr Sillous – such sharp claws would be awful useful for a surgeon – the leader took a swipe at her.

Maura was already moving.

Instinctively, the murmel shifted down and wrapped himself around her back, runner's positioning. Maura adjusted her balance to follow. She twisted, dodging out of the range of those deadly claws. Then she circled, hoping to spot intent before he moved again.

Korakay said, from behind her, "You have to fight him now, Crudrat. If you run away, every Jakaa Nova in Pikillacta will chase you until you're gutted."

"What!" *No running?*

"Coalition law permits them to hunt."

"Fantastic. Anyone ever tell you people that you're entirely insane?"

"Well, you only have to *fight* one of them," replied Korakay as though this were some kind of consolation.

No doubt as to which one. The hungry clawed Jakaa Nova

darted in and swiped at Maura again. The other two backed off and crossed their arms, claws retracted.

The alien was faster than Maura would have thought. Clothing and height seemed not so much of a hindrance.

This was a fight that seemed to interest people. Unlike when she'd sparred with Korakay, a small crowd began to form a wide semi-circle about her and the Jakaa Nova.

The alien swiped again, one, two, with each arm. *At least,* Maura thought, jumping out of range, *most of his fighting is predictable.* She unwound the murmel from her back and dropped him to the ground.

"Settle," she barked the command, without taking her eyes off of her opponent. Given the claws, this alien race was unlikely to use their lower body much in battle. So she dodged in past the man's next swing and delivered a sharp side kick to his stomach.

The alien made a noise like air escaping, more affected by her hits than a Kill'ki – but not that much more. Unfortunately, he also moved faster. Using his left arm, he clawed upwards, catching part of Maura's right bicep as she spun to the side. Her arms were unprotected by the Kill'ki skin which, while in the kitchen, she'd taken to wearing tied about her neck like a cape. His claws were sharper than any blade, slicing across the upper muscle of her arm easily.

Maura didn't feel any pain but she suspected she would soon. Problem was, she had no means to end this particular fight, no way to know her enemy's weaknesses. She glanced about frantically for Korakay, her only possible ally, but the Kill'ki had disappeared. Vanished into the crowd. Biskweet too, so maybe only one of them would be food.

Maura flipped away from the next strike and tumbled under the one after that. Claw dodging, instead of blade running. She wondered if they had a name for this kind of deadly dance in this end of space. She was finding it all a little less regular than a scyther, but pretty soon she had managed to suss the pattern of his hits. He was fast, a whirling flurry of flashing sharpness, but still avoidable once she knew what to expect.

They went on like that for a number of ticks. Maura soon gave up on trying to get any of her own hits in, just leaping and flipping and twisting out of the way of the claws. It became grotesque mockery of a run, inside a circle of alien faces instead of a tunnel. Maura was dripping blood from the gash in her arm, but hadn't taken any additional slices.

It was coming down to stamina, for they could have gone on like that forever, so long as neither was distracted and neither exhausted — the Jakaa Nova lashing out and Maura dodging away.

Strike. Spin. Strike. Flip. Strike. Twist.

A new rhythm for Maura to breathe to.

Then the murmel, safe she'd thought and hoped, screamed loud and long. But it wasn't a scream of dominance or a scream for attention — it was a scream of fear.

Maura broke her pattern at the sound. She glanced away in time to see one of the other Jakaa Novas spearing down at the little blue beastie with one long vicious claw. Distracted, she slipped in a little pool of her own blood and fell downwards, directly into her enemy's hand as he struck upwards from the hip — all five claws extended.

She heard a strange wet ripping noise as those deadly claws speared into her side and kept on going, lodging in and across her ribs.

15

---

*When the first humans, pure and unmodified, took to
the stars they found that the universe was empty but for
themselves.*

    ~ *On the Civilizing of Worlds* by J. Kilsen Slliurp

Maura hit the plaster floor solid and full body contact.

The claws jerked out of her side and someone swore in language she'd never heard. Melodic, lyrical even, but still recognizable as swearing.

All kinds of chaos came tumbling down after that.

Biskweet screamed, this time in full murmel rage. Maura was lying at just the right angle to see him leap out from under the claw of a Jakaa Nova and come charging to her rescue. He scampered across the intervening space and took up alpha posture next to her head. His fur fluffed all up and his tail lashing faster than she'd ever seen it move. He bared all his pointed little teeth at the enemy surrounding them, crowd and Jakaa Nova alike.

"Settle," she croaked at him, hoping the old command might convince him to run. Her brain was fixed on the fact that they wanted to eat him. There was still no pain. Surreal that, if she remembered right, hadn't she just been punctured five times in the side by some serious sharpness?

Biskweet ignored her.

"Settle," she said again, softer.

The murmel simply reared back and screamed a threat up at the Jakaa Novas, the surrounding hushed audience, and anyone else who cared to pay attention.

Disconnected, Maura figured she must be losing a good mess of blood. Still no pain but she couldn't quite feel her legs at all anymore. She tried to roll, to push herself up. Thinking better of that plan, she went to reach for the murmel, to force him away, but not a limb of her body was willing to respond right, proper, and according to instructions.

She waited to feel another claw-sharp slice, finishing the job. She thought harder and figured on it being teeth that ought to be come next. They'd said they liked to eat prey alive and she was still alive. Or she thought she was still alive. Could be dead. Might explain the numbness. Hard to tell, seeing as she'd never rightly been dead before.

There came a roar, loud enough to rival a murmel scream. Maura tilted her head back a bit to look, leastways her neck was still responding to commands. *Not dead, then.* All she saw was the faces of aliens all about her, and above them the ceiling that was no ceiling just the terrible void.

Quy broke through the crowd and swung himself to stand over her, one foot to each side of her body. Maura recognized those long furry legs. She was ridiculously grateful, mostly because she could no longer see the nothingness of space.

Quy was carrying a long stick in one paw with a bladed ball at its end. *Smart weapon*, Maura thought, *against a long armed, clawed opponent.* Her next thought to come about was, *Look at me with the two protectors, both of them over-much fuzzy.*

Then, rather inconveniently, and right when things were getting most exciting, Quy moved and the emptiness of space reappeared above her. At the sides of her vision the whole ice white world of aliens and stone began to fade, and she fell swiftly upwards into the blackness between the stars.

Maura awoke to a rip-roaring fight going on right about her head. Though not the physical one she'd half expected.

"You told me the testing would be safe! I can't believe this!"

Quy? Using the personal? And contractions? Couldn't be Quy, he never makes that mistake.

'"And you were to refrain from getting involved." That voice was female, also loud.

"What part of *bonded* did you fail to comprehend? She was lying there, bleeding, some idiot in kill strike, what was I *supposed* to do? You tell me."

Definitely Fuzzy. There he goes, using the personal again. Why so upset?

"You were to leave it be. The situation was entirely under control."

"Bonded," yelled Quy again. Louder.

"And she is absolutely fine, just look at her." That was a voice not given to yell. It was all settled into being calm and low.

"Fine! That does not look *fine* to me." Quy again, still at the top of his considerable lungs.

Maura blinked a bit. "What?" she tried to say, but not a whit of noise would come out.

Her pillow shifted slightly and murmured at her sympathetically.

"Biskweet?" she croaked.

A soft chitter of acknowledgement. *Well at least someone had emerged unscathed.*

A face with black and red eyes appeared above her and Maura flinched back. Dr Sillous clucked sympathetically. "No worries there, young Crudrat. Only me, not one of the youngsters. I've been patching you up, not taking you apart."

Maura couldn't help but think on what an enormous expense such medic action might cost. Imagine wasting it on her, a reject.

"Sorry."

"Goodness, whatever for?" The surgeon wanted to know. How did his eyes seem so kind?

Maura, practical to the last, said simply, "Slipping. This one should have remembered the blood."

The Patrona's face appeared next to her husband's. Her expression was calm, despite the arguing. "And so you should be. Imagine picking a fight with a bunch of young Jakaa Nova with not a single bit of proper training."

Maura held her tongue.

Quy was not so smart. He began pacing about the bed, all frustrated energy, his fur shivering slightly in agitation. "Those Jakaa were sent to pick a fight *with her*, not the other way around! And you know it. Really Aunt, couldn't you have tested with something a little less dangerous?"

Maura made the connection, finally. "That was a set up?"

Quy nodded, angry enough to be no longer playing whatever course his family had concocted for Maura to run.

"Quy, shut your big fat chew hole, you blithering little petulance," instructed his aunt.

Maura felt an odd sense of betrayal. Odd because they had not promised her anything, nor told her what form the games would take. "So these tests, they aren't announced? Did this one fail this last one, then?"

"Yes you did." The Patrona was not disposed to give false confidence to anyone.

Maura bit her lip. How was she supposed to test without even knowing what was required or how to pass?

Quy obviously agreed with that opinion. "It was an unfair test! She has had no cultural acclimatization. You could at least put her though the coalition approval and education regime, allow her to learn something before chucking her into the ocean without knowing how to swim."

Maura wondered what *swim* was.

The Patrona shook her head. The red fringe of her headdress swayed back and forth. "She is not some ambassador seeking treaty nor an envoy from a member world. The law does not allow for a petitioner to be assisted in any way."

Quy threw both hands up into the air violently.

Maura started at the movement. Dr Sillous bent over her, stilling her with those wide-tipped deadly hands of his. "Careful, try not to move too much, your side is still under gel."

"Why is this one not in pain?" Maura asked him, softly, while Quy and his aunt continued to argue.

"Jakaa Nova carry numbing agents in their claw tips. Genetic modification to extend hunt-time. According to the tinker records it made sense once long ago."

"You have *tinker records*?" Maura was amazed. That was like hearing the voice of the Wheel, right there, out loud – spiritually miraculous.

"Of course we do. So your Wheel's enhancers, most likely. They just don't talk about it. How do you think they know how to trigger those silver eyes of yours?"

Quy's voice, raised again, interrupted them. "But every petitioner in the past has at least known something about how our society works!"

"Then perhaps this should be a lesson to you. Pick your bond-mates more carefully in future!"

Quy went very quiet, and very angry. He also slipped back into use of the personal, a sure sign of upheaval. "I should like to think, Aunt, that you are not using my friend to punish me for acts of my own making and choosing. That would be dishonorable to say the very least."

The Patrona reared back as though slapped and bared her teeth in a snarl.

Dr Sillous sighed and interrupted them both. "My little sugar drop," he addressed his wife, "doesn't the law also state that equality must formulate the petitioner's starting point?"

"Husband, when I need your advice, it will be on matters medical, not legal. And I will ask you for it."

Dr Sillous gave her the raised eyebrow. Maura thought he was a remarkably tolerant sort of alien. She wondered what the Patrona was so afraid of. *What's it matter if I learn more of this world? I'm settled to live in it permanent and forever now, aren't I?* Maura thought to ask that question, but wasn't sure about giving offense. So many turns she'd been trained to keep her mouth shut, never speak unless addressed directly. It was hard to break that kind of habit.

Quy barely gave her the chance. He was already back to arguing. Sure was a champion arguer, old quoin Fuzzy. *Who'd have thought, when I fell on him out of the sky, he'd turn out to be such a talk-making machine.*

"Ah ha! See, even uncle agrees with this one on the matter. Why are you being so unreasonable about this, Aunt?"

The Patrona looked down at the small alien girl lying broken on her husband's operating block. Maura wondered what she saw. Shorter than the Kill'ki, hairless except for the blue on top, silver eyes, enemy made. Was that the issue? Kill'ki had been fighting Wheel off and on for generations. Or so the Wheel claimed. Mild skirmishes mainly, and always the loosing end of it, or that's what the Wheel reported. Maura wondered at the truth of that now, especially seeing as the Kill'ki had the Jakaa Nova on their side. She cocked her head, trying to wrap her brain 'round the suspicions inside an alien mind. *Manzanilla is a politician, and don't all those in power think the same, in the end?* Maura changed her thought tactics. *How would a sequensor think, faced with a Kill'ki on the block trying to climb into Wheel society?*

"She thinks this one is a spy," said Maura. She shifted her gaze to the Patrona without moving her head. "Don't you?"

Quy said, "No. Not possible. Really?" He lost most of his anger to amazement. "You mistrust this one's judgment that much?"

Dr Sillous said, "Not only *your* judgment. I've done a bit of anthropology in my day and from what little we know of them, the Wheel would never use a reject for anything, not even spying, but my suspicious little snowdrop here does not believe *me* either."

"She comes to us out of the void and unexpected. She has a strangely unique skill set, and looks more than she talks. She carries with her no technology either to offer in trade nor on her own person that we might use to find weaknesses in the Wheel. And you do not think any of this suspicious?"

Sillous shrugged. "She worries about allowing Crudrat here access to information."

Maura said ashamed, "You know this one can not read most words, right?"

The Patrona was unfazed. "Neither can we. Kill'ki have never had a written language. That is not the kind of information that concerns me."

"If you're that worried about her, why not take her through the education regime yourself? The Patron position is authorized to approve temporary coalition, is it not? You must have had the training."

The Patrona donned a very long-suffering expression. "Quy, I am Patrona of this entire city. I do not have time to shepherd your problem around."

Quy crossed his arms, looking militant. "Bonded, remember."

Dr Sillous looked at his wife. "And we *are* family."

"How do you consistently manage to drag everyone else into your mistakes?" The Patrona glared at her nibling. But it was clearly a capitulation and everyone knew it, even Maura.

Quy grinned.

Maura wasn't so certain about this change of approach. "Uh," she raised a querulously fingertip, "What was just decided?"

Dr Sillous explained kindly, "You are going to be attached to my wife here as soon as you are well enough to leave the slab. She'll explain to you the workings of Kill'ki life, and then you'll be tested."

The Patrona's expression said she didn't like this turn of events. Maura wasn't too sure about it either. Following around a highstock and keeping out of her way all shift wasn't Maura's idea of a pleasant run. Especially if that highstock was hostile.

She turned her gaze on Dr Sillous. The Jakaa Nova was

looking equally uncomfortable. Well, she supposed he was
going to eat it later for having sided with Quy in this.

Quy was the only one who was genuinely pleased.

Maura worried about letting him down and seeing him
bleed for it.

"Good that's settled," said Dr Sillous. "Now, the patient
requires rest. Both of you take any further," a pause, "*discussion* outside."

Quy and his aunt left. Out in the stone hallway, floating
back through the curtained entranceway, Maura heard them
raise up their voices once more.

"Do they ever stop?"

"You know he was fostered here for prequoin? They
drove each other to distraction, so she had him transferred to
a different city for quoin. Too much alike." Sillous picked up
a small round plastic globe and twisted something at the top.
"Now it is back to sleep with you." He passed the globe softly
under her nose. A strange smell wafted out, acrid as digested
crud but not quite so unpleasant. Just as Maura became interested in figuring out what it was, she fell asleep.

Despite her negative opinion of the Jakaa Nova, Maura grew
to genuinely like Dr Sillous over the next few spins. He had a
calmness about him either learned from his profession,
intrinsic to his character, or gained through marriage. She
found if she asked him a question, he was more than likely to
answer it and not be annoyed. *Miraculous.*

"How," she wondered one day, "did the Kill'ki ever
contrive to conquer your race?"

"I shall take that as a compliment. But actually, with their
wari training and their range of weaponry, the Kill'ki are a

match for the Jakaa Nova in a one-to-one fight. Such sparring is quite the sight to see. The Kill'ki, however, have better technology. But the Jakaa Nova were not conquered — that is Wheel coloring your question. The Kill'ki did, and will in the future, conquer some of their Coalition, but not us. We came in as allies. There was a lengthy adaptation period for both peoples, since we Jakaa Nova are a hot jungle genotype, and Kill'ki were made for ice. But it happened a long time ago and now there are bits of both in the Coalition."

The very idea of such open acceptance made Maura blink. "You truly are alien, in your thinking as well as everything else." She shifted a bit on the stone platform. She'd graduated to sitting up last shift, and Dr Sillous hinted she might be allowed to walk around later that afternoon. It couldn't come soon enough. Her muscles were not used to stillness. Biskweet was happy with her confinement. The murmel had taken up permanent residence on her feet, having been displaced from his role as pillow by an actual pillow. Dr Sillous's staff was spoiling him with ear scratches and bowls of flush. Currently, he formed a ball of blue in a nest of furs and blankets between her ankles.

Dr Sillous sighed. "You really do see us as entirely *other*, a completely different class of creature."

"It's difficult not to, particularly with the Kill'ki. They are so very furry."

"And you are a product of a narrow-minded culture, even if you lived on its outskirts."

"This one is trying to change the way she thinks."

"I've seen photos of your ruling caste, you know? Made a bit of study of it back in training. Some of them look pretty much alien to me."

"Yes, but they aren't, they are human."

Dr Sillous frowned, put down his quazi-scanpad and gave

her his full attention. "I don't think you are quite grasping the truth of the matter. We were all made once, triggered your people would say, but the Tinkers, what they started with was…" He left off mid explanation, reconsidered, then asked, "Didn't they teach you universe history on that spaceport of yours?"

"Reject, remember? This one thought you knew what that meant, medic. They taught me nothing from the moment this one rejected the implant. Learning is only possible with a chip."

"But you yourself have trigger traits, right? You must have been born into an elite family."

Maura gestured expressively at her silver slitted eyes.

"And the hair?"

"That's crudrat made."

"I thought they had some sort of educators or teaching devices for Wheel elite even when very young."

Maura wondered at his access to information. He sure did know more about the Wheel than she'd sussed about the Kill'ki Coalition. It made her think hard on all those security measures the armigers were always taking on. *Not so good, in the end.*

"Drones gave this one a bit of learning before chip-rejection, but this one is thinking such history lessoning were a tad less than reality. Why don't you speech on what rumors fly about the past 'round this part of space?"

Dr Sillous looked at the shift monitor reader attached to the cuff of his coat. "I suppose I could spare a few ticks." He checked about at his staff. A group of three, one Jakaa Nova, one little scaled greenish sort called Ooten, and one of the all-red aliens Maura had been amazed by during her first spin in the city. They all seemed to be busily occupied with important tasks. The surgeon settled on the edge of the stone plat-form near Maura's hip.

"Where to start? With the most relevant information, I suppose." He gave her a quick assessing look. "Genetically all of us here are compatible. Even you. There are a few species who have been tinkered beyond human breeding compatibility, like the Galoi, but none of those belong to our Coalition." When Maura still looked confused he added, "You know Manzanilla and I have a son? He's about your age, perfectly healthy, and fostered into the profession of his choice."

Maura wondered in amazement what such a creature might look like, half red-eyed furless Jakaa Nova, and half white fuzzy Kill'ki. Then she wondered if *she* was genetically compatible with these bizarre alien races as well. She wasn't particularly interested in that sort of thing, and it wasn't a pleasant idea. She hadn't yet even figured out how Kill'ki sex parts worked. She'd seen Quy naked, and he didn't seem to have any. She figured that this was a good question for a doctor.

"Where do the Kill'ki keep their, you know, bits." She gestured expressively.

The doctor didn't seemed inclined to laugh or be offended at the question. "Ice planet, remember? The males can retract their genitalia entirely into their body cavities for warmth and the females only develop breasts when feeding their young."

Maura blinked at him. *Very odd.* Then a fearsome thought struck her. "So if we are technically compatible, me being bonded to Quy doesn't imply any kind of a sex act, does it?" Not that Quy had tried anything, but it would be nice to know if he was entitled. Or if she was entitled, for that matter. Maura became rather nervous.

Dr Sillous looked repulsed by her question. Not a reaction

she had expected. "Quite the opposite, actually, bonded in an invitation to familial, not sexual, intimacy. Sex between bonded is taboo, tantamount to incest."

Maura breathed a sigh of relief. "Oh good."

"Don't find Quy attractive, huh?"

Maura wrinkled her nose. *An alien! Surely not. That seemed almost like fooling around with a murmel. Blech.* Since Maura was pretty sure Dr Sillous wouldn't like such comparisons, especially given his own preferences, she said, "Don't find boys that attractive."

"Ah, favor the female? Gender fluid? Third gender? Agender?"

That was more choices than she'd expected. Freedom from the Wheel appeared to have other perks attached to it. Options. Maura considered for a moment. Truth be told she hadn't ever thought much on the subject, it wasn't something that came up often for crudrats. There was that whole short life survival thing getting in the way. "Uh, no. Not interested in any of that at the moment. Thank you," she said primly.

The doctor laughed. "I would not be so fastidious for too long, if I were you. This side of space appreciates the exotic, and you are nothing if not exotic. Someone is going to ask to initiate you eventually."

"This one is barely thirteen turns, if that!"

Dr Sillous looked impassive. "Well, should you change your mind, I took the opportunity to sterilize you while I was making repairs. Like the wearing of jewelry, the Kill'ki do not permit breeding until adulthood."

Maura was pure confused by that. "But this one is a *reject*."

"So?"

"You didn't suss the body?"

Dr Sillous frowned. "*Suss* what?"

"This one is already sterilized. Has been since the implant didn't take. The Wheel does it to all rejects. Can't have a failure go about procreating. Not sanitary."

"What?" The surgeon rushed over to a side platform, picked up one of his not-quite-scanpads and poked at it for a couple minutes.

"Great space turds! They removed your whole blasted uterus!"

Maura wondered, if it was so important, why he hadn't noticed it missing. "Well, what do you do for the sterilize action?"

"Install temporary hormonal mod." He continued to stare at the digital readout. "That may be the most disgusting thing I've ever seen. And I've been through two wars. Look at the scarring." The Jakaa Nova's lip curled up in revulsion.

Maura opened her mouth to be offended and then shut it. She was feeling a bit like free float spaceside with no breather in this conversation. Best to quit while she wasn't too far behind.

"That will teach me not to check over all internal organs. Anything else missing?" Dr Sillous wasn't asking her. He was back in full medic mode, nose to the scanpad, wandering out of the room still prodding at it.

Moments later, Quy came into the lab for a chat.

Quy had been in to visit her every day and was getting used to suffering under the burden of Dr Sillous's revelations whenever he did so.

"Quy!" Maura said as soon as he'd settled himself cross-legged at the end of her bed. "This one found out the most amazing thing just a few ticks ago."

Quy was haplessly unwary. What Maura found amazing each day was generally an utterly mundane fact to him. "Oh, yes?"

"You male Kill'ki can retract your bits!"

"What?"

"You know, up inside. That's right nifty! Do you think they could make it so this one could do that with her tits?"

Quy winced. Sometimes Maura knew he found her phrasing too abrupt. Mostly it wasn't so bad, as Maura tended not to talk much but the other times...

"Maura!" no one else was in earshot, so he could use her real name. "We do not talk about these sort of things in such a forthright manner. You ought to take greater care."

"What things?"

"You know, sexuality and so forth." Maura thought Quy would have blushed but he hadn't the capacity.

"But you sure do start in on them young. Dr Sillous issued this one with sterilization. Said this one might need it."

Quy sat up straighter at that. "Was there a reason? Has someone been bothering you?"

Maura cocked her head. *Is this the bonded coming out? Why so protective?* "Nope, but apparently they will soon."

Quy bristled. "Oh will they?"

Maura went all prim on him. "You think they won't? Dr Sillous says this one is *exotic*!"

"Uncle Sillous talks too much." Quy sighed. "But he is probably correct."

Korakay came wandering in, shift break.

Maura was surprised. She hadn't thought they were that close, especially after Korakay abandoned her during the fight.

"Hello you three." Korakay included the sleeping Biskweet in her greeting. "How's it floating?"

Maura looked away.

The murmel raised his head autocratically, and received

the expected attention. Korakay scratched him under the chin. He groomed her arm hair gravely. *Deserter.*

Quy turned to look at his age mate. "Enjoying being out of the kitchen?"

"Rumor is, you took my place." Korakay didn't look up from the murmel.

Quy snorted. "Got into it nice and loud with the aunt over Crudrat here, and she took it out of this one's pelt in kitchen duty. Could be worse. Not sure how, but could be."

"Poor little cub, suffering in the land of food." Korakay was utterly unsympathetic. "How are you feeling there, Crudrat?"

Maura gave her a stony glare, silver eyes hard. *Much she cares!*

"Looks to be that you are in Crudrat's bad books." Quy was getting used to interpreting Maura's expressions. "What'd you do?"

"This one has no idea." Korakay seemed both confused and a little hurt.

Maura was thinking of Rees, always her tiny champion. "It's what you didn't do. In this one's part of space, a friend would have tried to help."

"I did!" replied Korakay, stung into using the personal.

"Who do you think came and fetched me?" asked Quy.

Maura bit her lip. "And she couldn't do it herself?"

"Not with a bonded in the city! It's not this ones place to step within bond," said Korakay, offended in turn.

"Even in such a dangerous situation as that, you had to fetch Quy? But I could have been killed while you were off looking for him." Maura could not get over the inefficiency of it.

Both Kill'ki shrugged.

"Bonded is bonded," said Korakay.

Maura sighed. *Weirdos.* She was beginning to understand why the Patrona had found her nibling's bond so aggravating. It sure seemed to inconvenience life. *Not to mention endanger it.* "Does the same apply in the opposite direction? Is this one bound to come to Quy's rescue every time he gets into it with someone?"

"Hardly," Korakay smiled, "you'd never have time for your own work! There never was a moment of breath that Quy here couldn't waste yelling at someone."

"Mostly the Patrona," added Maura.

"Yeah he is all over smart like that."

All insult seemed forgiven in their mutual abuse of someone else. Maura was pleased. She hadn't liked thinking badly of Korakay.

Quy didn't seemed to mind taking the brunt, if it mean Maura would stop glaring ice crystals at his age mate.

"Truth?" Quy looked serious.

Maura nodded.

"You do have to come if your bonded asks. Korakay took it on as tacit that you would have asked if you had known to do so. That's why she tracked this one down. This one knows to ask, although unlikely to do so until you are trained, already have the capacity, or need is great. Like in the whale on the way here."

Korakay perked up. In their long hours working together, she'd extracted very little from Maura on her past, or her journey out of Wheel space. Maura had operated under the assumption that since she wasn't sure what she was allowed to talk about, she'd best say nothing. It was a policy that always worked well for her.

"Sound's like there's a story in there," prodded Korakay hopefully.

Quy nodded. "Had her helping this one out by shooting fish, when we were shaking our way free of Wheel space."

Korakay settled in to perch on the end of the platform, still scratching Biskweet about the ears. "Well, this one just spent two shifts in targeting practice. Could be that gun schematics and firing solutions may drive this one space-crazy."

"You should get Crudrat to help you out. She was a remarkable marksmen for a first time gunner."

Maura went wide-eyed at the compliment.

Korakay was intrigued. "Oh yeah? So, tell all. This one did not know you two saw action." She looked at Maura accusingly. "Why didn't you say anything about it?"

Maura was confused. "You didn't ask."

"Terrible closed mouthed our Crudrat, isn't she?" complained Korakay to Quy.

"You don't say."

"Well?" Korakay looked hopefully at the two of them.

Quy told her about their space fight, without revealing too much about what Maura was doing with him, or why they were trying to get away from Wheel space. He relayed the fight itself in high detail, every maneuver and every shot. Maura would not have been so specific, but Korakay seemed to find every moment fascinating. Quy was exaggerating quite a bit, but as the two of them always seemed to come out sounding brilliant, Maura figured there was no point in correcting him. She dozed off, Quy's voice a pleasant hum of excited intonations, and only resurfaced when a whole new visitor wandered into the room.

16

*The once holy trinity of civilization was the Builders,
the Tinkers, and the Tailors. They did not work alone,
but they always worked best.*
    ~ On the Civilizing of Worlds by J. Kilsen Slliurp

Quy's voice went flat. "What are *you* doing here?"

Maura's eyes popped open just in time to see both Quy and Korakay rise and stand, arms loose but held away from the body, facing the doorway.

The Jakaa Nova who'd only recently decorated her insides with five very long puncture wounds stood frozen, pushing aside the curtain. He looked less fierce than he had in the plaza. Perhaps it was that he hadn't any friends backing his cause. Perhaps it was the sheepish smile on his face. He raised his hands, twisting them at the wrists twice to show his claws remained safely sheathed.

"This one has came to apologize." His voice was low and mellow, like Dr Sillous's – no danger to it at all. Maura could see, for the first time, why avoiding the word 'I' could be useful. Without his telling her straight, she'd found out his age. *Not yet adult. Probably a quoin like Quy and Korakay.*

"Are you here under the Patrona's instructions?" Quy wanted to know, not relaxing his stance at all.

The Jakaa Nova shook his head. "Under this one's own autonomy. This one was only supposed to scare the little blue. The extent of the injury was entirely unintended."

Maura noted that there was no denial of intent to injure some. Clearly he *had* been told to rough her up. She reassessed her opinion of the Patrona.

"Is she making you work in the kitchens for the mistake?" Korakay wanted to know.

The red-eyed youth gave her a long measured perusal. "It was thought, since Quy was already serving, perhaps this one best not go to work along side." He looked sidelong at Quy. The Kill'ki was shaking in repressed anger. "This one did not know she was your bonded. The Patrona never said anything on the subject." Clearly, he was annoyed at Manzanilla for that.

"Would you have resisted her instructions, had you known Crudrat had a Kill'ki protector?" Quy asked, tongue blade sharp and cutting.

"This one is not so much a coward." That made the Jakaa Nova angry enough for the tips of his claws to peek out from his fingers.

"Calm down, both of you." Korakay inserted herself deftly between the two. "No need for squabbling in the medical lab. You know Dr Sillous will have you both filleted and flat out on the butcher block if you mess about in here."

Quy sneered but backed off slightly.

The Jakaa Nova turned from the Kill'ki and came

around the stone platform to stand next to Maura's head. His stride was easy and balanced, no wonder he moved so fast.

Maura found it disconcerting to be near him again. She had to tilt back to look up at him. He stood that much too close. Her sliced ribs began to ache for the first time, as though they sensed his presence.

"This one must explain to you, little blue. The Patrona chose me to be your test *because* of my claw control. Normally, this one is known for only light bleedings, if any. But your fighting style was so strange, and that slip of yours so unexpected, this one was not fast enough to avoid injuring you severely. This one owes you recompense for the excess blood loss."

Maura remained silent. What to say to that?

"He is offering payment." Korakay explained.

Maura said, sadly. "This one has no chip, no way to receive or exchange credits." What good would payment do?

Now the Jakaa Nova looked confused. He frowned at her strange words.

Quy explained, "We do not have a pecuniary system in the Coalition. The Kill'ki ancestors abandoned the concept when they first took to the ice. We work on the principles of barter rather than coin. It makes matters much simpler, and helps build networks and relationships."

The Jakaa Nova curled his lip. "She thought this one was offering *money*? For blood? How barbaric."

"No crossgentors at all?" Maura was equally flabbergasted.

"Cross-what's-its?" Now Quy was confused.

Maura searched for the simplest explanation. "Those that sell product for a living."

"Oh, for certain, we have tradesmen and peddlers, but

exchanges are done through goods and services, not – what did you call it? – credits."

"Remarkable. Sounds cumbersome." Maura looked straight on up at the Jakaa Nova, evaluating him with her eyes. *Hard to suss in this alien place, what rich looked like. Is this dark red-eyed alien highstock? The Kill'ki equivalent of progenetor? How to tell?*

She asked him direct as could be, "Are you saying you owe for this one's blood? What would you pay for such a thing? What is equivalent value?" She pronounced the last carefully. It was not a space-tongue term she'd needed much before.

Quy cast his paws up in one of his favorite gestures. "Barter system, remember? The point, Crudrat, is what do *you* need in return?"

The Jakaa Nova gestured with one hand at Quy, as if to say, "Exactly!"

Maura frowned. What did she need? The Kill'ki housed her and fed her. She seemed mostly safe – when she kept her mouth shut and avoided Jakaa Nova. *What more to wish for in life?*

"Cost of the surgeon?" she suggested, hesitantly.

Everyone in the room, except the murmel, looked offended.

"Medical services are *always* provided by the Coalition. Especially during a testing," explained Korakay, in strict no-nonsense terms.

"Unless you do something really, really stupid," amended Quy, sounding like he spoke from personal experience.

Maura looked to her bonded for help. "What does this one ask for? What does this one need?"

"How about a couple of nice new weapons?"

"A change of clothes?" offered Korakay.

"A real pillow?" suggested Quy, having observed her and Biskweet's sleeping arrangement.

"A whale?" said Korakay.

"Whoa, there certainly is not enough barter for that," interjected the Jakaa Nova.

"Just because that's what you always want," said Quy at the same time.

"How about hair dye?" said Korakay.

They seemed as like to go on forever, back and forth – *who knew a body could collect so much stuff?* Half of it Maura had never ever heard speak of afore. *Some strange new definition of the word 'need.'*

She thought of those lonely pegs on her side of the big stone room she shared with Quy.

"This one supposes, clothing might be nice. Not that this one doesn't appreciate the pelt," she spoke swiftly, so as not to give Quy offense, after all it had once been a member of his family.

Quy said, "And this one is sure Great Uncle Raqchi there would appreciate a rest from daily wear."

"What would you like?" asked the Jakaa Nova, no other reaction.

Here was Maura, a *reject*, asking *him* to give her stuff. And he seemed ready to do it, just like that. *Amazing.*

Maura swallowed 'round the lump in her throat. "How about something more like what you are wearing?" She gestured with her chin at the Jakaa Nova's long tight shirt and trousers under the warm looking overcoat. Both were far tighter than Wheel modesty and fashion allowed, but what cared Maura for that anymore? She wasn't on the Wheel. Despite the tightness, the Jakaa clothing looked more flexible and convenient than her pelt, ragged shirt, and knickerbock-ers. *Bet I could run blades in something like that.*

"Ooooo," said Korakay, approvingly, "a full set of leathers, excellent choice."

Without flinching the Jakaa Nova nodded. "This one will send someone around to take your measurements this afternoon. It is a fair barter."

Maura looked a Quy. He was grinning fit to split the face.

She took a risk, turning back to the Jakaa Nova. "Your pardon, this one does not know the ways of the Coalition yet, please do not take offense. But may this one ask what you are called?" Maura glanced quickly at Korakay and Quy for hints that she should not have asked. They both seemed a little surprised but did not try to stop her.

The Jakaa Nova merely said, "This one is honored you would ask, after such a mistake. The barter must meet with your approval. You may call me Asherat."

Maura relaxed slightly and smiled in relief. "Very well then, Asherat, thank you. This one is called Crudrat." Emboldened by her success she asked tentatively, "May this one request a second barter?"

Everyone was surprised by this daring, even Maura. But again, neither Kill'ki tried to stop her, although Quy did say, "Careful there, bonded." Partly as a warning, but also, Maura guessed, to remind the Jakaa Nova that she had protection.

"You may ask."

"This one would like to better understand Jakaa Nova ways. Given the Patrona's approval, might you take a little time to instruct this one in the lore and customs of your people?"

Asherat blinked at her long ticks. Lids like rapid shudders over black and red eyes – *one, two, three.*

"Done," he said at last.

"And in return?" Quy asked, head to one side, interested.

"We shall leave the barter incomplete, for now, if you do

not mind? It is not a very great thing, that you ask. And it does us more honor rather than less. This one will have to think on the proper remuneration."

Maura looked to Quy. Wondering it it was bad thing, to leave a debt opened up like that. Quy shrugged at her.

"Agreed. And thank you again," Maura said.

The Jakaa Nova gave a funny little bow, not at all like those of progenetors, stiff and unfinished. "This one will return tomorrow to begin the instruction as bartered." With that he whirled around and left.

Korakay hooted with approval as soon as he was judged out of range. "Wasn't that beautifully done? You clever little thing. Hidden negotiating skills there, Crudrat — turning the barter around on him like that and asking nothing more than cultural tutoring. That's a nice little slap in the face considering cultural ignorance is, publicly, what started the whole fight. He is going to have a hard time coming up with an equal barter. The Jakaa Nova won't want to know anything about Wheel life. Too arrogant for that! This could be fun."

Quy was also ginning.

Somehow, Maura realized, ignorance of the system had worked in her favor this time.

Quy said, "Stars, he must have felt bad about bleeding you. Jakaa Nova leathers are high value. Worth more than a bit of blood, or so the furless tell me."

"They aren't," Maura swallowed, "made from dead Jakaa Nova. Are they?"

Korakay laughed. "Not to worry. They are perfectly respectable animal hide. The Jakaa home world habitable zone is mostly savannah, nice herding territory. Cows mainly?"

"Cow?" Maura was getting distressingly used to being unable to suss one word in ten.

"Big animal, four hooves, goes *moo*," explained Quy, unhelpfully.

Maura blinked. Alien humor?

"Don't forget tasty," added Korakay.

Maura grinned. "Is anything not tasty to you people?"

Dr Sillous wandered back into the room. "Nope," he answered the question. "Good adaptation that, the Kill'ki ability to eat just about anything." He glared meaningfully at the two furry aliens. They blinked wide black eyes at him, all innocence. "Speaking of which, shouldn't you quoin be off to the plaza? Second shift is almost over, you'll be wanting to eat before duty ticks commence. Besides which, visiting time is over for this spin, young Crudrat here needs her rest."

Quy and Korakay took his orders easy enough and bounced away, still grinning.

The next morning the Patrona turned up while Maura was eating first meal. Even the food for those slab-bound seemed to originate in the kitchen. Apparently, injury excused a body from hauling down plazaside between shifts, as well as from working those shifts. Meals were brought up to Maura special. *Luxury indeed. Imagine a crudrat not turning up to run blades because of a cut. Foreman'd have a license pulled in a single tick for no-show!* Here they sent her food! *Crazy.*

"I hear you had an exciting day yesterday." The Patrona settled herself gingerly down on an end corner of Maura's stone platform. She was wearing fewer than the usual number of necklaces, but more than the usual number of bracelets. *Significant?* Maura would have put her meal aside, but the huge Kill'ki gestured for her to continue.

The murmel padded over to their visitor expectantly.

The Patrona ignore him.

"You found out about the barter with Asherat? How?" Maura scrunched on a crispy wedge of potato.

"I am Patrona of this city, there is very little I do not know about it. That said, I was not overly surprised. I know he felt guilty and honor smudged."

Biskweet butted at her paw in an encouraging sort of way.

She continued to ignore him.

"This one is getting leathers out of the deal," said Maura proudly.

"And some cultural instruction, as well, I understand." The Patrona's face was impassive, Maura wished she could tell whether the Kill'ki approved or not.

"Only if it was permitted by you," she said, hoping to mollify.

The Patrona only nodded. "I find it an interesting tactic on your part. What made you ask for lessons?"

Maura shrugged. "So far all this one's problems 'round your city seem caused by ignorance. Yet ignorance be the most fixable problem a girl can have."

The Patrona was willing to accept such logic and allow the barter. "Jakaa Novas are notoriously cagey. You will hardly learn enough from a brash young quoin for a security risk. Especially, as you yourself are not talkative enough to draw him out."

Maura thought that was a fair assessment and wondered why the Patrona had revealed her logic.

"What did you think of kitchen duty?" First topic dealt with and Patrona approved, on to the next.

Maura was judicious in her answer. "Is it this one's business to like or dislike? There was regular food, merely for a lift here and a chop there and some kicking on the side. What's not to like?"

"My question exactly."

Maura looked at the leader of the city from under thick blue lashes. "Truth?"

The Patrona crossed her arms. "Truth."

"This one misses the running."

"Running?"

"Bladeside." Maura was enjoying being the one to cause confusion for once. "This one was one of the best. Five turns scraping the blades and nary a single cut. Not many 'rats can boast that kind of record."

"Are you saying you miss exercise?" The Patrona evaluated Maura more closely. Under the furs and textiles of the lab bed she finally seemed to understand how many muscles there were. All patronas had wari training. She could appreciate fitness whatever form it took.

Maura nodded.

"Did Quy not tell you, we have extensive recreational arenas in Pikillacta?"

A crease appeared between Maura's blue eyebrows. Had Quy said something? Not that she could remember. But then again, he'd never given her an actual tour of the city.

"How does it work?" she asked, figuring she was there for instruction, questions could not cause anger, could they?

The Patrona tilted her head back and hollered for her husband instead of answering.

Maura jumped. Apparently they could.

Dr Sillous glided into the room. "Yes, petal?"

Maura could not get over the fact that these two had produced an offspring together.

"When can she walk?"

Dr Sillous wandered over to the side of the room and prodded at one of the pillow stones. It slid softly out, and

after a few pokes with his spade-tipped fingers, projected a
three dimensional image of Maura's body up into the air.

He hummed over it for a few ticks. "You could take her
out now, for a short stroll, if you must."

"Excellent!" The Patrona ginned. "The best way to
answer your question, Crudrat, is to show you."

Maura smiled in relief. The Patrona had not been angered
by the questions. Hard to tell with highstock types, Wheel or
not, what would turn them vicious.

Dr Sillous helped Maura down from the platform. All the
furniture-stone blocks in this city were just that much too
high. Maura was beginning to hope, for the very first time in
all her ticks, that her tall triggers might actually kick in
further.

Dr Sillous handed her one of the strange blue jacket
things that he wore. Her knickerbockers and shirt seemed to
have vanished after the fight. She pulled it on, and wrapped
the same white pelt, an old friend now, 'round her shoulders. Biskweet looked very upset at this change of routine.
So far as he was concerned Maura in bed and everyone
waiting on them both was an ideal lifestyle. Why fuss with
it by getting up and dressed? His little murmel brain was
confused.

Maura, on the other hand, was thrilled to be foot solid and
upright at last.

"It shouldn't hurt you to walk about for a while. But you
will find you lack strength. Listen to your body and do not let
my wife drag you around the entire city in one shift. Pace
yourself." Dr Sillous instructed Maura but he was looking at
the Patrona. Manzanilla nodded her agreement.

Maura's legs did feel a bit shaky about the knees. Odd
since that wasn't the injured spot. *Wouldn't bet myself to run
just yet, that's for certain sure.* But the idea of getting off that

stab and away from medics, if only for a tick or two, sounded swift and good.

"I shall only take her to the recreation neighborhood. Then I'll bring her back directly after."

Maura was honored, a personal tour by the woman in charge of the whole city. Very highstock indeed. Was this what *education regime* meant?

She followed the Patrona out of the room, turning back when she reached the doorway.

"Coming?" she asked Biskweet, who was sitting in the center of her abandoned slab with his back to her, pointedly.

He flicked his tail.

Maura shrugged and padded after the Patrona out the door and down the hallway. Turning a corner onto a new stone hall, she caught a flash of blue, as the murmel skulked after them.

The Patrona lead them down a whole new series of stone hallways, ones that Maura had never seen or used afore now. The light creeping though the cracks was a warm yellow color, and the stones themselves were cut on the larger side.

"Does the size of the stones or the color of the light mean anything?" Maura asked, breaking silence.

"The Builders might have intended something by it, but we have long since forgotten."

"The Builders?"

"Did they tell you nothing of the dawn of civilization in your Wheel space?"

"Only from the Wheel perspective," admitted Maura, "and this one is beginning to suspect truth in Wheel words."

The Patrona spoke then, as though a sequensor, reciting Wheel scripture from memory. "And humanity took to the void in groups of three — the Builders, the Tinkers, and the Tailors. The one to change the state of things, the second to change the state of us, and the last to fit both back together again."

"You mean, this city of yours is as old as the Tinkers?"

The Kill'ki nodded.

Maura breathed a moment in reverence. "From the beginning of life."

"No, from the beginning of life in space."

They passed the usual range of alien life as they walked. Maura was mostly used to it by now. In deference to Maura's injury, the Patrona shortened her stride and kept them to the edge of the hall. The murmel stuck close to their heels. This caused a bit of a blockage, and frustrated huffs from every which way. When they realized it was the Patrona, greeting style turned to grave respect. One or two asked to *petition*. These Manzanilla put off with a curt, "tomorrow would be better."

She explained low and under her breath as they passed. "Those, the all red, they are Shosanshee, from an iron-rich dust-riddled high-temperature planet in the core quadrant of the Coalition. See how they have two sets of eyelids? That is for dust elimination. They respond well to frankness and fast talk, and are considered the least polite among us. Makes them difficult to negotiate with, but valuable in a battle."

They passed one of the smallish scaled aliens.

"Hydraborn, half aquatic race. My husband tells me they have a fascinating genotype."

Maura was intrigued. "Do all aliens look different because of the planet they came from?"

"Are you hypothesizing a kind of evolutionary biological determinism?"

Maura was defeated by such big words. The Patrona didn't seem to notice.

"It was the Tinkers. They were made *for* the planet, not *by* the planet. We all were." She looked down. "Well, not you. If you take my meaning."

Maura, who didn't, nevertheless nodded sagely. Aliens. Planets. Made. All very confusing and terribly muddling.

The Patrona led Maura and Biskweet through a side hallway, then down a ramp and around a corner, only to hit up against a mass of people come to a standstill near the end.

"What's going on here?" questioned the Patrona in a loud booming voice. Maura could see why such a feature as loudness might be useful in a city ruler.

Most in the group turned around to look at her.

"Details!" insisted the Patrona.

Someone near the front yelled back, "Quy's gone up against the Jakaa Nova in the sparing ring for bonded damage. Should be a good match."

Maura was aghast. She didn't know what this meant exactly, but it was clearly her fault. She was getting mighty sick of this bonded business. "But there was a barter, this one thought it was all forgotten."

"My blighted little wart of a nibling would seem to feel that he has a claim as well." The Patrona began elbowing her way through the crowd. "Blast it, can't he stay out of trouble for more than ten ticks?"

For lack of anything better to do, Maura scooped up Biskweet and followed. She was starting to feel a little weak and her heart was pounding something awful. She hoped that wherever they were going it boasted a place to sit down.

It did, in excess.

The Patrona paused once she'd pushed through the masses. She looked down at Maura's gape.

"You could catch snow in that mouth of yours. Welcome to the recreation court."

The place was huge – could have eaten the crossgenetor

arena two times over and still been hungry for more. It had the open top invisible domb that seemed to indicate a public place. Maura didn't look up, not sure she would ever be comfortable under vacuum and stars. It was no trouble not to, there was so much else to see.

They'd entered top side of a massive amphitheater, which must be carved down into the great ball of ice upon which the city rode about through space. It was all stone, massive rows of benches formed tiers and tiers down to a central area. That center bit was divided into four.

"Those are the courts. For display events only, there are plenty of practice areas, warm-up rooms and so forth through those doorways there." The Patrona pointed half way down the rows of benches where the great circle was dotted with curtained exits leading into rooms and hallways underneath the one they'd come in on.

Manzanilla led Maura down a set of long stairs between bleachers. By the end of them Maura's side was starting to ache and her heart was all a flutter. She was going to ask to sit, when the Patrona directed her to do so, at the very last row of stone before the courts. Maura collapsed gratefully, the murmel scolded them both and then set off to explore. He ambled atop the walls 'round courtside, tail lashing for balance. Those same walls made for a good long drop below Maura's feet. Such a thing would keep anyone but a crudrat from leaping down, and even Maura would think hard on such a trick – the plaster floor at the bottom looked awful hard.

There below her was Quy, faced up against Asherat, armed with a bladed-ball on the end of a stick and a fierce expression.

17

Kill'ki always carry. The Jakaa Nova don't have to.
That's what we call 'an advantage.'
   ~ Coalition proverb

"Well at least he chose a sensible weapon," commented the Patrona.

"What's it called?" asked Maura.

"Mace."

The two seemed evenly matched. Asherat with his claws and his speed and Quy with his mace and his attitude.

"Aren't you going to interfere?" Maura asked the Patrona, after they'd sat and watched the two go at it for a while. She seemed remarkably relaxed about the fact that her nibling was near to being skewered.

"Not my place."

"But you're Patrona!"

"This is not a political matter."

Asherat lashed out with one arm. He then twisted around

Quy's answering hit to come in close and strike forward with the other, low toward the Kill'ki's leg.

A palpable hit. Red blood seeped out and into Quy's white fur.

Maura winced. Her own injury ached in sympathy.

It obviously wasn't severe, for Quy barely flinched, and neither stumbled nor slowed his answering strike.

"That is the unfortunate problem with fighting a Jakaa Nova. One never knows when to stop, for the injuries do not hurt, and one's opponent never wants to finish a good fight. Even to win it."

As the Patrona spoke, Asherat drew another five red stripes onto Quy's other side.

Maura was uncomfortable sitting and watching. She'd never left Rees to fight alone, allowing Quy to do so seemed unfriendly. She snaked out a stealthy hand and lifted one of the Patrona's many knives from its belt sheath. She was a little surprised that the Kill'ki didn't notice.

Asherat took another slice at Quy, catching one cheek with two of his claws. Red blood beaded the white fur once again. Quy seemed to be getting the worst of things.

Maura tested the weight of the knife in her hand. The Patrona's eyes were fixed on the fight below. It made Maura wonder about the amount of crime in this city.

Quy stumbled to one side, swinging the mace up in a high arc, bringing it down slightly too slowly.

Asherat had time to dart in, slice once more, and get out with nary a scratch. He was fast moving for such tall bones.

Quy fell to his knees. The wounds may not be paining him, but Maura knew from personal experience he had probably lost most of the feeling in his limbs.

Asherat circled the now kneeling Kill'ki, pacing about like a murmel strutting alpha victory.

Next tick and Maura jumped right on over the wall top, testing out exactly how far down that drop was and exactly how hard the plaster floor at the bottom.

Very far and very hard, as it turned out.

She somersaulted the landing. Her side screamed at her. Her legs were sluggish, but they worked well enough. Fast as Asherat moved, Maura was still crudrat faster, injured or no, and he was still no scyther blade. Plus she had surprise as an extra weapon.

She didn't want to kill him, so with lack of any other option and assuming he was basically biologically similar to herself, she ducked in. Twisting fast as light, she stabbed the dagger down to the hilt in the meat of the Jakaa Nova's backside. Without breaking her stride, she flipped out of range. He hadn't even noticed she was there, until he fell.

He set up quite the howl, part surprise part pain, clutching as his backend and glaring at her.

Maura came to stand over him. The crowd in the stands above was in an uproar.

"Foul!"

"Dishonor!"

"Unbalanced!"

Maura didn't know what to do. This was clearly not one of her better choices.

"Apologies, Mr. Asherat," she said, haltingly. She was feeling a bit dizzy and the roar of the crowd wasn't helping. She swayed slightly and she'd lost her pelt during the jump — the cold was back.

Quy was looking at her with an expression of dumb fascination. Maura would have found this amusing, had she not become worried by the near violent dislike coming from of the crowd above them.

She looked at Fuzzy. "This one thought, as bonded, this one was duty bound to help. Is this not right?"

Quy only blinked at her. He looked like he felt blurry.

Asherat, who'd stopped howling and was lying on his side clutching at his rear, started to laugh in pained little spurts. "Quy, what *have* you gotten yourself into with this one? She's nothing but stealth and innocence and backward dealings. You bonded a countervail?"

Quy gasped. "Shut your mouth!"

Maura looked from one to the other, wondering if they would start in with fists next. But they were both all talk, neither of them looked to be moving up off the ground anytime soon.

Quy shifted a paw to his thigh. It came away covered in blood. He looked more annoyed than anything else. He glanced up at Maura. "Crudrat," he said real slow as though teaching space-tongue to a babe, "this is not the kind of fight that allows interference. Plaza brawling is one thing but this was a set match."

Maura sat down all a sudden like. Her legs had taken their own vote and elected to stop working. "Fight's a fight, what difference does it make *where*?" It seemed her mouth didn't want to stopper up, for once. It had kept too much in until now. "Why does everything have to be so confusing? Oh, hello Biskweet." The murmel jumped down into the court, sniffed at the fallen forms of Quy and Asherat, and then wandered over to stand next to her. He gave her a look that said, *If you will insist on these kinds of shenanigans, I'm no longer coming to your rescue.*

"Quite right," agreed Maura. She continued her diatribe. "And why does it have to be so cold all the time?" She lay back. "And why are you all so opposed to a good solid ceiling?" The stars crowed in on her. She turned her head away from them and found herself staring into the red and black eyes of the Jakaa Nova.

"I do hope this doesn't damage our barter," she said fuzzily, "I could really use some proper clothing."

The young man's face was drawn with pain. "Certainly not, a deal is a deal."

"Oh," said Maura, "Good." And passed out.

This time when she woke up she was in the larger of the med labs, the one with lots of stone platforms, instead of just the one slab. On those extra platforms lay Quy on his back and Asherat on his stomach.

She heard, as she surfaced, the two former combatants chatting softly and amicably. It was a low rumble of voices that, at first, was quite restful.

"She sure can talk a whole lot of nothing when she wants to," Asherat was saying.

"This one didn't think she had it in her. That was the first time she spouted more than two sentences in a row," replied Quy.

"And all of it complaints."

"Wasting words is almost as bad as wasting fights, and you people do too much of both," said Maura sitting up. She took stock of her limbs. Everything seemed to be working fine despite her exertions.

The two looked at her, having not a jot to say at such an accusation.

Dr Sillous glided in. He gave them all a calculated glare. Then moved from one slab to the next checking bandages and three-dimensional body read-outs.

The murmel followed him in and trailed him about next to

him, with an air of haughty officiousness. He was clearly upset with Maura for causing a fuss. *Outside of enough*, was his attitude. *I'll stick with Dr Sillous now. He feeds me regular and doesn't get himself near killed every other tick.*

"I've got all three of you tidied up nice and neat, and you should be released end of this shift. Yes, even you Crudrat. After which I expect to see *nothing* of any of you for a good long time. Is that clear?"

All three of them attempted contrition. They weren't convincing.

Dr Sillous snorted and snapped the stone panel back into the wall with an angry thunk.

He looked at Maura. "Crudrat, your instructor is here." Then he stormed back out, in a very elegant and refined way, of course.

Biskweet stayed behind, but despite Maura's coaxing, sat with his back to all three of them in the middle of the floor.

The Patrona came and loomed over Maura. "You have been out a whole shift. At least it gave me a chance to get some real work done. I'm also getting a good sense of what ought to be done with you."

"You are? This one thought to be stuffed in the kitchens for good long ticks." Maura sighed.

"Why would you think that?" wondered Quy. "The whole idea is to get you settled into a *real* profession."

"Kitchen work is a *real* profession, you nutless husk. Besides which, that may have been *your* idea Quy, but in reality you've just stuck us with another massive problem." The Patrona paced about, back and forth. She nearly tripped over the murmel. Biskweet decided to sacrifice affronted dignity on the altar of safety, and leaped to settle at the foot of Maura's platform.

"Now my bonded is a problem?" Quy narrowed his black eyes.

"Quy, *you* are a problem." The Patrona rounded on him.

Asherat snickered softly at that.

Everyone turned to look at him, reminded of his presence.

"Should he be hearing this?" asked Quy.

"You have chosen to make this his concern." The Patrona paused and examined at the three of them lying before her. "I take it you have settled your difference of opinion, even with the Crudrat's interference?"

"Satisfactorily," said Asherat.

"Be fair, Aunt," said Quy, "she didn't know she was doing anything wrong."

"And yet I believe that, even had she known, she would have still done the same." The Patrona looked to Maura for confirmation.

Maura shrugged. "That depends. Were there restrictions on the fight? Could Quy have died down there?" She looked at the Jakaa Nova.

"It was a fight to first fall, not to the death, so extensive damage was unlikely."

Maura turned back to the Patrona. "Had this one known this, then it is unlikely this one would have interfered."

"But not impossible." The Patrona swirled about the room, robes flying, the fringe on her headdress jiggling in agitation.

Maura was moved to annoyance. "This one never agreed to live by your mysterious code in total."

"You see?" The Patrona sighed. "There really is only one possible profession for her."

Quy sat up straighter in his bed. His fuzzy white face suddenly looked desperate rather than angry. "You can't possibly have completed the testing already!"

"Sometimes a role is obvious from the start, and no great amount of time is needed." The Patrona went to stand next to him, looking strangely sympathetic.

Quy pleaded. "But she still has had no enculturation, no true instruction as to our ways."

"I do not see that will change her behavior or personality all that much."

Quy looked even more desperate. "Please, Aunt, give her a chance. She might be *wari* material. Don't be so hasty."

The Patrona looked Maura up and down. Maura, who barely made a protest, who sat silent and contained and observant. "She stole my knife, nibling."

Asherat looked uncomfortable. "This one really should not be here right now."

Manzanilla looked over at his prone form. "You also do not agree with my decision?"

"It is not this one's place to have an opinion, Patrona."

"But?"

"But, despite what this one once said," he looked at Quy, "she has bartered well. Her behavior has been driven by confusion not malicious intent. She has prospects and possibilities you should not abruptly disregard on account of prejudice."

Quy gasped at this.

"That will teach me to ask an honest opinion from a Jakaa Nova. You'd think thirty years of marriage to one might have taught me something."

Maura was charmed by Asherat's support. She grinned at him.

He winked back at her.

The Patrona sighed. "All of you, try to look at this from my perspective. She fights, yes, but not directly, and by her own admission is better at running away than anything else."

Maura nodded at that.

Quy glared at her.

The Patrona continued, "She looks Wheel and she acts it, despite that culture's obvious flaws. She will never fully integrate into Kill'ki society, no Wheel person ever could. She hasn't the openness of spirit. Even her speech is cagey. Even now, as we talk back and forth about her future, she merely sits, watching. She will remember what she is told, but can she apply it? I hardly need tell you what profession caters to all these personality markers."

"It is unfair!" insisted Quy. "This one petitions for six more days of testing. She should at least be fully healed before you render judgment."

The large Kill'ki sighed heavily. "I always knew if you bonded you'd be impossible over it. You are correct of course. I concede the point. Besides which, my judgment will affect you too, nibling, and I think you should have time to prepare."

Quy looked appalled at that. "Is this one under testing as well?"

"In a way."

"Fantastic," said Quy, with feeling.

His aunt shook her head, the headdress wobbled precariously. "I'll return next shift to continue your instruction, Crudrat. Much good it will do you."

With that she left the room.

Quy let out his breath in a loud *whoosh*. "She sure has her mind fixed about you, bonded."

Maura could only agree to that.

Asherat looked at both of them, his red eyes sympathetic. "This one is deeply sorry for you both." To Maura he added, "This one shall take this into consideration as your leathers are constructed. Modifications will have to be made."

Maura bit her lip. She could only draw one possible conclusion from this discussion. "Is this one being sent to prison? Or the mines? Or something?" The atmosphere inside the medical lab had become very depressed.

"Worse," gloomed Quy.

There's worse?

"Killed?" she practically whispered.

"Countervail," said Quy, quiet and somber-like, as though this explained everything.

At which point Korakay walked into the room.

"You always come visiting." Quy was still annoyed by his aunt enough to snap at anyone. "Don't you have work to do?"

Korakay snickered. "You only say that because you don't want me to see you all weak and injured. Poor little cub." She patted him on the foot in a manner Maura was sure he found annoying.

Quy winced. "Thanks for that, friend."

"Any time you want abuse, you just come to me."

"Wait," interjected Maura, as it looked like they'd just leave that word hanging, with no support, and use Korakay's entrance as an excuse to move on. "What's *countervail*?"

Korakay was startled out of her good humor. "Why would you be discussing such a thing?" She looked from Asherat to Quy to Maura. "Well, this one sure stumbled into the wrong conversation. Here this one finished her shift, and thought she'd check up on the murmel and little blue here, only to find you two have been at it as well. And what are you all doing? No cheerful talk of the latest textiles, or the dinner menu, no you'd rather depress yourselves with terrible prospects."

She settled at the end of Maura's platform, petting the murmel.

Quy explained. "The Patrona wants my bonded to go for

countervail. Her mind's made up. She's dead set against the Crudrat, has been from the start."

"Wonder why?" replied Korakay sarcastically. "She is, after all, *your* bonded. You've never caused the gens anything but trouble. What'd you expect?"

"Well…" Quy didn't get a chance to finish his sentence for Maura was fed up.

"*What. Is. Countervail?*" Maura's voice, sharp and shrill, cut through the conversation like a blade.

"Wow," said Asherat, "the lady's got some impressive wind emitters when she chooses."

Quy blinked in amazement. The murmel looked very impressed.

"Countervail is what the Kill'ki do with cowards." Only Korakay would be so blunt. "Countervail is where we put the dishonorable. Those who cannot live by a warrior's code. Those who cannot bond to the greater community. It is our best solution when there are no others." She spread her big paws in a sort of shrug.

Asherat added, "They are the infiltrators and the spies, the subterfuge makers and the assassins."

Quy said bitterly, "They are wari's rejected and unworthy. The psychopaths."

"But they *are* useful." Korakay may be blunt, but she was also less emotion riddled about the word than Quy.

Less with negative, and more with concern.

"They *are* needed," added the Jakaa Nova.

"They just aren't much liked or respected," Korakay again.

Quy and Asherat looked at Korakay curiously — there was an edge of bitterness to her tone.

"This one has a brother who had to take to the vail," she said.

Maura processed this information and breathed a long held sigh of profound relief. "Oh, is that all? No problem, then. This one is used to all that stuff. Sounds like being reject, made to run and hide all ticks." *Gloriously familiar.* She actually smiled.

The others appeared perturbed by this reaction.

"You know, the Patrona's own son went in for countervail. Voluntarily. Or so goes the family doggerel," said Quy.

"He told us he was going for fostering!" said Asherat, shocked.

"That's right, you were friends." Quy looked guilty. "This one should not have said."

Asherat tilted his head to the side. "No, it makes sense. He would suit the lifestyle. Remember, we Jakaa Nova are more open to the vail. We're less particular than the Kill'ki about how we fight. So long as we *get* to fight."

Maura made the connection. "You're on about the Patrona's son with Dr Sillous?"

"You would think she'd be a bit more forward thinking about things, given that," said Korakay

The others nodded.

Maura asked for clarification. "His having gone to become a countervail, that's *bad*?"

Quy shrugged and looked pointedly at Asherat. "It certainly would be an embarrassment to the gens, should it become common knowledge."

Asherat merely rested his cheek on the slab. "This one will not tell."

Maura was beginning to understand. It was just like when a progenetor child rejected the implant. No one was ever happy. Perhaps the Kill'ki were not so different from the Wheel after all. Countervail was obviously the Coalition's form of reject.

Would it be as all-over bad? she wondered. *Couldn't possibly. Nothing could be all-over bad in this floating ice city, where they put food out for anyone to take. Nothing.*

"The Patrona wants this one to take on a countervail position? Or train for one?"

"Looks like, despite all logical objections." Quy wrinkled his nose.

Korakay stood and came up to put a hand on Maura's shoulder. It was meant to reassure but Maura started. No one had yet touched her in affection. "You will do fine there," insisted the Kill'ki.

"Does this one have to *do fine* or is just surviving good enough? This one seems to be best at just surviving."

"To tell you the truth, we don't know. Countervails keep themselves to themselves."

"Will Biskweet be allowed with me?"

"You could claim him as a symbiotic necessity. No one knows all that much about Wheel rejects, even Dr Sillous. They might not question."

Hearing his name, the murmel squeaked at them.

"Your first priority," insisted Quy, "should be to convince my aunt that you are better than countervail, that you have other virtues. Push to become wari instead. You have a little time, it might be just enough."

"How's that done?"

"Quy, the Patrona is awfully stubborn." Asherat spoke as though he knew this from personal experience.

"It *is* possible." Fuzzy was petulant, as though he knew how unlikely Maura was to convince the Patrona against a preferred course of action.

Maura was tired of being ignored. She took a breath to yell again.

Quy raised a paw. "No need. How's it done? Well, you must *act* more like a wari."

"You must be strong, and tough, and direct, in both speech and action," said Asherat, proudly.

"You must fight with honor," added Korakay.

"And you must not run, or dodge, or flip about the way you do."

Maura's head bounced amongst the three of them as they talked.

"You must not give insult unless you are in the right."

"Even then, politeness is your best first choice."

"You must show the Patrona that you are willing to learn."

Asherat added, "That you have a personal code of ethics. That you are a noble person with grounding in pure rationality of purpose."

"But," said Maura, "This one has none of those things. This one does not even know what they are." *Why,* she wondered, *is the world always trying to make me into something different?* She was bound to disappoint these people. Alien or not, she had come around to thinking of them as friends. She hated to disappoint them. She'd been better off with only the murmel and Rees, as least they only expected her to be a crudrat.

"The only thing this one is good at," she insisted, "is running and dodging."

Quy shook his head. "Nonsense. You showed excellent strategic thinking when you broke me out of prison on that ghastly spaceport of yours. You took to the whale's guns like you were born targeting. Korakay has been training on that instrument for days now and you are still better than her."

"But that was all in aid of running and dodging," insisted Maura.

"Space it Quy, you really do have a countervail on your hands. Your aunt is right." Asherat looked at Maura with interested, if slightly censorious, eyes.

"How many times," muttered Quy, looking like he wanted to leap off the slab and strangle the Jakaa Nova, "does this one have to tell you to shut your mouth?"

"Stop it, both of you," Korakay spoke staccato in her annoyance. "We've got to help Crudrat here. What is it that makes someone *not* a countervail?"

The three went back to brainstorming.

Maura tried to pay attention, but she couldn't keep the refrain from her traitorous mind. Once again, someone was insisting she become something she was not.

18

Want sympathy? Go to your bonded. Want help? Go to your gens. Doctors are for healing.
~ Coalition Proverb

During the next shift all three were discharged from Dr Sillous's stone domain. Maura figured she'd miss the surgeon So far he was the only full-on sensible person aboard the floating iceberg.

It turned out she didn't see much of any of them for the next six spins. True, she saw Quy at night, but she was usually exhausted down to the bone, and could manage no more than a few words before collapsing onto her mat. Sometimes she saw Korakay or Asherat during shift breaks, but the Patrona was always near, and they seemed nervous about casual talk in proximity to the highest-stock in Pikillacta. Asherat still came to instruct her on Jakaa Nova ways, but only for a few ticks each spin, and always with Manzanilla there, testing her. It was limiting.

The testing was, frankly, odd. Mostly Maura trailed after
the Patrona on shift duties. This took up all Maura's ticks,
every shift. She no longer worked the kitchens. She missed
the snacking, but not a lot else. Instead, first tick of first shift
she had to show up at the Patrona's den and spend the day
with the leader as she went about her routine.

As a result, Maura was learning much on how a space city
was run. She was pretty certain she could now make her way
about every nook and cranny of the whole icy place. But she
didn't quite suss where the testing came in. She did as she
was told, and tried to remember the tenets her three friends
had thrown at her in the medical lab. Showing willingness to
learn was no problem, for she was. But to be openly bold was
against her nature. Her physical abilities were secret
weapons, best hidden behind a veneer of quiet timidity. She'd
not had to fight again, with honor or without, but given the
general scuffling of the Kill'ki, she'd no doubt another fight
would come soon. That it, too, would be a test. She was
unflaggingly polite, to the point where the Patrona began to
look on her with a diplomat's suspicion.

Maura didn't mean too, but she overheard the Patrona
discussing her with Dr Sillous. The massive Kill'ki could not
find fault with her small blue shadow, but was convinced that
fault was *there* in that air of quiet reserve that proved Maura
was always watching, always waiting, always seeking weakness, counting the seconds, measured and alone.

She said, "It is not wari. Nor is it any other profession I
can source. Only countervails keep such consistent stealth
and secrecy. Only countervails keep such stillness in their
souls."

Dr Sillous murmured something in reply that Maura
couldn't hear. He must have asked after Maura's curiosity.

"I instructed her to ask about anything, no matter how

silly or trivial. But her questions are not the questions one expects of a newcomer. She wants to know: Where does breathable air come from? How does the invisible ceiling work? Why are there invisible ceilings at all? Why is the city on ice? Where did the ice come from? How cold is our home world? Where is our home world? How big is the Coalition? Why are we Kill'ki in charge of other races? Why did others join? Was it voluntary?"

Dr Sillous replied, "These are all valid questions, indeed. Many with interesting answers."

"But they are not the questions envoys normally ask. Crudrat does not ask about the workings of the government, or the etiquette of the culture, or the relationships of individuals to the group. She did not care to hear of mythology, or religion, spousal unions, or child rearing. She wants none of the stories that form the tapestry of Coalition life and society. It is as if she sees only the loom, and not the textile upon it. An observer, not a participant. No interest in integrating. It is weird."

Dr Sillous said, "Perhaps is is her culture?"

"Or perhaps she really is a spy."

Maura was stung, until then she had no idea of the impression she gave to others. *I merely enquired of what interests me. A right certain mistake.* She did not think that even her questions might get tested. But after that, she did try to direct them more towards the tapestry of Coalition life, as the Patrona had called it.

"Does anyone know anyone else's true name? Do you even have them?" she asked at one point, figuring that had to count as culture.

"Of course. They are shared between close family members. They can be used with closed circuit transmission in times of great need, but only then. Gens honor demands an instant response to a name summons. I know Sillous's, for example." She paused and frowned. "And Quy's."

Maura processed this. In telling Quy her name, had Maura somehow made him family? "Does it work in one direction? If this one told you her name, would you consider us related?"

"No, names must be shared, like a completed barter. It is unacceptable to place a debt in one direction. That is why it is done so rarely."

"So what would you do?"

"I would forget that you had told me."

Regardless of the Patrona's opinion, Maura felt like she was learning what she wanted of the way the Kill'ki arranged life. More, she was learning how differently things fell out here than in Wheel space. People could switch professions, for example. The Kill'ki allowed for the jumping of spokes! One of the most taboo moves anyone could make back in Maura's home space and here they shrugged it off like it was nothing.

Asherat did his best to help Maura understand interpersonal relationships between different Coalition species, but mostly what she got was an impression of danger, that her words could cause violent actions, and were more likely to than not. Especially with the Jakaa Nova.

"Though, we mostly like you now," insisted Asherat, "at least, us Jakaa quoin."

Maura wondered if it was a good thing, to be liked.

She thought she was adapting well enough. But Quy's face, when she found a few ticks to tell him of her gleanings before bed, seemed ever more worried. The Patrona seemed never likely to warm towards her. Though she unbent enough, by the third spin, to scratch Biskweet about the ears.

"Well, I will say something for you, young Crudrat." It

was Maura's second to last spin companioning the Patrona around the station. Manzanilla had become enough comfortable with Maura to forget the crudrat was there, once or twice. That, too, obviously worried the Patrona once she realized her mistake. "You are not easily distracted, nor do you formulate quick judgments."

"Thank you, Patrona." Maura did not know what else to say.

"But you are terribly sly. You can't hope to hide that fact from me. Crafty, even. It is not," the Kill'ki paused, as though space-tongue were failing her and she could not source the right word, finally she came up with, "respectable."

That night Quy called a council of war in their room. Korakay and Asherat joined him and all three were waiting for Maura when she got off shift.

"Tomorrow is your final bout of testing," said Quy, by way of greeting and explanation.

"Physicals," added Korakay, wrinkling her nose. "We all have to go through them at some point."

"It is going to be very intriguing," added Asherat. "They've had a taste now for your unique fighting style, but this one has a feeling you may still surprise them when it comes to the other tests."

"What other tests?"

"You know we can not tell you that." Korakay looked sad. Maura sighed.

"But we can give you these," Asherat tossed a pile of fabric and some other heavy material at her. It thunked into her hands, scaring Biskweet off of her shoulder. He leaped onto one of the stone platforms and immediately began an embarrassed washing.

Korakay went to placate him.

"What is it?" Maura turned the stack over, spilling parts onto the cold plaster floor.

"Your barter, remember?" The Jakaa Nova settled himself lounging, stomach down, on Quy's sleeping mat. He pressed his fat fingertips together, rested his chin on them and looked up at Maura with eager red eyes.

Maura had, in fact, forgotten. She also hadn't realized until that moment that she probably owed Asherat a blood debt for knifing him. He still could not sit down comfortably.

"Asherat, does this one owe you further barter for, you know, the mistaken puncture?"

"Very politic way of putting it, dear," complimented Korakay with amusement.

The Jakaa Nova huffed, seeming a little embarrassed. "This one has added it to your debt."

"Oh, very well. You'll let this one know, when it's pay-up time?"

Asherat nodded. "Might be soon."

Maura looked to Quy.

He shrugged at her. *Not his problem, apparently.*

Maura unfolded the leathers. They were the most beautiful things she'd ever clapped eyes on. Maura had seen some of the greatest triggered faces of the Wheel trot about spaceside. She'd seen denizens of the highest families, with their smooth skin and sculpted lips. She'd seen exotic clothing and rich tapestried fabric, cut to perfection and draped over bodies that matched. But nothing equaled the leathers in her hands. These belonged to her.

They were a soft deep chocolate brown with piping the same electric blue as her hair. There were also four sets of some thin silky wearables, dark blue, and clearly meant to be donned underneath.

"Wow," she breathed, awed.

"Try them on," encouraged Asherat, delighted by her reverence.

Without pause, Maura stripped out of her old crudrat rags.

"Whoah there," said Quy, turning his head away sharply.

Korakay squeaked and covered her eyes.

Maura had forgotten, nudity was taboo, even amongst friends, in this part of space.

"Ha!" Asherat, unlike the Kill'ki, hadn't bothered to shield his gaze and seemed the only one not particularly upset. "This one *told* the others your nipples could not possibly be blue!"

Maura blinked at him. *Why would they be? And why were the Jakaa Nova discussing my nipples?*

Clearly, it was not an appropriate thing for Asherat to say, for Quy, who usually yelled first, hauled off and punch Asherat, hard and without warning.

The Jakaa Nova collapsed forwards, but didn't jump up and return the hit, an admission to being in the wrong. He propped himself back up. "Sorry, Crudrat."

Maura hurriedly donned the silky under things — a set of very short knickerbockers, and a sort of shirt with tiny sleeves.

"We thought you would like a couple pairs of liners," explained Asherat, "Given this is likely to be your only set of clothing for a while, and you'll need time to wash one set and wear the other."

Maura nodded. The Kill'ki in particular, but everyone 'round this side of space, were rather obsessive over cleanliness. They had things called *dry baths* that they put simply *everything* into, including themselves, most every day. It had been made clear to Maura, from the very start, that she was expected to do the same. She didn't mind. It wasn't an unpleasant sensation. But her old shirt and knickerbockers, never in the best of condition, did seem to object. They were becoming thinner and thinner and more and more ragged with each successive wash. She suspected they'd been held together by crud and dirt until that first cleaning, and were now dying of shock. These liners, she suspected, were better designed to be cleaned regular-like.

She pulled on the leathers. They fit perfectly from neck to ankle. Better, they were deliciously warm and supple, like having a second very thick skin.

"Well," wondered Quy, "how do they move?"

Maura flashed him a grin. Then, without warning, she did a quick back hands-down flip, using up most of the space in the room. The leather creaked a little but otherwise barely protested.

"They'll break in soon enough, especially if you go about doing that kind of thing." Asherat looked impressed by her simple trick.

"They're wonderful," said Maura fervently. "No one has ever given me anything so lovely afore. They're really mine?"

"Who else would they fit?" wondered Korakay.

Maura went over to Biskweet and offered him a leather-clad arm to sniff. The murmel stuck his fuzzy nose up close. Then he stuck out his blue tongue and licked.

"Ew," said Maura, pulling her arm back, "stop that."

The murmel apparently needn't have been told, he made a funny little face and sneezed. Then he went back Korakay's petting.

"They'll be great for tomorrow," prophesied Quy. "Speaking of which, we'd better get our little blue here to sleep. She's got a long couple of shifts coming up."

Korakay and Asherat took the hint and left for their own nests.

Maura stripped out of her new favorite possession, well her only real possession, and snuggled back under the Kill'ki pelt. Eventually, she even managed to sleep. Biskweet did not approve of her restlessness.

Things were certainly different the next day. *Odd different.*

Maura showed up at the Patrona's office first shift in her new leathers, fixed to be shiny, to find the Patrona impatiently waiting for her.

"Oh, there you are. Finally." The headdress quivered in repressed annoyance.

Maura refrained from mentioning she was there at the same time as she had been every first shift for the last five spins.

But the Patrona had already directed her attention elsewhere, at the murmel dogging Maura's heels.

"*You* cannot come this time, for you cannot be allowed to interfere," she told him severely.

Biskweet twitched his whiskers at her.

"Put him in there for the shift." Manzanilla pointed to an empty quy hutch that incongruously occupied one corner of the room. It had obviously been brought in special.

Maura nodded and scooped up Biskweet. The murmel seemed a bit surprised but curled himself about as though expecting a tunnel run.

"Sorry, old boy," Maura said, unwinding and depositing him carefully inside the cage. There was a good solid latch but Maura knew that murmels were known for getting into or out of wherever it was they were least supposed to be.

Biskweet gave her a very offended look from behind the tiny bars of his prison.

"Follow me," said the Patrona, without giving Maura the chance to explain about murmel escape-artist skills.

The moment passed, Maura shrugged and fell silently into step behind the Patrona. The Kill'ki led the way down a now familiar trace towards the recreation courts.

The Patrona was strangely talkative. Well, more talkative than normal, which was still more than Maura thought natural. "Do you know why we Kill'ki take any able-bodied and interested peoples into our Coalition?"

Maura hadn't thought to wonder. It was so very different from the Wheel policy. She'd figured it was just part of the Kill'ki being Kill'ki.

"It's because we are such a warlike race. Many wari die at every turn. What you have seen here on Pikillacta is all peace and trade, but there are worlds not so ready to join our ranks. There are other empires, like the Wheel, who do not agree with our policies or our existence. It is not only in our everyday lives that Kill'ki bicker and fight. The real danger is when the wari are called upon to fulfill their duty to the Coalition."

Maura nodded as some kind of response seemed to be called for. The Patrona was looking at her with a glare composed entirely of hard edges.

"Our military is difficult to join, because it is so very elite. But we Kill'ki have always prided ourselves on even-handed treatment of any genotype that would try. Why do you think we respect the Jakaa Nova, for all their fire and brash-ness? When given the choice of tribute in tax, labor, or mili-tary service, every single Jakaa Nova has chosen service. And gotten in."

Maura wondered why the Patrona was speaking these things. She looked to her face, curious.

Manzanilla was worrying her lower fuzzy lip with sharp teeth. She was deeply concerned over something.

Maura said, trying for reassurance. "This one will do what she can, to the best of her abilities, regardless of your preferences or Quy's hopes."

The Patrona looked at her, startled. "And my husband wonders why I am so set on this course."

Maura paused. "Since we are like to end this thing soon, might this one speak frankly and in her own voice?" Quy had said the personal was allowed on very special occasions.

The Patrona nodded.

Maura took a deep breath. It didn't suit her to speak long winded. But the Patrona seemed to need some kind of reassurance, and the truth was the only thing Maura knew that might help. Maura's truth — her way of seeing things. She didn't like to see the Patrona questioning herself. By-and-large, her decisions appeared to be good ones. The Patrona may be many things – quick to anger, verbose, mistrusting – but Maura had seen her over the past turns expertly handle the toughness the city chucked at her. She was an excellent ruler, so far separate from the progenetors and their cruelty, or the sequensors and their ruthlessness as to be called some other name than *ruler*. Maura wanted the Patrona to understand that.

She used the personal. She let much of the Wheel accent re-enter her space-tongue. "I've never afore had chance nor choices given me as though they were mine by right. I've never eaten a meal regular-like. I've never had garb not all-over rags. I've never gone walking through crowds and been *seen*. I've never had highstock treat me fair and to the face. What you do not seem to suss, Patrona, is I could go right on to die down there in those courts of yours, and still you'd have given me more value than anyone else. No matter what you think of me, I have felt nothing but honor from you, and I could not be more grateful."

The Patrona winced away from her words, as though they hurt. "Now I understand what Sillous sees in you." She sighed. "Very well then, let us see if you can prove my choices or the weakness in them."

19

Worth is a measurement of *value* against *use*. Although weapons are good too.

~ Coalition Proverb

The Patrona took Maura into a room, probably the smallest Maura had seen in Pikillacta that wasn't for waste disposal. It was filled with stuff, more objects in one place than she'd yet encountered, as the Kill'ki seemed to prefer life sparse.

It took her a moment to realize that it was set up like the cockpit of Quy's whale.

She looked at the Patrona. "You know this one can't pilot, right?"

"Yes. However, my nibling insists you are a dab hand at sinking an enemy ship, so I agreed to test for proof. It is not a skill considered relevant to countervails, but highly prized in wari. I shall be interested to see if that little barnacle of a relative of mine was lying. If you would please take the gunner position."

One of the green scaled Hydraborns appeared next to the Patrona in the doorway while Maura seated herself. At least with her new leathers the seat wasn't as cold as it had been first time 'round. Otherwise everything was much the same, except the walls were made of stone.

"This man is called Eeaa. He is Pikillacta's best piloting instructor, and will test your targeting ability. I'll return at the end of the shift to take you to the next exam." With that the Patrona vanished.

Maura looked up and nodded to the Hydraborn politely.

This was the kind of test that Maura had expected from the first. This was more like those vague memories of before chip rejection, when progenetor teaching drones dictated life.

"Note that the controls are all in the same place as in your prior whale experience." The Hydraborn had a high fluting whistle of a voice.

Maura nodded, and reaching forward flipped the projecting screen up into its table position.

Eeaa pressed something outside the door of the room and the screen came to life, generating that familiar three dimensional sphere, a snub-nosed blip of green at its center with its cone of red emanating up from the top.

"Everything is simulated, but it will seem exactly as though you were in a space battle."

"Umm," Maura hoped it was permitted to ask questions, "the stone walls aren't going to go invisible all of sudden, are they?"

"No. The simulation does not extend to whale skin."

Maura reached down to the two targeting coils dangling from the base of the screen, and slid one around the forefinger and the other the thumb of her left hand. "Is that what the walls are called, whale skin?"

"No. It's what they are." Eeaa seemed very brief about speech-making. Maura admired that.

"What?"

"Did no one tell you? Perhaps it's not so grand to the Kill'ki but it *is* the pride of my planet and our greatest contribution to the Coalition. You know we have a mainly aquatic home world? At the depths of our oceans live massive beasts, able to withstand great pressure, akin to the whales of ancient Earth Core. We turn their carcasses into space-faring ships."

Maura had thought the ribs of Quy's skiff looked like to old bones. Apparently this was, in fact, exactly what they were.

"You mean, this one was riding 'round space snug inside a carcass?"

"Yes." The Hydraborn took no offense at the term.

"Well, there you have it." Maura fiddled with controls on her fingers. Aliens be alien. "Shall we move on?" She'd rather not stick her noggin too long on this somewhat disgusting revelation.

"By all means. Testing commencing. Now."

Hundreds of little blobs of yellow light zoomed into and out of the display area.

Mauras hand began to tingle. She shoved it into the sphere and pinched at the enemy fighters.

Catching the blobs between thumb and forefinger was still difficult. But she managed it, about half the time. She didn't have Quy's encouraging presence, nor his little tips as to where the ship would tilt to next, but she also didn't have weightlessness mucking about with her stomach. She found it not so hard, in the end. Eventually, as with the real ship, she ran out of ammunition, and the simulation stopped.

"Interesting performance. Are you quite certain this is only your second time in the gunner seat?"

Maura nodded.

"Interesting," he said again.

"It wasn't so exactly like to the real thing."

"No?"

"Too much gravity and none of the smell. You know, that metallic nose tickle? This one remembers it vividly from when Quy first turned on the targeting coils."

"Do you? We Hydraborn have poor nasal sensors, I had no idea the simulator lacked this detail. It is usually used for training those who have never been in battle before, and it is rare for a seasoned wari to return to the simulator and notice a flaw. Thank you for telling me."

"What do I do now?" Maura stripped off the coils and stood up.

"The Patrona will be back shortly. I shall give her my report. Then you will continue on to your next test."

Maura nodded. "Thank you for your supervision."

The green-scaled man nodded curtly and disappeared into another room.

Maura waited.

Eventually, the Patrona reappeared. She had added more jewelry in the interim, and switched her headdress for a larger and more impressive one.

"Eeaa tells me you did very well for a first timer." She looked like she'd rather not believe such a report. "For once my nibling appears to have neither lied nor exaggerated. Remarkable. I will take these results into consideration, but you should know my decision is also based both on your previous informal testing over the last few spins, and those exams that are still to follow."

For the next test they made her fight.

Maura was not much surprised by this. The Patrona led her in and down to one of the four main courts of the recreation area. Turns out there *was* an easier way down than jumping, stairs right through a hole in the plaster floor, off to one side.

Maura trotted on down them alone and came out into the pit and chaos.

It was all about *what* they made her fight.

Animals. Not little food creatures like the kitchen quy. Nor useful smarts, like the murmel. But big, nasty teeth-riddled things, which looked more into hunting human than feeding or helping them. Four of the critters waited for her, all interested in Maura-meat. She turned fast to get back up the stairs but someone had capped over the entrance and there was nowhere to go but front-ways.

She hadn't even a weapon. For a people that seemed pretty obsessed with sticks and knives and the like, the Kill'ki were remarkably unwilling to give her any.

Maura did what she was best at. Ran. She flipped forward, up over the charging beasties and took off straight across the court. The beasts wheeled about and chased after her. They had big, heavy haunches, coarse thick fur, and a good deal in the claw area to go with the teeth. They were also prone to slobbering.

Maura took in the space about her. *A big open square of a room. High walls on all sides, no good hand-holds, a few stone platforms to one side, and a wide expanse of plaster floor. Nothing to use as a weapon.* Not that she was sure it was a right mind set, simply to kill a critter for following its nature. Even if that meant following her.

She made for one of the stone platforms and jumped on top of it.

The four animals charged, all those teeth and claws heading her way, and Maura stayed as long as she dared, crouched atop the stone, luring them forward. They hurled themselves at her. At the last possible tick, she dove into a somersault, a long arc over their heads, and sped away again across the plaster floor. She peeked back. In their tumble and haste, they'd managed to knock the massive stone block over and toward the wall.

Maura dashed around the court, noting she'd drawn a bit of a crowd watching from above. There were no ticks to go about recognizing faces or count how many were watching. She ended her mad dash back atop the knocked over stone platform, balancing on its side.

The four creatures hurled themselves at her, snarling. *Not so bright, these beasties.* She jumped over them once more, this time not bothering to dive, just propelling herself up and forward in one massive leap, and began the lap again. Given her stamina, and their stupidity, they could probably go about repeating that pattern all shift.

But they'd hit against the platform hard enough the second time to slide it a good handsbreadth across the plaster floor. Not quite up against the wall, but enough for Maura. She went for one last lap — got up as much speed as she could, the creatures chewing away at the air beyond her heels, and spun the wall at the far end of the court. It was one of her favorite blade moves, placing one hand to the tunnel side, and flipping vertically feet-over-head, around the hand.

It certainly confused the critters. They balked, stumbling up against one and other and the hard stone, giving her a good head start as she charged back across the court directly at the tipped-over platform. Getting up real momentum, she used the platform as springboard to propel her up against the wall, touched down one, two, three, steps up, and just managed to grab the top of the wall with one hand. It was enough for a crudrat, she could hoist with the other hand and pull herself right up and over the top.

She was suddenly face to face with a group of very surprised looking spectators. Not knowing what else to do, she scanned the crowd and made her way around to where the Patrona sat. Dr Sillous, Quy, Korakay, Asherat, and number of others were all perched near her.

"Unusual approach." The Patrona was noncommittal and grave.

"Now I see where you get all those muscles and calluses," said Dr Sillous thoughtfully.

"How are the leathers feeling?" Asherat was clearly trying not to look impressed.

Maura could be wordy about that. "Brilliant! No pinching, no folding over or hiking up, nothing loose to get caught, no movement restriction. A bit indecently tight," she paused at his annoyed look, "by Wheel standards," she hastily modified, "but really brilliant."

Quy, typically, was angry. "You didn't even give her a weapon," he accused his aunt.

"That was not part of her test," replied the Patrona. "Considering she stole the first knife she used. Penalties are my province and I choose to enact them in this instance."

Clearly, the Patrona was still bitter about that.

Quy narrowed black eyes at his aunt, but held his tongue for once.

"We will have to take a few extra ticks to set up the modular test. Given your unusual ability to simply climb out of the court arena." The Patrona sounded annoyed.

Maura wondered how else a body was to get away from beasties. Seemed a bang up solution to her. *Have I failed again?*

The Patrona signaled three wari to come over. Maura recognized them as Quy's semi-cousins from her very first day in Pikillacta. She hadn't seen them since, but all three looked much the same — all over white, with different lengths of fuzz, and black skin where kill markings were shaved into face and shoulder. They wore the same Kill'ki wrappings in bright colors, and the customary amount of wari weaponry and jewelry.

The large female stepped forward, her gold necklaces jangling melodically. "Your orders, Patrona?"

Maura felt a terrible sweating panic – was she up against these three fully trained armigers for the next test? *And me – not a weapon and not a lick of skill. I don't stand a chance.*

"Remove all lifts and portable obstacles from the modular arena," instructed the Patrona.

The three nodded.

"Follow us," said the smallest one to Maura with a grin.

Maura moved to do so, and as she did, Quy slotted a metal stick-like object into her left hand. Without looking at him or reacting in any way, Maura, all hidden movements, slid the rod up her tight leather sleeve.

"It will be fun to see how you take to narrow dimensions. I enjoyed that last show, by the way. A bit short, and a bit tame, but certainly *different*." The small wari had an expression suggesting he really had enjoyed it and wasn't just talk-making.

"No one has ever simply leaped out of the court before," said the medium sized wari. Maura wasn't sure if his tone indicated awe or disgust.

Despite her fears, the three warriors merely led her down and around to a different court, and then left her to her own devises while they moved furniture. The new court was quite small, or so Maura was thinking, until the three disappeared 'round the end of it, proving it was no end at all but a bend. They returned carrying one of the massive stone platforms, which they pushed into the holding area near Maura. She was impressed by their obvious strength. They proceeded to do this several more times before giving Maura three little waves, one from each, and disappearing back the way they'd come in.

Maura moved forward into the court, cautious. She needn't have bothered, no one and nothing was in there with her. The area was constructed out of a series of very high walled passages, and Maura took a quick jog 'round and about to try and get the lay of it. Not a lot to work with, no hand holds, no easy way out, and she simply wasn't tall enough to run up a wall that high without a platform to aid.

Why did it always come down to height? Too tall for crudrat, too short for Kill'ki.

Maura slid the weapon Quy had given her out of her sleeve.

In the stands above, she heard the Patrona shout, "Quy, you didn't!" and string of attached profanity.

It was a long metal stick thing with a stiff knobby switch halfway up. She clicked the switch up, carefully, and a wicked little blade shot out one end. Maura rather liked it. It had the same length and heft as her old crud scraper from tunnel time. She whirled it about a bit for testing, swinging it behind her head and under her arms, as if she were scraping a blade. *Nice.*

Still nothing happened.

Maura got tired of twirling the weapon and crouched to rest, staying alert.

She was beginning to wonder if anything would happen at all when a soft thunk sounded. She stood.

Still nothing.

Eventually, three opponents rounded a bend in the passage before her — one Jakaa Nova, one Kill'ki, and one of the all-red Shosanshee. *Two sets of eyelids*, Maura's brain reminded her proudly. Much good such knowledge did her now. She realized she'd never asked the Patrona – or Quy, or Asherat, or Korakay for that matter – how to best fight any of the aliens that now surrounded her. She'd been so concerned with getting along, with not intruding or getting herself noticed, she hadn't even wondered what their weaknesses were – or their strengths. An armiger would have asked. A wari would have asked. Was that, too, a failing mark against her?

The Patrona was right — Maura was no warrior. But Maura did know enough about the Coalition by now to realize that the three now blocking the way before her weren't yet full warriors but still quoin. Which was more training than Maura had, but still was, the Patrona probably felt, closer to fair. Or perhaps it was in the testing rules.

They each held a pair of nasty looking knives made of some kind of sharpened stone, one in each hand.

Maura did the only thing she could. The only thing she was good at. She used crudratting against them and moved – straight at them.

At the last second she twisted to one side, skittered partway up the wall, and leaped out.

One. Two.

She stepped from the head of the Shosanshee, to the shoulder of the Kill'ki, catapulting herself from there forward into speed. Six stone blades slashed at her, one hit her ankle, but skittered harmlessly off the leather. A good barter indeed, she really had gotten the better end of that deal.

Two of the quoin took off after her — the Kill'ki and the

Shosanshee. The Jakaa Nova went in a different direction, obviously intending to cut her off.

There was a nice long stretch to pick up speed and gain some space. While Maura did both, she also slid the trigger switch on Quy's weapon, and heard it sink back inside itself again. She tucked the metal rod back up her sleeve, at the same time thinking she'd love a few pockets in these leathers of hers.

She'd learned the lay of this maze-like court, and had a pretty good idea where the Jakaa Nova might pop up again if he were coming around to head her off. So she grabbed at next corner with both hands, swinging her legs around the bend first, into the passage, and hit the Jakaa Nova running towards her with both feet, hard, to the sternum. The quoin *oophed* and fell back against the wall.

Maura dashed on, not waiting to see if he stood again, or if his companions would stop to help, trip over him, or manage to keep going.

She ran so fast 'round the next corner, she had to slap her hands and rebound away from the opposite wall. In front of her was a T in the passageway — two choices of direction. She took neither. Instead, she judged from the footsteps that those behind had caught up to her just enough. She took a quick dash up the wall, and pushing off and up with all her strength, the big muscles in her thighs screaming, flew into a long back dive over their heads. Ending in a twist, she landed facing back the way she'd come and sped off again.

There had been only two behind her. The Jakaa Nova was still separated from the others.

'Round the next bend she saw him coming at her. She put on a quick burst of speed, dodged to the side, leaped up, placed both hands to the side of his face, and shoved down, as though he were a beltway rail Maura wanted to vault over.

Maura used the Jakaa Nova's own body to brace against, and ran sideways, parallel to the floor, along the wall, all the while shoving downwards, leveraging pressure to compensate for lack of physical strength. The Jakaa Nova reeled to the side, and Maura ran on.

No one was following. Which meant the other two were also trying for a frontal approach.

Maura met them coming at her just after she made that realization. She ran toward them, without pause. They both took up some kind of fighting stance, low, grounded, balancing on the balls of their feet. Armigers only knew weapons and wari seemed the same. Maura intended to go at them with her body as the weapon. *Bet they're not used to that.*

She dove at the space between them, doing a side flip through the small gap, tilting so her front fist and back foot whipped, one after the other, into the nose of the Shosanshee as she passed through, the shorter and more accessible of the two.

The Kill'ki made a grab for her, dropping one knife. It shattered with a high tinkling sound on the plaster. *Glass knife, not stone?*

Maura squirmed her way out of her grip, blessed the leathers again, and ran on.

Around several corners and down a few more straight stretches and Maura gained a good deal of velocity. She'd also thought up a plan.

All three aliens appeared before her once more — the Kill'ki at the front and the other two flanking her. *Good,* thought Maura, *she's the tallest.*

Maura ran forward, trying not to look at the knife the Kill'ki held, a shifting rapidity of sharpness. She charged directly at her, as though to use her for another wall run, but at the last moment, swerved to one side. Maura used the Kill'ki's knee, hip, waist, and shoulder with her left leg, and the wall with her right, to tic-tac straight up. At the quoin's shoulder, Maura shifted balance over, her right foot coming against the top of that fuzzy head. For a split second she was entirely balanced on top of the Kill'ki and then she sprang, landing atop the wall.

20

When there is nothing else, countervail.
    ~ Coalition Proverb

After that, it was all easy. Maura ran along the wall top, narrow, but not a challenge since they were about the same was the metal beams 'round her old spaceport's tag end. She jumped over the passageways below, smooth and simple, balancing the landings perfectly. She made her way, one after the next, back over to the stands where the Patrona, Quy, and the others sat, mouths slightly open.

She took up stance, all self-conscious, before them. *Now what?*

She seemed to have drawn quite a crowd this time. A number of different aliens were gathered, having watched her tightrope over wall-tops towards them. Everyone was all agog, except Quy. Quy had seen her run the beltway. He had some small notion of what a crudrat could do.

Maura handed him back his unused weapon.

"Crudrats don't use blades, we dodge them." She looked to the Patrona, and said, rather bold and daring, "Running a scyther is *still* harder."

Dr Sillous recovered speech first. "Are you saying that any Wheel-made crudrat could do," he paused, "*that*." He waved his spade tipped hand at the partitioned court below.

Maura gave this question some serious consideration. She'd been the best in her sector. And some other 'rats suffered from lack of innovation — not many would think to turn the run itself into the fight. "Most could suss to it, if told how," she finally said, trying for honesty, "But not all have the noggin to think it up to start."

"But can they all twist, flip, and jump about like that?" Korakay was looking mightily impressed.

Maura shrugged. "What, that? For certain. Whatcha all think crudratting was *about*?"

The Patrona seemed at a loss, but for once something Maura had said obviously made her really think, instead of only get annoyed. "And these are the same crudrats who, when they become too big and strong, are unwanted? Like you were when my nibling found you?"

Maura nodded.

"And what, exactly, happens to them, if some pustule of a Kill'ki doesn't come along and inadvertently provide them with other options?"

"What *exactly* happens?" Maura hesitated.

"Yes. What *exactly*?"

"This one can only speak to her own spaceport."

"Good enough for us." Dr Sillous leaned forward slightly looking very interested. "Quy remembers the coordinates, right Quy?"

"Of course," replied Quy looking offended.

"Well," Maura frowned. Then she spat it all out in one go

— her future as might-have-been. "Generally we get our licenses pulled. That's the little chip that allows a reject to work the scythers. Once that happens, we're air wasters. Armigers – them's like your wari – will hunt a body down. If they feel like it. Mostly they don't much care, so they leave a reject be. There's no way and nowheres to nosh. Some of us make it through spins begging for scraps, but since they shut off the crossgenetor arena, them's scarce pickings. So we look to starvation and death within a turn."

The Patrona and Dr Sillous shared some sort of significant, if surprised, look.

Maura shifted from one foot to the next, nervous, and turned to Quy. She'd thought this was a known thing. She'd thought she'd made it clear, what life was like for her kind. *Guess not. Guess maybe I should do a bit more talking once in a spin or so.*

Quy raised his eyebrows but did not explain what was happening.

"It would be an excellent countervail recruitment base," said Dr Sillous to his wife, after a long moment.

"A very dangerous recruitment process though. Imagine, pulling agents out of Wheel space, training them up, taking them in, then sending them back when active."

Maura was seized with a sudden shock of real hope. First time in all her ticks. She could go back for Rees! She looked to Quy. *They* could go back for Rees? They could get him out. They could get others out. The very idea made all the tiny hairs on her legs stand up.

"That would be wonderful trick, though," she said, unguarded for once in her life.

The Patrona frowned. "Worth the risk?"

"If they could provide this kind of quality skill," Dr Sillous gestured once more at the maze of a court, referencing

Maura's spectacular performance, "And the Wheel just *murders* them." His voice was rich with disgust.

"'Tis not murder," said Maura, all honestly.

"Murder through neglect is still murder."

"But murder has to be done to a *person*."

Quy jumped in to explain, "Crudrat is trying to say that rejects aren't real people, not by Wheel standards. Right?"

Maura nodded, she'd thought that was obvious.

"You mean, they're like animals?"

"Worse. Animals are useful. Rejects that can't crudrat have no purpose at all." Maura was beginning to think the Kill'ki would never understand this concept.

"This one is surprised they don't use you rejects for food," interjected Asherat.

Maura raised her eyebrows. "This one is, too, now that you speak to it."

Most everyone else looked a little sick, except Dr Sillous. He and Asherat shared a Jakaa Nova's irreverent amusement.

"It is an interesting idea," said the Patrona, sounding like Eeaa the Hydraborn. "No, not the cannibalism. I will give it some serious consideration and perhaps bring it before the Council of Cities at the next potlatch. For now, however, we have more pressing business."

She stood. "I have made my final decision."

Oh, thought Maura, *so quickly as that.*

The Patrona straightened up tall, which was mighty high, and fussed at the robe about her shoulders so it fell perfectly. "It has not been an easy one."

"Yes it has," said Quy sullenly, "You had your mind made up from the start."

The Patrona did not get angry with him. For a change.

Dr Sillous gave Quy a grave look. "You are already imperiled by breaking the testing strictures and handing your

bonded a weapon illegally. Though *she* did right and
refrained from using it. It is time for you to be mindful of
your tongue, son of my brother-in-law."

Quy, unused to being admonished by his uncle, sat back
cowed.

The Patrona continued. "The petitioner, Crudrat, received
scores on her targeting test that were unexpectedly high. Plus,
she recognized a sensory flaw in the simulation system that
no one else has ever remarked upon. The first, is a mark of a
wari, the second a mark of an engineer. Nevertheless, in her
questions and her social relations, the petitioner remains
essentially disconnected. Her interests are in observation
rather than understanding, stealth rather than confrontation,
and these are marks of a countervail. In her physical tests she
has performed unlike any other petitioner, it is hard to
measure the worth of one who instead of beating a test,
merely avoids it. But that, too, marks a countervail, choosing
options that are neither wrong nor right, but just evasive."

The Patrona paused. She turned to address Maura directly,
rather than the crowd.

Maura faced her, head tilted back to see her face. Behind
the ruler's massive headdress stars twinkled in endless black.

Manzanilla said, "It is possible that you might socialize
and integrate fully into the Coalition, but it is my assessment
that it is not your origin culture but your nature that has lead
to these test results. There would always be the chance that, if
you were wari, you would slide too easily into subterfuge and
individual action." She looked at her nibling. "Even you must
admit to that, Quy."

Quy, Korakay, and Asherat were all looking gloomy. It
was a particularly odd expression on the face of the Jakaa
Nova.

"This one has failed her testing," Maura realized.

"There is no failure, there is only fit. You do not fit a wari life." It was Dr Sillous who explained, all kindness.

Maura looked about. "This one could have told you that. This one may be reject, but there's nothing but progenetor genes floating her body, no armiger at all."

Quy looked ever sadder.

The largest of the three wari semi-cousins stepped forward and clapped her paws together six slowly measured times. "The Patrona will now render judgment."

Manzanilla cleared her throat. "Given the social and physical test results, her small size, and relative youth, Pikillacta will accept the petitioner, Crudrat, into the Kill'ki Coalition on the condition that she undertake formal training to become a countervail."

Maura bowed her head. Despite what Quy thought, it couldn't be that bad. *At least they don't want me dead. And if they find use for other former crudrats too, some part of my ticks here have been well spent.*

"Of bloody course," spat Quy.

Without looking at him, the Patrona signaled with one massive paw. Bracelets around her wrists jingled together.

Once more the largest of the three wari semi-cousins moved to join them at the front and clapped her paws together six times. "The Patrona will now render judgment," she repeated.

"Child of my brother, quoin, called Quy in the City of Pikillacta, called Xeegan in the city of his birth, called Fuzzy by his bonded." Someone snorted at that. Maura felt guilty – *how'd that gotten out?* "You, too, have been under testing and are called to judgment."

Quy started violently, and jumped to his feet, coming to stand next to Maura facing the Patrona. He looked very, very nervous.

"As is the law, we cannot separate a bonded pair prior to adulthood. Given good reason, the Coalition can break the bond, for the benefit of the whole. In this instance, it is my judgment that the bond stand. The pair will profit from continued association."

Quy looked suddenly hopeful and surprised. "This one did not know that law existed. Is it strong enough to overturn your previous ruling and keep Crudrat here with me?"

"Silence," said the large semi-cousin.

Quy snapped his mouth shut.

The Patrona looked infinitely sad. Maura wondered, for the first time, how old she was. "After much consultation with the rest of the gens, we have decided, Quy, you are to accompany your bonded."

Quy reeled back slightly, mental shock as physical blow. "What?"

"Oh no," said Korakay softly.

As though she had not heard his shocked exclamation, his Aunt continued. "You have disobeyed the strictures of quoin orders once too often. I will not list the sum total of your transgressions, but today alone you chose to assist outside of approval in the testing *and* interrupted a judgment in session. Though you have lived amongst the Coalition all your life, it was your bonded, a stranger to us and a counter-vail by nature, who knew enough not to accept your assistance."

"Aunt, what are you doing?"

"You are undisciplined. You are also a good fighter and you might have been a great one, like your mother. You are an excellent pilot. You are certainly neither the sly nor stealth personality prototype that chooses countervail."

"Exactly!" said Quy.

"But if nothing else, the countervail field boasts the most

discipline of any in the Coalition. It has been decided that you would benefit from this aspect, regardless of tested fit."

"No!" Quy roared. "You can't do this."

"I think you will find that I can. The decision of the gens is final."

Quy's eyes were desperate. Maura's plight was forgotten with the threat to his own future. "But all I ever wanted was to be wari!"

His aunt sighed, relaxing her stance and rubbing the back of her neck under the collar of her robe with one paw. "Then you should have taken to that life with greater caution and behaved like a wari."

"But…"

"There are no choices left for you, my problematic little nibling."

Maura saw real regret and affection in the Patrona's gaze.

"All your options have been spent. You have used all your goodwill barter with the gens and must be on the receiving end of its authority now."

"Please," said Quy, voice soft.

The Patrona swallowed, dipping her head forward slightly. "I too have no more choices." She took a breath. "You are hereby stripped of the title quoin, and all the authority and rights thereby connected. Your personal whale will be repossessed by the gens unless you can dispose of it before your departure. You will leave at the end of this shift."

"Request barter," said Asherat instantly, upon hearing that little gem. He was the only one who seemed unperturbed by this whole turn of events.

Quy recovered from his shock long enough to say, "Not on your red-eyed life." He turned to look at the crowd, some sympathetic, some nodding approval. He rubbed at his eyes briefly. "Korakay," he said, strength back in his voice, "want a skiff? Good condition, hardly used."

His friend looked up, there were tears in her eyes. "Barter accepted. It will have to be left unfulfilled. You know this one does not have enough to trade for a whole whale yet."

"What good would barter do where we are going anyway?" said Quy starkly. He lifted the keycard from about his neck. Maura hadn't even known it was there, hidden in his fur, and tossed it to his friend. Korakay caught it deftly and ceremoniously pulled it over her own fuzzy head.

Maura was beginning to feel worse and worse. That she had got herself into this countervail thing was all to the truth, and fine with her. But to drag Quy along with her?

"This one is vastly sorry," she said to him.

Quy straightened his back. "This one is not so mean as all that. It is not your fault, it is my own misdeeds. This one knew there would be consequences, there always are. Just not what form they would take. This one's birth mother approves?"

The Patrona nodded.

"As the universe wills it, and as gens bid, so it be done. This one will do as ordered. It will be nice to see this one's cousin again, if nothing else."

Maura recognized that as a little dig, to remind the Patrona that her own child was already set to be a countervail. Already a shame on the gens.

Manzanilla winced. "Perhaps they will curb that razor tongue of yours as well."

"And perhaps they will twist it to better use." Dr Sillous smiled softly. It was as though he knew something his wife did not. As though this wouldn't be so bad.

Maura took courage in that.

"Judgments have ended for this shift." The Patrona sagged down to sit, looking tired.

Quy whirled about and marched rapidly away, his long furry legs eating up the distance.

Maura wondered if she should follow him.

Dr Sillous stood and patted Maura's shoulder. "This is a positive thing, you will see. My wife makes good decisions, hard ones, but good."

"And the other crudrats? Will you really do a mite for them?"

"She said she would consult with the council, and you can rely on her keeping that word. But you must understand that the decision to recruit intentionally from Wheel ranks will rest, in part, on how well you do in this new life that she has selected for you."

Maura took a sharp breath. She was testing for the saving of all crudrats? Maura vowed then and there to be the best counterveil the Kill'ki never knew to want. "Then this one shall do brilliantly. And the murmel, would you, perhaps, look after him?"

Dr Sillous shook his head. "We are not so cruel as that. You will be allowed to take him with you. I have noted in your medical records that you have an emotional symbiotic relationship with the animal, and you are not to be separated."

Maura did not know what to say. "Thank you." Then she remembered what she was supposed to say at that kind of favor. Thank you wasn't enough. "This one owes you barter."

The surgeon smiled, white teeth flashed. "I would consider it settled if you would say hello to my son when you get there. Remind him that it was his choice, and he need not cut us off, nor be ashamed. I, at least, would like to hear from him once in a while."

Maura nodded. "Of course. By what name is he called?"

Dr Sillous shrugged. "I do not know. New place, new name, what you are called is earned or given, not taken with you. It is the Kill'ki way. And we have not heard from him since he left."

"This one will do her best," said Maura wondering how many half Kill'ki half Jakaa Nova there could be. She turned to go, worried about Quy.

"Wait!"

Asherat and Korakay stopped her.

"Best if this one goes after him," explained Korakay.

Maura nodded. If Korakay thought so. She'd known Quy longer, after all.

That left Asherat standing next to her. "You know, this one has never seen anyone move like that. A real test of the leathers. This one thinks you will do remarkable things as a countervail."

"Thank you."

"As you are to leave very soon. Shall we walk?"

Maura nodded. She checked quickly to see if she should say goodbye to the Patrona. But the ruler was leaning her head heavily on her husband's shoulder, looking so sad. Maura could not bear to approach. Perhaps she would come to see them off.

Maura walked with Asherat toward the recreation area exit.

"We have an unfinished barter, Crudrat. You can't leave such business incomplete without acknowledgement that it will remain so from both parties."

"Oh, of course." Maura was ashamed, she had forgotten about that. And he had been so helpful, with the leathers and the talking.

"This one is terribly sorry. What would you ask?" She

hoped it was something she could give him quickly, or perhaps defer until later.

Asherat actually looked a little embarrassed. "This one's friend, the Patrona's son, he is a mixed species. He finds things difficult, being neither Kill'ki nor Jakaa Nova. This one would ask that you be kind to him, when you meet. Not judge on appearances or attitude. He is shy."

Maura raised blue eyebrows. "Unusual trait for both Kill'ki and Jakaa Nova."

Asherat snorted. "Too true. So you will accept this as barter completion?"

"Gladly, but it does not seem like enough. Simply to be kind to a stranger."

"You have not yet met him."

"Do *you* know what name he goes by?"

"No, this one did not even know he had gone countervail until recently. But Quy knows him by sight, of course. What is that horrible noise?"

They reached the entrance to the Patrona's rooms, where a *very* angry Biskweet was busy shrieking his little heart out from behind bars even a murmel could not escape.

Maura let him out of the hutch. He streaked away, deeply offended.

They walked slowly on, Asherat talking inconsequential words.

They found Biskweet, ruffled and grumpy, back in Maura's sleeping quarters. Quy was also there, ruffled and grumpy.

Korakay was looking frustrated. "This one has shift down in engineering in about three ticks. Good luck." She gave Maura a quick hug before she left. Maura wasn't sure if that was luck for the journey or luck dealing with Quy.

Asherat also turned to go. "It has been interesting to know you, little Crudrat."

"Likewise," replied Maura. The tall youth stooped, took her shoulders in booth hands, and touched his forehead to hers. "Remember our barter."

Maura said nothing.

A tick later, he had gone.

"He likes you," said Quy, shaken out of his melancholy by this surprised realization.

Maura grimaced. "Would you stop?"

Quy shrugged. "You will have to get used to it eventually. But no point in pushing, this one will already have to fend off suitors, without you responding favorably." He grinned a sudden flash of teeth. "I guess it's not so bad that this one goes with you considering someone has to keep an eye on you."

"Are you sure?" Maura sat down next to him, worried.

He tilted his head to the side. "Truth between bonded?"

"Truth."

"We all swim the seas before us, this one just stopped looking where he was going."

"And some of us ain't never seen the sea."

Quy's smile went sad. The murmel, having decided to forgive at least Quy if not Maura, came wandering over and began grooming the Kill'ki's arm.

"Locillor," said Quy softly.

"What?" Maura was confused.

"My name or record, it's Locillor."

He'd started using the personal pronoun.

Maura was silent, processing for a moment, thinking back to the Patrona's lessoning on Kill'ki ways. Shared, the Patrona had said. *Names are to be shared.* He already knew hers of course, but he'd never once used it publicly or privately. So she said, "And mine is Maura Am Vern. So, a great white alien beastie is now my family?"

Locillor/Quy/Fuzzy sighed. "Better that than no family at all, I suppose."

"Too true." Maura bumped his shoulder with hers. "Won't be so bad."

He looked funny. Maura thought he must be realizing at last that he'd basically adopted a strange blue-haired Wheel child. Then he looked at her even stranger little blue murmel busily licking away at his arm fur. "They have no idea what they are in for, Maura Am Vern, do they?"

Maura didn't realize to how touched she'd be, hearing her name in full out of someone else's mouth after so many spins of *Crudrat*. She thought on her testing, how surprised they all were when she simply did crudrat doings, and the way Fuzzy always got into trouble, and the murmel's loud and wily little ways.

She sat up straight, looking dead ahead. "No they don't."

fin

AUTHOR'S NOTE

Thank you so much for picking up *Crudrat*. I hope you
enjoyed Maura's story. If you would like more from the
Tinkered Stars universe, please say so in a review. I'm
grateful for the time you take to do so.

I have a silly gossipy newsletter called the Chirrup. I promise:
no spam, no fowl. (Well, maybe a little wicker fowl and lots
of giveaways and sneak peeks.) Find it and more at...

gailcarriger.com

ABOUT THE WRITERBEAST

New York Times bestselling author Gail Carriger (AKA G. L. Carriger) writes to cope with being raised in obscurity by an expatriate Brit and an incurable curmudgeon. She escaped small-town life and inadvertently acquired several degrees in higher learning, a fondness for cephalopods, and a chronic tea habit. She then traveled the historic cities of Europe, subsisting entirely on biscuits secreted in her handbag. She resides in the Colonies, surrounded by fantastic shoes, where she insists on tea imported from London.